the right kind of trouble

Trouble
Book Three

christina c jones

Copyright © 2015 Christina C. Jones
Cover art by Christina Jones
All rights reserved. This book or any portion thereof may not be reproduced or used in any manner whatsoever without the express written permission of the publisher except for the use of brief quotations in a book review.
This is a work of fiction. Any similarity to real locations, people, or events is coincidental, and unintentional.

acknowledgements

To my family, my friends, my readers, and my AWESOME beta readers, thank you.

one
...
Lauren

I FELL in love in the library.

At least… as much as you can with someone you've never seen before, or spoken to, and don't even have the privilege of knowing their name. I was dreaming anyway. With a face like that, I had to be.

He had bright, expressive, *intelligent* eyes, the kind that noticed everything, the same color as the "espresso" polish on my. My gaze skated over to the lean arm he was using to hold himself up, his toned bicep flexing against the arm of his tee shirt as he pressed his palm flat to the table. I was laying down, my face pressed against my arm, textbook and notes in front of me. He was above me, in my personal space, leaning across my table in one of the private study rooms.

He smelled like… *books*.

In my ear, I faintly heard one of my favorite singers admonishing a soon-to-be former lover, and I wondered why the music seemed so low. He pulled my other earbud from my ear, and smiled. "So the sleeping beauty awakes."

I blinked once.

Twice.

A third time.

I wasn't dreaming at all.

I let out a quick, quiet gasp as my heart started to race from being in such close proximity to him, whoever the hell he was.

He was a cutie... an everyday fine, with skin the same rich golden-brown of caramelized brown sugar. He had the kind of strong features I loved on a man— wide, prominent nose, strong jaw, thick eyebrows, and full lips that curved into an easy smile. The smile, and the eyes, and the whole smelling-like-books thing... he was sexy, so much so that my nipples turned into hard little peaks in my bra.

I need to get out of here.

I sat up quickly, wiping my mouth with the back of my hand while I prayed I hadn't been drooling. He chuckled as he straightened, standing to his full height once he'd laid my earbuds down on the table.

"I'm sorry," he said, stepping back as I frantically began gathering up my books to shove into my bag. "You seemed to be sleeping so soundly... I hated to wake you up, but the library is closing, so—"

"What?!" I stopped with my notebook half in, half out of my backpack to look at him. "Closing?"

He wrinkled his brow. "Yeah... it's eleven o'clock. *After* eleven actually. Like I said... sleeping soundly, and all of that."

"Elev— at night? Eleven at night?"

A thick, heavy feeling of dread settled over my chest as the weight of that realization hit me. His eyebrows pulled even closer to the middle of his forehead in concern, but I tuned him out as I hurriedly finished packing my bag and slung it over my shoulder, then snatched my cell phone from the table.

"I have to go," I mumbled as I skirted past him toward the door, so fast that I walked right out of one of my ballet-flat style shoes.

"Slow down, Cinderella. I'm sure the ball—or wherever you're headed in such a hurry – can wait." He smiled at me again, and a feeling I could only describe as warm and fuzzy pricked my skin, until I remembered I had somewhere to be.

Shoving my foot back into my shoe, I ran my fingers through my hair, brushing the kinky coils away from my face. I gave him a little half smile, thanked him for waking me up, then hauled ass for the front door.

Outside, I groaned at the blackness of the sky and pulled out my phone. My fingers shook as I unlocked the screen, then navigated to *Terrific Tech* in my phonebook and hit the dial button. I could already hear my manager fussing at me, but her fussing was the least of my worries. I hoped my ass wasn't about to get *fired*.

I stopped on the sidewalk, hugging myself with one arm. With my free hand, I pressed the phone to my ear, silently praying while I waited on someone to pick up.

"*Terrrr-ific Tech*, open til midnight on Fridays and Saturdays to service your late night electronic needs. How can I help you?"

I grinned at the sound of Mina's – my friend, roommate, and coworker – voice on the other end of the line. "To service your late night electronic needs? You know that sounds like a sex-toy shop slogan, right?"

"Only to your under-sexed behind, Lauren," she quipped back, a smile in her tone as she realized it was me. "What are you calling up here for?"

Lifting a hand to massage the back of my neck, I groaned, tipping my head back to look into the sky again. "To beg for my job. I'm like six hours late for my shift."

Mina scoffed. "*You*? Late? Lauren, that's not funny. You weren't even supposed to come in today."

"I come in *every* Saturday, what are you talking about?"

There was a pregnant pause on the line before Mina cleared her throat. "Uh, you do realize it's Friday, right?"

"No it's n— hold on." I pulled the phone from my ear and swiped my notification bar down to look at the date. Sure enough, there it was –Friday. My shoulders sagged with relief, and I closed my eyes as I brought the phone up to my ear again.

"Lo, you still on the line?"

"Yeah."

"Where are you?"

I looked back at the library, watching as the downstairs lights began to shut off, then looked ahead, *way* ahead, at our dormitory-style apartment building. The walk to get there wouldn't even take a whole ten minutes, but I was exhausted. "Just left the library. I ran out of there like I was on fire, thinking I'd missed a shift tonight."

On the other end of the line, Mina sighed. "Please take your confused ass to the apartment and get some sleep."

"I *got* some sleep," I groaned, a fresh wave of embarrassment hitting me as I thought about the handsome stranger who'd woken me up. Had my mouth been open? Had I been mumbling things in my sleep? "I went to the library right after class, at like three this afternoon. I remember getting interrupted my some random guy around four, but the next thing I remember after that is waking up to get kicked out of my study room so they could close up."

"So… you're telling me you fell asleep studying?"

"When *don't* I fall asleep studying Mina?"

She sighed again. "Good point. Get off the phone. I have to go look like I'm actually working until my shift is over in thirty minutes, and *you* need to get your butt in the bed. Bye."

Mina didn't wait for a response before I heard the distinctive click of the phone in the cradle, followed shortly by phone chiming to let me know the call had ended. I started walking again, toward my dorm.

Blakewood State University had a beautiful campus, obvious even at night. The sidewalks were well lit for safety, but the lights did double-duty, showcasing the gorgeous spring landscaping in the dark. My eyes fell to a long row of neatly trimmed, bright pink azaleas, and my heart grew heavy.

My impromptu nap had made me miss an opportunity to talk to Harper.

She was probably oblivious to it. Her little almost-four-year-old world was occupied with preschool, a puppy, and paternal grandparents this weekend, plenty of things to be distracted enough not to miss mommy. But mommy certainly missed *her*.

I sighed, kicking a stray rock in front of me down the sidewalk as I continued my trek to the shared apartment I called home. I made a mental note that a video call to my baby girl would be the first thing on my agenda for the morning.

By the time I made it to my front door, I felt a little better. I took a shower, changed into comfortable shorts and a tee shirt, then sat at the desk in my room with a salad and my *Systems Analysis and Design* textbook. I dipped a slice of cucumber in a puddle of vinaigrette then popped it into my mouth, leaning back in my office chair as I munched.

My book was open, but my thoughts were elsewhere, back in the library with the cutie who woke me up. I'd never seen him before, but Blakewood was a big school, with a majority black campus population. Seeing someone new wasn't exactly surprising.

Besides, I was pretty actively *not* looking for cute boys. Looking at cute boys is how I ended with Harper. Well... Mekhi and I were doing a lot more than *looking* at each other to conceive Harper, but my point remained.

No boys.

I didn't have the time.

Go to class, make perfect grades, go to work, go home and study, get some sleep. Go back to class, pass the tests, don't be late for work, don't forget to study, make sure you talk to Harper, and don't forget to do your homework. Don't forget to turn in the homework, don't miss class, don't put off studying, but you should probably take that extra shift at work, and today is important to Harper, the puppy's birthday, so don't forget to call before her bedtime.

Oh, and don't forget about those perfect grades.

But I wasn't supposed to complain. I preferred to think of Harper as more of a blessing than a mistake, but to pretend that getting pregnant at sixteen was an ideal situation was silly. Mekhi and I messed up, so it was up to us to be responsible for our child, and we did our best.

We were lucky enough to have parents who were willing to do what they could to give Harper the best chance at a good future. They took turns caring for her while Mekhi was off in the air force, and I went away to school.

It was a sacrifice on all parts, and something I didn't take lightly. I attacked school full force, took as many Advanced Placement classes as I could, and applied for every scholarship I was qualified for. I took courses at the local community college before I officially enrolled as a freshman at BSU, and I took advantage of the ability to "test out" of as many courses as possible. I took full course loads for fall, spring, and summer semesters, and as a result of all of that, I was now classified as a *senior* in college, coming up on my twenty-first birthday in a few months.

I was tired.

I was really, *really* tired.

But I shouldn't complain. I was doing what I needed to do, whatever I possibly could, to eventually provide as well as possible, as *soon* as possible, for my daughter. Nothing else really mattered.

Not sororities, no social life, and no cute boys who smelled like books.

But I wasn't complaining.

I finished off my salad, and forced myself to stay in my chair instead of searching out something to fulfill my sweet tooth. Regular exercise was another casualty of my crazy schedule, so I depended on walking to class and being on my feet at work to balance the not-that-healthy diet I maintained. Snacks were pushing it.

After a long swig from my water bottle, I pushed my empty bowl to the side and tried to focus on my book. We had an exam on Monday, and I hated being unprepared, but as I stared at the pages, the words began to swim together in a blur. I closed my eyes, hoping to clear my vision, and the next time I opened them, Mina was in front of me, impatiently shaking my shoulder.

I lifted my head, carefully peeling the delicate vellum of my book pages from my face. Mina shook her head, sending her thick curtain of bone straight hair swaying around her shoulders as she watched me unfold myself from my slumped position at the desk.

"What time is it?" I asked, yawning through the question as I stretched my arms over my head.

"A little after midnight… I see you fell asleep with your head in a book, *again*."

I gave her a wry smile, then stood up, keeping my hands on the chair for balance until my feet were steady underneath me. She followed me to the other side of my small bedroom, where I flicked off the lights then crawled into the bed, burrowing underneath the covers. A few seconds later, I scowled as she pulled the blankets away from me, taking them with her as she pushed the switch to illuminate the room again.

"Uh-uh girl. Last week you told me you were coming to this party with me. Get your ass up and get dressed."

I lifted an eyebrow, then really looked at Mina, noticing that she was out of her work uniform – lime green polo and khakis – and in skinny jeans and a cropped tank top that showed her pierced belly button.

Shit.

"Mina… come on, now. Weren't you just telling me to get some sleep?"

She sucked her teeth, propping a hand on her hip. "Yeah, and you obviously got it, from the way you were snoring into that book."

"I don't snore," I scoffed, to which she shot me a mischievous little grin.

"Wanna bet?"

I rolled my eyes, then rolled myself onto my back, propping my arms behind my head. "Not really. Seriously though… you know I'm not about to go out, right? When do I ever?"

"Um, that's exactly why I want you to. And you said you would."

"Was I fully awake?"

She shrugged. "Doesn't matter. Get your ass up."

I sat up, crossing my arms over my chest. "Mina… if I get up, it's not gonna be to go out. I need to study."

Mina growled, and made a gesture in the air like she wanted to choke me. "*Goddammit*, Lauren. Are you ever going do anything besides sleep, work, and study?"

I tipped my head to the side. "I'll do something besides sleep, work, and study when you stop making me regret the decision to split the rent. How about that?"

Silence reigned between us for a short moment before Mina curled her lip in mock disgust. "You are one *evil* smart bitch, you know that?"

"I love you though," I quipped back, blowing her a kiss across the room. She caught it, then smacked it to her butt as she turned for the door.

"Love you too, it's the only reason I stick around!" she tossed over her shoulder as she left – with my blanket.

I groaned, then flopped back onto my pillows, staring at the ceiling for a long time after she left. The textured paint seemed to swim before my eyes, morphing into a question that had haunted me long before Mina posed it.

Are you ever going to do anything besides sleep, work, and study?

Was I?

Could I?

Was I even allowed to do that?

I mean, Mina was right. I was only twenty years old, and my older sister, Bianca, had previously offered a similar sentiment as well. I was still young. Even though I did a good job – or so I thought – suppressing the desire to "have fun" it was certainly still there. I wanted to do a little underage drinking and dancing with people my age, experience the things my college peers were doing. I didn't want to be Little Miss Responsible all the time, the stick in the mud.

I wanted to… *live.*

I ran my tongue over my teeth as I thought about it for a second, then called out, "Mina, you gone yet?"

"Touching up my makeup as we speak," she yelled back.

I thought about it for another moment longer, then sat up, climbing out of the bed. I jogged to the open door of her bedroom and stepped inside to find her standing at her bathroom vanity with a tube of lipstick in her hand.

I called myself being casual as I leaned against the doorjamb, watching her in the mirror as she pressed the vibrant purple color to her lips. "So… who's hosting this party?"

Her hand stilled, and she moved the lipstick away from her mouth as her eyes shot up to mine. A little smile spread across her face as she lowered it back into the tube, then replaced the cap. "Alpha Phi Alpha. They usually keep it pretty clean. Party ends at three." She stuck the lipstick back in her makeup bag, then zipped the pouch closed. "So… whatcha gone do, Lo?"

I looked at her reflection, then looked at mine, suddenly feeling lightheaded with the pressure of making a decision. When I didn't answer after a full minute had passed, she shook her head, giving me a sympathetic pat on the shoulder as she squeezed past me in the door.

"Wait," I said, catching her by the hand and pulling her around to face me. "I…" I pushed out a heavy sigh, then squared my shoulders, holding my head high. "Help me find something to wear."

two
...
Lauren

IT TOOK me just under fifteen minutes to decide this party wasn't my scene.

My realization started with the "security" check at the door – a pat down by a guy in a black and gold lettered shirt, where the skimpier dressed girls got the more thorough "searches". It was pretty ridiculous, but I submitted to getting felt up under the guise of making sure I wasn't armed, then shot a *look* at Mina.

She paid for both of us to get in.

Per usual for this frat – according to Mina – the party was happening at a little off-campus event center called The Warehouse. It was my first time there, and I was already confident it would be my last, mostly because it more than lived up to its name. The building itself was rudimentary, the finished state of the walls and floors questionable. The few windows were blacked out, and big industrial grade fans whipped overhead, stirring around the not-quite-cool-enough air put out by one – maybe two – AC units propped in the windows.

The heavy thud of bass from the speakers rattled my chest and thundered in my ears, pumping popular rap into the room at an obscene volume. I cringed at the sight of so many of my female peers with so few clothes on—not because I was on any type of "be classy, not assy" nonsense, because screw that, wear what you want. I turned up my nose because it was hot, and when it got hot people got sweaty, and all these half-naked sweaty people... *Gross.*

"Why are you frowning?" Mina asked, putting her mouth right up against my ear for me to hear her. Before I could answer, she yanked me backward, away from the dance floor so I wouldn't get my shin kicked in by a group of girls in pink and green doing a "party strut" in a line.

I pulled back so Mina could see my face, and frowned harder, shaking my head. "I don't think this is for me," I mouthed, to which she shook her head and laughed.

"Can you give me an hour?" she asked, clasping her hands in front of her. "There's someone that I want to talk to, and he swore he would be here tonight. Let me find him, chill for a bit, and then we can go home, okay?"

I gave her a deadpan expression, and when she started to squirm under my gaze I finally rolled my eyes and nodded. "*Fine.* An hour, and then I'm going home with or without you."

Mina gave me a bright smile, and then disappeared into the crowd, leaving me alone. With every song, it seemed like the partygoers got a little more hype, a little more drunk, and the building got a little more stifling until finally I had to seek refuge with the other "lames", against the wall. After a bit longer, even *that* wasn't enough separation.

I slipped my phone from the pocket of my skinny jeans and checked the time.

Damnit.

There were still forty minutes left in Mina's hour, and I wasn't going to renege on giving her that time. Instead, I found my way outside, where a makeshift patio had been set up. Ten or fifteen people were gathered under the covered part of the area to smoke something that definitely wasn't cigarettes, but downwind of them, there were seats in the fresh, warm spring air.

A slight mist of rain was falling, but I didn't care. It felt good, revitalizing and cool against my skin, so I sat down on a varnished wood bench and propped my head back, letting the minuscule drops hit my face.

I should have stayed my behind in the bed. Thick crowds and loud parties had never been my thing. Not in high school, not freshman year, and certainly not *now*, when the idea of studying was honestly more appealing than where I was now. If I was boring, or a nerd for that... so be it.

Closing my eyes, I silently wished for the next forty minutes to pass as quickly as possible. As tired as I was, sitting there with my eyes shut quadrupled the risk of me falling asleep. From out here, with the refreshing mist in my face, the muffled, steady beat of the bass from inside the building was almost like a lullaby. My eyelids grew heavy, and the sounds around me began to dull into a rhythmic hum.

"So do you just sleep everywhere you go? Is that your thing or something? Just get comfortable as hell, wherever?"

My eyes shot open at the sound of a male voice, and a moment later, I was watching as the boy from the library sat down on the bench beside me, close enough that his jean-clad leg touched mine. My mouth was too dry to speak, so I just stared.

He had a short fro, chunky but tamed, tapered low on the sides. A cool haircut, for a cool, book smelling boy. But, as I kept staring, I realized "boy" probably wasn't accurate. He didn't have facial hair, but a faint shadow of stubble told me it was because he shaved, and he wasn't baby-faced by any means. Young, but not a boy. Nothing delicate about his features, with those brilliant eyes, wide nose, and full lips. A legitimately sexy *man*.

He sat back, casually draping his arm behind me on the bench, like we knew each other. I still couldn't remember how to use my tongue. Not to talk, or to shove it down his throat, which is what part of me wanted to do.

But no boys.

Fine... so what about a man?

Holy shit...I had to stop staring.

I turned my gaze to my hands, and he chuckled in response, enveloping me in a smooth, rich tone that definitely wasn't boyish. He sat forward, leaning so he could see my face. "Am I bothering you? If so, I'm sorry. I don't mean to—"

"No!" I said, too eagerly. I pressed my lips together and sat back. "You're not bothering me at all."

He smiled, and I had to look away from him again, because I wanted to climb in his lap and stare at that smile for the rest of the night.

"So what, you're just bashful or something?"

I shook my head, still not looking at him, defying my denial of being shy.

"Okay, so what is it then?" he asked, nudging my shoulder with his. "Wicked stepmother told you not to talk to anybody at the ball?" I bit my lip to keep from smiling at the Cinderella reference, but turned to him as he continued. "Is getting ready for this party why you were in such a hurry you damn near ran outta your shoes?"

I sucked my teeth. "Hell no. For this wack party? These frat parties are really not my preferred vibe."

The corners of his mouth twitched in a suppressed smile as he leaned back, draping his arm over the bench again. "*Damn.* Wack ass party, huh?"

"Definitely wack. All hot and stuffy, bootleg security, gross drin—" I stopped mid-sentence, covering my mouth as my eyes landed on the front of his black tee. Greek letters, printed in gold. Underneath, in white block letters: Security.

I swallowed hard. "You know... I—"

"Don't sweat it," he said, laughing again. "Truth be told, these parties aren't really *my* thing either, but everybody pitches in for the cause. The frat tells you they need somebody on the door, mixing drinks, keeping the music going… you do what you have to, right?"

"Right," I nodded. "Like working security. You weren't the one on grab-ass duty at the door, and you're sitting out here in one spot with me. So… I don't know if you're doing a very good job at this security thing."

His eyes went wide before he broke into another smile that I had to look away from. "You're going to put me on the spot like that, huh?"

I shrugged. "I mean…"

"Okay, okay." He ran his tongue over his lips, then sat forward again until we were shoulder to shoulder. His voice lowered, not exactly a whisper, but low enough that he had an excuse to speak right into my ear, the minty coolness of his breath tickling my neck. "Tell me this… do you feel secure right now?"

My lips parted over a quick, silent intake of breath, and I turned my head to meet his gaze. His mouth wasn't smiling anymore, but his eyes still were. Bright, and inviting, and waiting for my response.

"Yeah." That little truth came out in a breathless whisper before I realized it *was* a truth, that yeah, I felt secure. I felt good.

"Then it sounds like I'm doing my job." He nudged my shoulder again, and the contact made goose bumps erupt all over my skin, and an unfamiliar tightness blossomed in the pit of my stomach. I wanted to look away again but I couldn't, like my gaze was magnetized to his. "What's your name, pretty girl?"

"Lauren," I said, automatically. Just earlier that day, I'd given one of the campus boyfriends – one of *those* guys, who was fooling with so many girls that he was all of our man – a hard time about telling him my name, but I felt no such inclination now. I would have told this guy anything he wanted to know.

"Nice to meet you Lauren. Everybody calls me Ty." He

extended his hand toward me, and I returned the gesture. His larger palm engulfed mine, his skin pleasantly warm, humming with energy, making my heart race even faster.

"Nice to formally meet you as well."

I slipped my hand away from his, tucking both of mine into my lap as I silently willed myself to stop acting so wet behind the ears. Ty was just a boy—a man. He was just a man. A very, very sexy man, but still. No reason to freak out, and get all weird.

"So, *Lauren*. Parties aren't your thing, so what do you like to do? Besides sleep and study?"

I shrugged. "I don't do much else. Don't really have time to."

"Heavy course load? I saw your books… looks pretty serious. Those are senior level courses, right?"

"Right. And I have job, at Terrific Tech, so that keeps me pretty busy too."

And plus a kid. You know, the tiny humans that tend to take up a lot of your time.

I thought it, but didn't say it out loud, and immediately felt guilty for it. *Hiding* Harper… is that what I was doing right now? Ty was saying something about Terrific Tech, and how hard it is to maintain a job while keeping up your grades, but I wasn't listening. I felt a little sick… but was I doing anything wrong? I mean, I barely knew this guy, we were just sitting here talking. I didn't owe him every – or any, honestly – detail of my life, but consciously *not* saying anything didn't sit right.

I nodded, agreeing with his assessment of balancing school and a job, and the next time he stopped to let me speak, I said, "Yeah, so I'm doing all of that, school and work. And I have a little girl, almost four years old now."

His eyes went wide in surprise, and I waited to see how he would extricate himself from the conversation. Would he suddenly remember something he had to do, would his presence be needed in the party, would he—"

"There you are!"

I looked up to see Mina, her expression pinched in annoyance, walking up to where Ty and I sat on the bench. "I've been looking for you, I thought you left without me. You ready to go? It's past an hour, and people are starting to leave." She looked at me, then suddenly, she realized Ty was not only there, but that we'd been interacting. Understanding crossed her face as he glanced up at her with a smile, and she shot him a grin back, then cringed at me.

"Sorry, Lo. I can give you guys some—"

"No," I said, springing up from my seat on the bench. "It's fine, I need to get home anyway, get some sleep. I'll see you around, Ty."

Before either could respond, I grabbed Mina's hand and led her around the building toward the parking lot, where people were starting to make their way to their cars.

"Who was *that*?" Mina asked as she pressed the button on her keys to unlock the doors. "Did I see that right? *You* were talking to a man? And a *sexy* one at that?"

"Whatever Mina." I climbed into the car and clicked into my seatbelt, ignoring her continued teasing as she started the car and we began the slow creep to get out of the parking lot. I caught a glimpse of Ty, helping direct the hectic flow of traffic to funnel people onto the street, and immediately looked away. There was no point in entertaining that fantasy.

First of all, he was a young, handsome guy. I highly doubted he was interested in doing the whole single mom thing. Secondly, I had no business thinking about him like that anyway.

"Lo," Mina said, as we finally turned onto the main street. "Why are you acting all secretive? What's up with you and that guy?"

I shook my head. "Nothing. I've told you before, I'm all about my grades right now. No boys."

We pulled to a stop light, and Mina turned to me, her face illuminated by the lights from the street. "Lauren, sweetie… he didn't look like a *boy* to me."

three
. . .
lauren

AN INSISTENT CHIME in my ear pulled me out of my sleep. As I felt blindly over the surface of my night stand, I mumbled *"Just a second"* into my pillow, as if it would carry through to the person on the other end of the line. When my hand finally made contact with the phone, I lifted my head to look at the screen and smiled. I sat up, sliding the green icon across my screen to answer the call.

"Your hair looks funny mommy."

My mouth dropped open in surprise, but then I laughed at Harper's failing attempt to suppress her giggles. She had her little pink-glitter-polished hand pressed to her mouth, her round cheeks flushed red with effort.

"Good morning to you too, silly chickadee," I said, lifting my hands to my head. I'd taken a quick shower, then fallen into bed with no efforts at preserving my hair for the next day. Now it was sticking straight up, in a tangled mess I would have to tend to before I could even think about leaving the apartment.

"G'morning mommy. Puppy got in trouble."

I gasped, widening my eyes in feigned shock. "Not your sweet puppy, oh no! What did he do?"

Harper looked around, her sweet face suddenly growing very serious as she brought the phone closer to her face. "He went pee-pee on Gamma's couch," she whispered. "He had to go outside."

"Ohh, that's not good baby. What did grandma say about Puppy's future?"

I knew for a fact that "Gamma" – Mehki's mother, Tanya – hadn't wanted anything to do with a dog in her house, but she hadn't quite yet mastered the ability to say "no" to Harper's tears. The simply named "Puppy", a fluffy white Pomeranian, might be looking for a new home after such an incident.

Harper obviously didn't share my concern, because her face broke into another smile. "Puppy got to go live with Pop-Pop to learn not to piss on people's furniture."

I blinked one.

Twice.

A third time.

"Say that again, baby?"

Harper groaned. "*Puppy* is living with *Pop-Pop* to learn not to *piss* on people's *furniture*." She gave me a deadpan look, as if to say "did you catch it this time, slowpoke", and I had to bite my lip not to laugh. Mrs. Tanya must have been really mad.

"Chickadee, mommy doesn't want you using the word "piss", okay? Let's stick with pee-pee for now."

"But Gamma—"

"Harper..." I lifted my eyebrow at the phone, knowing that even from a screen, my "look" held the same power of persuasion. "I don't care what grandma said, she's a grown up. I'm telling you that I don't want *you* using that word. Okay?"

Harper's eyes went a little wide, and she nodded her head. "Okay mommy, yes ma'am. I sowwy."

"It's okay baby," I smiled. "Now, you were quick to tell me

about Puppy getting in trouble, but how has *your* behavior been?"

She brightened up immediately at that question, giggling so hard that she was barely able to get out any words.

"Calm down, chicky. Mommy can't understand what you're saying."

"I got a medal, mommy!" she repeated, speaking clearly this time. "For good ba-hay-vor at school, and I wasn't whispering at nap time!"

I doubted the veracity of that, but I let my baby have her moment and clapped for her. "Good job Harper! Mommy is so proud of you!"

"Thank you! Love you mommy gotta go!"

Before I could even respond, her pretty little golden-brown face and mass of curly hair were gone from the screen, and the call had ended. I shook my head and chuckled as I glanced at the time, knowing that she "had to go" to get her morning Doc Mcstuffins fix.

Sure enough, a few moments later when my cell rang with a normal voice call from her grandmother, I could hear Harper belting out the theme song in the background.

"Good morning, Mrs. Tanya," I said, smiling into the phone as Harper finished singing.

"Good morning sweetheart. I see Harper abandoned you for Doc this morning."

I laughed. "Yeah, second-class-citizen here. She's still not giving you any trouble is she?"

"*Never*," was the immediate response. "Harper is a sweet child, no more trouble than her daddy was at this age. And speaking of Mekhi…" – I rolled my eyes at her attempt at subtlety – "He's coming home for a few days here soon. I'm sure Harper would love to have her mom and dad with her at the same time."

Right.

Harper would love to have me and Mekhi at the same time.

Mmmhm.

To Mrs. Tanya's credit, it was probably true that her little heart would burst with joy at the prospect, but there was another angle. It wasn't exactly a secret that Mekhi's mother wanted the two of us to get back together, and raise Harper as a nuclear family. Neither she, her husband, *nor* Mekhi and my own father seemed to understand that Mekhi being a "good guy" wasn't compelling enough for me to marry him.

Mekhi and I had been friends since we were ten, and that developed into a relationship in our very early teens, which developed into… a baby. He was the only boyfriend I've ever had, my first and only partner in sexual experience. I wasn't comfortable with the idea that he was the beginning and end, especially when, as an adult, I couldn't say with certainty that we'd ever had real chemistry.

He and I broke up shortly after Harper was born. We were always arguing, constantly stressed and at each other's throats, and as teenagers, neither of us felt like it was worth the hassle. We were committed to our baby – not each other, and I shed no tears over the end of the relationship.

As young adults, we got along well as friends and parents, but we were hardly ever physically in each other's presence. He'd joined the Air Force at eighteen, and got 30 days of leave time per year. I scheduled my time with Harper around his, mostly. Our families came together for holidays, and that was it. Certainly no time to develop romantic feelings – despite Mrs. Tanya's best persuasive efforts.

I hurried her off the phone as quickly as I could without being rude, promising her I would think about trying to see Mekhi when he came home.

I thought about it.

No.

Tossing the phone onto my nightstand, I stretched my arms above my head and my legs in front of me, trying to shake away any lingering fatigue. I needed to get my butt up. I had an exam bright and early Monday morning, and until then, the library would be my best friend.

I *could* study at home, but there was something about the academic energy that flowed in the library that seemed to make me absorb everything better. I felt smart when I studied at the library, like there was no *Business Statistics* question too complicated to answer, no system database too complicated to unravel. I *never* doubted my ability to successfully complete my MIS – Management Information Systems, a sort of hybrid Business/Computer Science degree – coursework when I was there.

But of course, thinking about the library made me think about Ty.

That very first interaction with him was seared into my mind in clear-cut detail. Opening my eyes to look right into his, staring back with an intensity that felt like he was looking into my soul. And then last night, when he'd touched me... I shivered a little, then fell back onto my pillows with my eyes closed. It was pretty pitiful, that the mere memory of a shoulder bump and a hand shake had me throbbing between the thighs.

Mina had called me under-sexed yesterday, and it was painfully true.

Well... depending on who you asked.

My father, for example, if he knew such details of my life, would probably think that I was having the perfect amount of sex.

None.

A part of me agreed with that sentiment, because in the long list of things I needed in my life, another child didn't even make the list. And sex leads to babies, right?

Of course, Mekhi and I hadn't exactly been careful, because we were stupid teenagers. The gravity of "forgetting" a condom hadn't hit us until those two pink lines showed up on that little plastic stick. These days, a low dose birth control pill accompanied my morning vitamins, although I wasn't doing anything to need that kind of protection.

For one, I was too damned busy to maintain any semblance of a relationship. Between work, school, and Harper, I didn't have the free time for trips to the movies and late night phone calls, and I wasn't into the social-media centric relationships that many of my peers seemed to be into. Plus, even though I'd recently encouraged my older sister into a fling that ended up being much more, I wasn't really down with casual sex.

But, hormones.

I was great at keeping them at bay, typically. I got my fair share of male attention, but by and large, they came at me completely wrong, with corny lines or blatant disrespect. It was like a day to day game of Battleship, figuring out the perfect response that would allow me to walk away from rejecting an advance without getting called a bitch, or otherwise verbally – or God forbid, physically – attacked. But those encounters left me dry as a bone anyway.

For me, it was the ones like Ty that made it hard to maintain the strength to keep my legs closed. Laid back, smart, sexy without seeming like he knew he was.

And there's the whole smelling like the fresh pages of a brand new book thing.

Yes, *that*.

And that smile.

And those eyes.

And those lips.

And… damn I was pitiful.

1. I didn't even know Ty. He'd offered me nothing but conversation, and I was ready to start coaching myself on not having sex with him.

2. He probably wasn't that interested in me like that anyway. He hadn't asked for a number, email, nothing, and now that he knew about Harper...
3. I was at the library when I smelled him, and I basically fell asleep in my textbook. I was all messed up in the head about a guy who smelled like books, when it probably wasn't even *him*. Silly ass.

I climbed out of bed and went into the bathroom to brush my teeth and wash my face, so I could get a trip to the library in before I reported for my shift at the store. When I was done, I dressed and packed my backpack, making sure to include my laptop, then headed into the kitchen to grab a granola on my way out.

I found Mina sweating at the counter, still dressed in active wear from her morning workout.

"Tough run this morning?" I asked, turning my back to her as I opened the cabinet.

She grunted something under her breath, but didn't lift her head until I was facing her again. "Tough isn't the word. Torturous. Overwhelming. Exhausting. Something more like *that*."

I shook my head, and gave her a sympathetic smile as I peeled the wrapper from my granola. "Marathon training getting to you?"

"*Getting to me* isn't the—wait, I did that already did that, didn't I?"

"Yep."

"Okay. Well, *yes*. The marathon training is kicking our ass. Why did I think I could do this again? Why did I want to do this?"

I swallowed my mouthful of oats and raisins, then grinned. "Because a certain dark chocolate somebody with locs runs marathons."

Mina's head shot up. "Girl... I have no idea who you're talking about..." she said, eyes darting from me, to her hands, then up to the ceiling.

"You're a horrible liar," I laughed. "Do you really think I don't know you were running behind Austin, and that's who you were trying to meet at that party?"

She cringed. "Why would you think that? That boy's parents named him after the city they live in. What would I look like with Austin, from Austin, Texas?"

"Oh girl, please." I sucked my teeth. "Don't try to cover it up. It's a little suspicious how you suddenly became a runner when he told us he was going to participate in the charity marathon for the school."

Austin was a senior, like us – Mina and Austin were both older than me, 23 and 22 – and another one of our coworkers at Terrific Tech. Mina had been crushing on what she referred to as his "African warrior" appeal since he started work there last summer. I had no idea why she was faking like she wasn't interested with me, of all people.

"Wait a minute," I said, narrowing my eyes. "You said, the marathon training is kicking "our" asses... did you run with him this morning, while you're sitting here lying to my face?"

"I...yes. I did." She shrugged at me, her expression contrite. "But seriously, Lo, don't get all mushy on me like you did when I first told you I liked him. I found out today that I probably have like, zero chance anyway."

I screwed my face into a scowl. "Um, why the hell not? You're beautiful, smart, funny, sweet, what's not to like?"

"Apparently," she started, turning on her barstool to reach down and begin removing her shoes, "Austin doesn't like "shallow, superficial" girls. And I mean... hello?" She swept her a hand in front of her, indicating her perfectly sewn weave, perfectly arched brows, and perfectly coordinated running outfit, down to the matching shoes. Any other time, she would have a perfectly made up face as well.

"He actually said that to you?"

Mina nodded. "Yeah. Well... not like, to *me*, as if he were talking about me, he was just talking in general. But it was seriously like a slap in the face, and I still had to run two more miles with him. I'm pretty sure those were my fastest miles ever."

I wanted to laugh, but her expression was such a mask of disappointment that I suppressed the urge. I tossed my breakfast wrapper in the trash, and followed her into her room as she tossed her shoes into the closet, then began stripping off her sweaty workout gear.

"Mina, if he didn't intend it personally, you shouldn't take it personally. I mean... you're not those things. You're one of the sweetest people I know."

I wasn't just saying that to make her feel better either. As appearance obsessed as she was, that preoccupation didn't extend further than herself. She wasn't mean or bitchy about the way other people looked, and as fixated as she was on always – her words – "being ready so she didn't have to *get* ready", she wasn't afraid to get dirty... she just wanted to take a long, luxurious soak to get clean afterward.

"Thanks for the vote of confidence Lo, but I'm not that convinced. At least my abs will look great this summer though, right?" She tossed a smile over her shoulder as she stepped into the bathroom, but her eyes gave me sadness. I didn't have a chance to say anything else before she closed the door, and I took that as my cue she wanted to be by herself. With a heavy sigh, I left her room, grabbing my backpack and phone on the way out of the apartment.

The weather was nice, so I took my time on my walk, and fifteen minutes later, I walked through the front door of the library ready to work.

four
...
ty

I FELT her before I saw her.

Like we had somehow already gotten on the same wavelength, I lifted my eyes to the main doors of the library as they slid open for Lauren to walk in.

Flawless, rich brown skin, a lush, thick fro of kinky-curly hair, big brown eyes that held a maturity that didn't match the youthfulness of her face, and pretty, kissable, full lips that curved into a smile as she spoke to another library patron. Lauren was a natural sort of sexy, the type that snuck up on you, well after your brain had registered "prettiness".

I closed my book, because I already knew there was little chance of me focusing with her in the same building. The library was crowded this morning anyway, and I was being hounded with constant interruptions. Directions to this, instructions for that... all part of my job, but still distractions from the studying I needed to do. I couldn't complain about that though, not when I was dropping what I was doing to creep on Lauren.

Two giggling – most likely freshmen – girls approached the desk, and I smiled because I smiled at everybody, but that sent them into another round of loud giggles. By the time they actually asked me a question and I provided an answer, Lauren was well out of sight.

Damn.

I flipped my book open again and tried to focus, but the words weren't making any sense. Again, I snapped it closed, abandoning it to pull the steady-growing pile of books from the return drop, neatly arrange them on a push cart, then head for the shelves, leaving my coworkers to handle the front desk.

The task of re-shelving books held two purposes. First, the required focus would help me clear my thoughts enough that when I went back to *Modeling of Integrated Information Systems*, I would actually be able to get something done. Secondly… it would take me past the windowed study rooms, where I would be able to catch a glimpse of Lauren.

Or so I thought.

To my disappointment, she wasn't in any of the rooms, and I'm pretty sure I had a scowl on my face as I shoved *Pot Liquor: A Guide to Cooking Modern Soul Food With Love, by Charlie and Nixon Graham* back onto the shelf.

"What the hell did that cookbook do to you?"

A warm hand slid up my arm, and I turned to look into the face of evil.

I mean… Jamila.

As always, she looked good. Glowing caramel skin, honey-blonde tipped locs resting on her shoulders, and pretty hazel eyes that made her look sweet.

Look sweet.

"What can I do for you Jamila?" I asked, pushing my cart along without waiting for her to answer.

Behind me, she sucked her teeth, then quickened her stride to catch up to me. "What's with the formality? Are we really not past that yet?"

Not really.

"*Ty,*" she sang, dragging out the "y".

I hated when she did that shit.

She slid her hand up my bicep and underneath the sleeve of my tee shirt, then hooked her arm around mine, using it to pull herself close. I rolled my eyes, but didn't push her away like I wanted, because we were in the middle of a crowded place. Instead, I gently extricated myself from her grip, dodging her attempts to hook me again.

"*Goddamnit,* how many arms do you have?" I backed away, holding out my hands to keep her back. "*Fucking octopus,*" I muttered under my breath, which earned me a scowl.

"Don't be an asshole, Tyson. I just want to talk to you, is that a crime?"

I blew out a heavy sigh, then turned to her, giving her my undivided attention. "What is it, J?"

She raised an eyebrow at me, then glanced around at the people walking past. "Can we like... go somewhere? Speak privately?"

"You came and found me at work, so say what you need to say."

I crossed my arms and stared at her, making sure to keep my expression blank. Goal: make this shit as uncomfortable as possible for her.

"*Ugh,*" she groaned, glancing around us again. "I was wondering, if you wanted to grab something to eat, and—"

"No."

Her mouth dropped open, and she looked at me as if I'd said something in a foreign language. "What do you mean, *no?*"

"Well, I mean a negative answer, used to express refusal or dissent. A denial of—"

"*Tyson!*"

I smiled innocently, like I didn't know why she was upset. "Yes, J?"

"Could you cut the dictionary bullshit? You knew what I meant."

"Honest mistake," I insisted, rocking back on the balls of my feet. "I didn't realize you heard *no* often enough to understand the meaning. Figured it seemed like a foreign language to you."

Jamila huffed, rolling her eyes as she pulled a handful of locs away from her face, tucking them behind her shoulder. "You're *not* funny, Ty. If you can act like an adult for two seconds, I'd like us to make plans. We can sit down over a meal, and discuss… *us*."

There was a short moment where neither of us said anything. She was waiting on my response, and I was waiting on the punchline, because hell no. "You can't be serious right now, if you think there's an *us* to talk about."

"Well, I was hopi—"

"You shouldn't."

Those words left my mouth and hung in the air between us, until Jamila shook her head. "Ty… I don't understand why you're doing this to me. It's been almost six months, and people are starting to talk. They're asking about the wedding."

I shrugged, giving her a look of complete disinterest. "You say that like I should care. But I don't."

That seemed to sting her, and for a second I felt bad, until she held up the backside of her hand up to me. "This used to *mean* something to you," she said, using her other hand to point to the two carats of diamonds in a white gold setting, a purchase I now affectionately referred to as "stupid tax". I'd never asked for it back, nor did I expect her to give it. It *did* surprise me to see it on her hand, but knowing that was a satisfaction I would never give her.

I glanced at the ring, then looked back at her with a wry smile. "It used to, yeah. But you fucked that up, didn't you J?"

She scoffed, then dropped her hand. "Fuck you, Ty."

"I hope you have a wonderful day. Thanks for visiting the

library at Blakewood State University, hope to see you again soon," I called to her retreating back as she stomped away. Over her shoulder, she flipped me off, and I chuckled, then turned back to my task of re-shelving books.

∼

lauren

It was stupid.

Really.

Like… insanely stupid to be bothered that a guy who wasn't my boyfriend – hell, he wasn't even a friend… hell, I barely even knew him – was talking to another girl.

Girls.

Like, plural.

So maybe the gigglers didn't count. He had to talk to them, had to be nice, because he was at work. In the library. As in, Ty worked at the library. As if he needed any other points in the sexy category for me.

But the other girl, the gorgeous one, with the locs. *That* girl counted, definitely.

I couldn't hear their conversation anyway, and tried not to look, but what was I supposed to do when they were right in front of me? I cursed the people taking up the private study rooms – if I was in there, I wouldn't have to witness this – and tried to mind my business.

Tried.

I was relieved when she finally walked away from him, and fully aware of how crazy it was to feel that way. But he was fine, and I wanted him, and even though nothing would ever happen between us, a girl could dream, right? And his arms… exactly how much book shelving did one have to do for biceps like that?

I tore my gaze away.

I had to stop looking at him, before I got caught being a weirdo. I could wish for, and fantasize, and imagine, and – shit, where did he go? While I was visualizing what Ty might have underneath his royal blue BSU tee shirt, he'd slipped away from my line of sight, and of course I felt a little disappointed. But what I *needed* to do was get back to my work.

In the three years since Mekhi and I stopped being a "thing", I could count on one hand – to be specific, three fingers – the number of guys I'd been intensely attracted to, to the point of distraction.

There was Wes, in my senior year of high school, who was so quiet that everybody else thought he was weird, but really his home life was so fucked up that school was solace for him. He didn't want the rest of us interrupting his peace. Well... not us. Them. He liked *me*. He kissed me one day, out of the blue, in the closet beside the teacher's lounge. The next day, he and his mother moved away, and I never saw him again.

The summer between freshman and sophomore year, there was Reggie, from the football team, who I tutored for the computer science class he was making up so he could play next season. Brilliant at his chosen athletic, but just plain lazy with academics. He was gorgeous though, mahogany skin and broad shoulder and big hands, and he always worked hard to impress me. He was another one of those "everybody's boyfriend" types though, so I wouldn't let him touch me. But I certainly *looked*. I was a huge BSU football fan that year.

And then, there was Ty: a potentially huge crush, happening way too fast, with no assistance from him.

"You know, you're really living up to this Cinderella thing, with the way you keep running away."

My heart leapt somewhere in the vicinity of my tonsils at the sound of Ty's voice in my ear, and the pleasant warmth of his breath on my skin. I swallowed hard, tempered my facial expression into something like neutral, then glanced his way.

"It's rude to interrupt people when they're studying. You know that, right?"

I had no idea why I chose such a pissy response, but I turned my eyes back to my screen, willing the rise and fall of my chest into a slower rhythm. Ty didn't need to know he made my heart race. Beside me, he chuckled a little.

Because of the way he was sitting, straddling the bench-style seat, he was turned in my direction. Any attempt to calm myself was lost as he moved closer to me, and the heat of his gaze against my face just made adrenaline pump faster.

"What if I'm not interrupting?" he asked. When I looked at him again, his eyes were bright with amusement. "I'm helping you study."

I couldn't keep the skepticism off my face. "How exactly are you helping me?"

"I can point out a problem with the code you're writing."

Frowning, I looked to my computer, where I'd been practicing writing several code snippets from memory for one of my programming language classes. "You've been sitting here for two seconds, and you've checked my code? How do I know you're not just trying to make conversation?"

"Because," – he covered my hand, which was still on the laptop's touchpad, with his. Our gazes met, and he smiled. "I'll show you the error." I held my breath, unable to make my eyes leave his face as he guided my hand. Instead of the smoothness of the day before, his jaw was covered with a thin layer of hair. But rather than making him look scruffy and unwashed, it made the compulsion to touch him even harder to ignore than it already was.

"Right here," he said, tipping his head toward the screen to direct my gaze there. Reluctantly, I turned my attention to what he was showing me, and sure enough, I'd typed the wrong thing.

I ran my tongue over my teeth, then looked back at him. "Um... how did you find my mistake so quickly?"

He shrugged. "I've had this class, plus all the ones after it."

"*Really?*" I lifted an eyebrow, not in disbelief, but genuine surprise. "What's your major?"

"Information Management Systems. PhD program."

My eyebrow went higher. "PhD program? Seriously?"

"What?" he asked, the corners of his mouth twitching, threatening to smile. "I don't look like the type or something?"

Well... no, actually. Of course I wasn't about to say it, but he *didn't* look like the type. He seemed too cool, I guess, for a PhD in science. And too young for it as well.

"Ummm..."

Ty laughed, and my heart skipped a few beats.

"It's aiight, I know I'm not the typical twenty-five year old, whatever that is."

Twenty...five?

Ty kept talking, but my mind went somewhere else. Twenty-freaking-five, while I was twenty. Was that too old for me? As long as we were both in the same decade, that was fine, right?

"So what's *your* major?" he asked, as I shifted focus back onto his words. "I'm gonna guess it's something IT related, since you're coding, right?"

I nodded, swallowing hard to wet my suddenly dry throat.

Twenty-five.

Grown.

I'm barely not a freaking teenager.

"Yeah, MIS. Management In—"

"—formation Systems. Yeah, I know. You get tired of having to explain it every time, don't you?"

Again, I just nodded, feeling like a bobble-head.

"That was actually my major in undergrad too. Masters in Computer Science, then straight into this program, which is... can I tell you a secret?"

"Yes," I said immediately, just above a whisper.

He smiled, then leaned toward my ear. "I'm really fucking sick of school."

I pulled away from him, giggling as I met his eyes.

"But you can't tell anybody that, okay?" he said, touching my hand. "Everybody thinks I love BSU so much that I can't let it go. And don't get me wrong, I *do* love BSU, but really... I'm just tryna get this shit over with so I don't have to come back. You feel me?"

"I do." I gave him a little smile of affirmation instead of nodding, then slipped my hand away from his, into my lap.

"What about you?" He propped his elbow on the table, resting his head on his knuckles. "You said you were a senior, right? What's next for you? Going for the Master's?"

I shook my head. "Nah. Not yet, at least. Once I finish undergrad, I'm hitting the pavement, looking for a real job."

"A real job? You're saying Terrific Tech isn't a real job or something?"

"Ehh, not exactly," I giggled. "It's fine for now, for part time, when I'm splitting the rent. But I want to use the degree I've busted my ass for. And of course, take care of myself."

"And your daughter," he added, smiling. Immediately, I felt heat creep up my face, and for the second time in two days I was glad for my deep brown complexion. If it weren't for that, I would have turned bright red. "You know you didn't have to run off like that last night, right? What did you think, I wouldn't want to have a conversation with you because you have a kid?"

I shrugged, not meeting his eyes. "I don't know. Sometimes people get weird about it."

Ty scowled a little. "Why? I think it's pretty dope, personally. A kid, work, school... which I'm going to assume you're pretty good at since you're always studying. You're balancing all of that and don't look like you're about to lose your mind or pass out, so I'd say you should be proud. You had your little girl at what, eighteen, nineteen?"

I swallowed hard. "Sixteen."

"See? You're out here beating the odds, fucking up these people's statistics," he laughed. Relief started hammering away at the nervousness in my chest. Until his expression changed. He went from amused to baffled, as if he were working something out in his head. "Wait… didn't you tell me your daughter was four?"

"Almost, yeah."

He narrowed his eyes. "So, if you had her at sixteen that makes you…"

"Twenty."

I was back to whispering for some reason, and couldn't help the razor sharp stab of hurt in the pit of my stomach when he shifted away from me. It was just a slight shift, so subtle that he probably didn't even realize he'd done it.

"Twenty," he repeated, in a stifled tone, like the word was uncomfortable in his mouth. And why wouldn't it be? A twenty-year old mother of a four year old wasn't exactly a *comfortable* situation.

"I've gotta get to work." I closed my laptop without saving my work, then shoved it back into my bag. I was already up from my seat, swinging the strap over my shoulder when Ty snapped out of whatever little trance he was in, and stood.

"Hey, I'm sorry I interrupted your study time."

I tipped my head back, looking up him. He had one hand shoved in his pocket, the other lifted the rub the nape of his neck.

"No big deal," I replied, shaking my head. Waiting for him to get out of my way.

He lifted an eyebrow. "I don't know… you kind of needed it, you fucked up that code." He smiled after that, trying to lighten the air.

I didn't laugh.

"Yeah, I know that code up and down. I only messed up because I… never mind." No way I was about to tell him I messed up because I was distracted, watching him interact with the girl with the locs. "I'll see you around."

I eased around him, not giving him a chance to respond before I was halfway across the library. I couldn't get out of there fast enough, and as I swept through the big glass double-doors, it felt a little like déjà vu: running from the library to get away from Ty.

∼

MINA WASN'T HOME WHEN I GOT BACK TO MY PLACE, SO I FLOPPED across my bed, covering my eyes with my arm. Why did I feel so awful about Ty's reaction to my age? He hadn't even said anything, but still. Just that little subtle movement, the compulsion to get away from the teen mom in case it rubbed off on him, made my eyes sting.

I pushed out a heavy sigh, then dropped my arm to stare up at the ceiling. I did that so much you'd think I knew every line and bump by now, every variation in the texture. And that was... pitiful.

Rolling onto my stomach, I snatched my phone from my nightstand, unlocked the screen, and navigated to my dialer. From memory, I punched in ten numbers, then pressed the button to initiate the call.

"Hello?!" Bianca answered breathlessly, just before I was about to give up and end the call. On the other end of the line, she giggled, and despite my foul mood, I smiled. I knew exactly what that giggle meant – she was with her boyfriend, Rashad. They were probably cuddled together, in one of their beds or on one of their couches. Flirting, touching, loving on each other like normal people did. The kind of thing I wanted to do.

But Ty thinks you're undesirable, so... blah.

"Lo, are you there?"

"Yeah," I replied, shaking my head. "Sorry, I... I got distracted. Are you busy with Rashad? I can call later if you—"

"No, no. He's actually leaving right now. I can talk. Are you okay?"

I blew out a little sigh, then sat up. "Yeah. No. I don't know," I whined. "I..."

"It's about a boy, isn't it?"

"How do you know?"

Bianca laughed, on the other end of the line. "Because you never get flustered about anything else. You're pretty damned good at articulating yourself Lo, so when you can't..."

"Got it," I said, fighting a smile of my own. "Yes, it's a boy. Well, I guess I can't really call him a boy, since I found out today that he's twenty-five."

She sucked her teeth. "You say that like it's old."

I didn't bother to suppress my smile over that. Ty was actually the same age as Bianca, so it wasn't that I necessarily thought it was old, it was just older than me.

"Anyway, what's going on? What man has your little panties wet girl?"

"*Eww*, B!"

"What?" she laughed. "If you're all tongue-tied it's because he turns you on, don't be embarrassed. Spill the beans, what's his name? What's his sign?"

"His name is Ty, and I don't know his sign, but he's an Alpha, he works at the library, he's in a PhD program in the same field as me, he has a little mini-fro, beautiful brown eyes, beautiful brown skin, and his biceps... *lord*."

"You are so far gone, Lo." I could hear the smile in her voice as she spoke. "Nerdy, but cool, and fine too? Poor you. Have you been out with him yet?"

I sighed, again. "No. I just met him yesterday, but we keep bumping into each other. We've only talked for a little bit. But he's too old for me anyway."

"What?" Bianca sucked her teeth. "You're twenty, he's twenty five. That's not a big deal. Besides… you're not exactly a "typical" twenty year old, sis. Hell, you're more mature than a lot of thirty-somethings I know."

I knew Bianca meant that as a compliment, so I suppressed the sigh I felt in my spirit. There was no way she could know how deathly tired I was of hearing that I was *so* mature for my age, and *so* different from a normal twenty year old. For someone who craved a little more freedom, and a little less responsibility, it made me uncomfortable to accept accolades for simply making the best I possibly could of the situation I'd created.

"It's not just that," I continued. "I told him about Harper, and he lost interest. So there's that."

For a moment Bianca was quiet. "Lo, are you sure you didn't misunderstand?"

"I… no."

"Okay, well, don't jump to conclusions."

"I'm pretty comfortable with that jump, B. If he was interested, he would have asked for a number, an email, something."

"Not necessarily. Maybe he's nervous."

I scoffed. "No. You haven't met this guy. Three times now, he's been completely comfortable approaching me first. He's charming, smooth, never without something to say. If he wanted me, he would have made it clear by now."

"Okay, well fuck him," Bianca shot back. "If he really thinks you're not good enough because of my gorgeous niece, he can swallow a bag of dicks. There are plenty of sexy, eligible men on that campus, Lauren. And *you* are friggin' gorgeous, smart, and dope as hell, so who's next? Are you even ready to date? I thought you said you were off that, until you were done with school."

Sliding down from the bed, I walked over to my closet to retrieve my polo and khakis for work. "That declaration still stands. It's probably for the best that he wasn't interested, because I need to focus on finishing out this year anyway. Ty was going to be a distraction."

There was another long pause on the line, a key indicator that Bianca wasn't buying what I was trying to sell, but she didn't push it. She pushed a different button instead. "So what are you going to do," she asked, "when you finish with school, and you start working, are men going to be a distraction then too? Are you going to put off dating a little longer, so you can get a strong foothold at your job, and then a little longer so you can get that promotion, and even longer while you work hard for another one? Put it off until Harper graduates high school? College?"

"Seriously, B?" I huffed. "You act like there would be something wrong with focusing on Harper, focusing on my career, instead of dating. You know, getting a man isn't some magic key to happiness."

"Oh *pleeeease*, Lauren! If nobody else knows that shit, *I* know it, so save your little soapbox rant for somebody else, okay? Get a boyfriend, a girlfriend, marry your damn self, I don't care, I just want to see you happy, and we both know what that means for you, you've told me about it a million times. A man, a house, Harper and a little brother. Rejection of traditional gender roles in the home, and an even split of the chores."

I chuckled a little, then blew a puff of air out through my nose. "It's not realistic though. Maybe in a perfect world."

"Maybe in a perfect world what?"

"Maybe in a perfect world, sexy men who work part time at the library while they go for their PhD won't be disgusted by the whole teen mom thing."

"*Ugh*," Bianca growled in my ear. "It makes me want to smack you when you get like this! Any man you give the time of day should feel privileged to have your attention. You hear me?"

"Yes, B. I have to go, have to get ready for work."

"Okay, but did you hear me?"

Even though a smile teased the corners of my mouth, I rolled my eyes, and let my exasperation come through in my voice. "I *said* yes, damn! I hear you, I'm flawless, got it. Bye."

"Listen to that Nicki and Bey, *Feeling Myself* a few times in row before you take your ass back to the library."

"*Okay*," I giggled. "Love you B."

"Love you Lo."

I hung up with a grin on my face, but it was quickly stripped away with a glance at the time. I pushed away thoughts of Ty, feelings of inadequacy, and everything else other than getting my ass to work.

five

・・・

lauren

AUSTIN AND MINA *would make gorgeous babies.*

That was my first thought upon walking through the door of Terrific Tech, with just a few minutes to spare before my shift was supposed to start. Austin was helping a customer pick a new camera, but he lifted his chin at me in greeting as I passed him on the way to the back.

I stowed my purse in my locker, but kept my phone since we were encouraged to google things and find better prices, whatever we could for good customer service, and made my way back to the front.

As far as jobs went, I considered myself lucky. Aside from being on my feet for the whole shift, the "work" aspect was pretty light. Talk to customers about computers, TVs, cameras, video games, cell phones, whatever they were looking for, answer a few questions, and sometimes make a sale. Usually? Easy-peasy.

My conversation with Mina came to mind again as I checked in with my boss, and when she asked what section of the store I wanted today, I chose the cameras.

"What are you doing here?" I asked Austin as his customer left our checkout counter with a full bag. "And where is Mina? She's supposed to be on shift today."

He shrugged. "I thought maybe you'd know. She called in, said she needed a mental health day."

I really did try not to roll my eyes at Mina's dramatic ass. I was 99% sure she was at a spa right now, treating herself to a full body everything they offered. When I put my gaze back on Austin, it registered to me that he was *really* concerned, and waiting on me to respond.

"I'll text her later," I told him, nodding as I bent to start organizing the locked camera shelf. "But I'm sure she's fine. Probably school stuff getting to her, you know? Maybe she just needed to catch up on studying or something. I mean, she was fine at you guy's run this morning, right?"

Austin scoffed, then pushed a hand through his locs. "That's... subjective."

"What do you mean?"

Shoving his hands into his pockets, Austin shrugged again. "I don't know. It's like, at first we were having fun, you know? But then, out of nowhere, she got really quiet, and it was like at the end of the run, she couldn't get away from me fast enough. I don't know what I did or said, or..." he pushed out a slow breath, and his frustration was so palpable I felt bad for him. "Anyway... you're coming through to kick it Friday, right?"

"Come through to kick it where?" I asked, standing up. Austin wasn't quite as tall as Ty, but I still had to tip my head back to look into his handsome face. Good-looking, definitely, but not as appealing as Ty.

Wait a minute – was I really going to judge everybody on a scale of *Ty* to *Not Ty* from now on?

"I'm having a little get-together at my place," Austin explained, then glanced over my shoulder to speak to a customer coming through the door. When he turned his attention back to me, he lowered his voice. "You should come. And maybe... bring your friend."

I lifted an eyebrow. "Austin," I said, fighting the urge to smile, "If you want Mina to come to your party, why don't you just ask her?"

"Huh?"

I sucked my teeth, then playfully pushed his shoulder. "You're not fooling anybody. Talking about *maybe* bring my friend, knowing damn well she's the one you actually want to see."

Austin kept up his serious expression for about two seconds longer, then broke into the slow, easy smile that had Mina swooning the first time he flashed it at us.

"Aiight, so maybe I *do* really want Mina to come."

"So, why not just ask her? I'm sure you guys have a shift together this week, or aren't you running again?"

He cringed. "I don't know. It was a little uncomfortable."

"Why?"

"I guess I just... I like Mina, a lot."

"So what's the problem? *Tell her* that!"

"I *can't.*"

I scowled. "Why the hell not?"

Hands still shoved in his pockets, Austin lifted his shoulders, then dropped them in defeat. "Mina is one of those girls you have to be a certain type of guy to get. And *I'm* not that type of guy."

"And what type is that?"

"One with money, status, *swag*, all that shit," he answered, counting them off with his fingers. "Not a college kid only here on scholarship. Like, don't get me wrong, I'm not like down on myself or anything like that. I'm a good-looking guy, make good grades, I can fuck up a track meet, I do my best to treat people right. But chicks like you, Mina, a couple others on campus... that's just not enough."

Frowning, I sucked my teeth. "Says who?"

Austin scoffed. "Says everybody."

47

"Well, everybody is wrong." I crossed my arms over my chest. "I can't speak for anybody but myself, and I've been friends with Mina long enough to know this goes for her too: we don't give a shit about money or status. We can earn our own money, gain our own status. We aren't here for a husband, we're here for an education. Finding a boyfriend is just... a bonus."

"Oh," Austin nodded. "So, it's not because I don't have money, she just doesn't like *me*."

My eyes went wide. "What? No, I... Austin, look. Mina walks around here like she's the bomb, because she believes that she's the bomb—"

"Because she *is*."

I grinned at the look of reverence on his face, then nodded. "Right, because she is. But she's still just a normal girl at heart, just like the rest of us. I know you think she's –"

"Out of my league."

I laughed. "Sure, Austin. Out of your league. But sometimes you have to take that risk, shoot your shot. How can you say she doesn't like you if you haven't given her any indication that you like her?"

"I... but..." he stopped, then shook his head like he was disgusted. "Do I sound as bitch-ass out loud as I do in my head right now?"

I pursed my lips. "Well I wouldn't use *bitch-ass*, but..."

"Ah, damn."

"I'm playing!" I said, gently slapping him on the arm. "Seriously, you don't sound weak, you sound like a guy with a crush, not trying to be all ridiculous and macho. It's endearing, Austin. You're a good guy, you're handsome, and tall, and buff, you run fast as hell, I saw your name on the dean's list when it came out, and you're funny. And employed. And you're not corny. *That's* your swag. Trust me, you don't have to be "big man on campus" to get Mina's attention. Just be yourself. Okay?"

He gave a long sigh, but the tension in his shoulders seemed considerably lighter, and he turned back to me with a smile. "Okay, Lo. Thanks for the pep talk."

I smiled back. "Any time."

"So… you gonna ask Mina about coming to kick it Friday, or nah?"

Rolling my eyes, I headed away from him to help a customer. "Nope," I tossed over my shoulder. "Ask her yourself!"

∼

THE MORE I THOUGHT ABOUT AUSTIN AND MINA, THE MORE CERTAIN I was that there was a lesson in there for me. Like… how was it that encouraging Austin to let *Mina* tell him what she wanted instead of letting himself be ruled by false perceptions came so easily to me? Isn't that exactly what I was doing to Ty?

By the time I made it in from my afternoon shift at the store, Mina was home. As soon as I walked through the door of our apartment, I was assaulted by the delicious scent of pizza sauce and melted cheese.

Mina looked up at me with a smile as I locked the door behind me, and my stomach grumbled for some attention as I watched her pull a slice of pizza from a box on the counter. "Hey Lo! You hungry? I can't eat this by myself."

"Uh, hell yeah," I answered, tossing my keys, purse, and phone onto the table. "My stomach thanks you."

Mina laughed, then sat down at the counter as I fixed my plate. "Soo…," I said, after swallowing a bite. "Mental health day?"

Across the counter, Mina cringed. "I had to. There was no way I could look at Austin today after this morning. I needed a massage and a pedicure to bring my mood back up, so there was no way I was going in."

"You're serious aren't you?"

"Dead serious."

Shaking my head, I sat down beside her. "So I talked to Austin today," I said, then bit into another mouthful of pizza as I watched her from the corner of my eye.

She froze, just for a second, then absently began picking the hunks of sausage from her pizza, lining them up in the middle of the slice. "Oh. What did you guys talk about?"

"You know, the usual stuff," I said, shrugging. "Cameras, parties, swag…. You."

"Me?!" Mina gave up pretending to be disinterested, grabbing me at the shoulders to turn me towards her. "You talked to him about me?! Come on, Lo! You didn't tell him I—"

"*Oh my God*, would you relax?" I giggled as I moved away from her grasp. "I didn't tell him anything you said. He thinks you're out of his league."

Mina drew her head back in surprise, lips parted. "Are you serious?"

"*Dead* serious. He likes you, but he thinks he's not cool enough or rich enough, or something. He thinks you're high maintenance."

She lifted an eyebrow. "I *am* high maintenance."

"Duh," I said, then took a long drink of water from the bottle I'd grabbed. "But that doesn't mean you're only attracted to guys who can buy you shit and improve your "status"."

"I'm actually repulsed by those guys. They're usually so arrogant, and gross. Him *not* being like those guys is part of why I like him. He's laid back, and cool, and *sweet*, you know? Not like in a gross way, but just…" She sat back in her barstool, letting her eyes drift closed. "He's *sexy*. I would wrap my hands in those locs and just—"

"Okay, I get it," I giggled, pinching her leg to get her to open her eyes. "I don't need to hear your little Austin from Austin, Texas fantasies. Unless he wears a cowboy hat or something silly in them."

Mina smirked. "Running shoes. *That's all*."

"Ewwww!" I pinched her leg again, then wrinkled my nose. "You nasty, Mina."

She sucked her teeth. "Whatever girl. Running shoes, timbs, makes no difference, as long as he knows to work with some leverage."

"Oh my God, I'm about to leave," I said, laughing. "Anyway, I only told you any of this because I don't know if I convinced him. If you want Austin, I think you're going to have to up your flirting, so he understands you're serious, not just being friendly."

Mina nodded. "I think I can arrange that."

Before I could respond, my cell phone started ringing from the other side of the room. "Give me a second," I said to Mina, then did a light jog to grab it. Looking at the screen, I wasn't particularly surprised by *who* was calling, but the fact that he'd decided to initiate a video call confused me. Still, I pressed the button to answer, holding my phone up so I was in view of the camera.

"Mekhi?" I said, lifting an eyebrow. It was definitely him on the other side of the screen, he just looked… different than I expected.

Even back in high school, he was handsome – beyond handsome, actually. Sexy, slanted eyes, thick eye lashes, wavy hair that he kept cut low, and the most perfectly shaped lips I'd ever seen, all wrapped in creamy, caramel-toned skin that was a mixture inherited from second-generation Jamaican immigrant mother and pacific-islander father. He'd had a baby face back when we dated, but now it seemed like every time I saw him, a little more of that "babyness" was gone, slowly replaced with grown man.

"How you doin', Lauren?" He licked his lips after he asked that question, and for the first time in… *years*, the sight made my heart race. It was a compulsion of his, always licking his damned lips, ruining their perfection with dry skin. Now though, it seemed like he'd solved that problem. They were looking quite... *kissable*.

What... the... hell...? Why am I looking at Mekhi like this?!

I answered my own question when I *really* looked at the screen again, and realized he was shirtless. He'd used his computer to place the call, so the web cam was picking up shoulders and biceps and abs and an air force tattoo on the right side of his chest, and Harper's name on the other, across his heart. Obviously I saw him at least every few months, and talked to him at least once a week, but I'd not had occasion to see Mekhi with no shirt on in... again, *years*.

The skinny kid I'd called my boyfriend three years ago had blossomed.

"I... I'm fine," I answered, shaking my head to snap myself out of my trance. "What about you?"

He scrubbed a hand over his face, then leaned back in his chair. "Shit, tired. But looking at your pretty ass face got your boy feeling energized," he chuckled. And I blushed. What the hell was happening?

"Mekhi, what are you talking about right now? What are you doing, what's up?"

"Nothing's up. I just wanted to see you, that's all. I mean we talk about Harper, and occasionally we cross paths, but really I barely see you."

Pushing out a little sigh, I sat down on the arm of the couch, keeping the phone in front of me. "You're in the military, of course we don't see each other often. You're across the country right now, with limitations on when you're able to go home."

"I know, that's why I'm doing this now. It's been what, six months since we laid eyes on each other? That's not the norm."

"Our situation isn't *the norm*, Mekhi. You're off doing the military thing, I'm up here in school, Harper is with our parents. None of this is conventional, we're just making the best of it."

Mekhi laughed. "Lauren, *relax*. I agree, we're making the best of it, so I placed a video call, so I could lay eyes on my kid's mother. Is it wrong of me to want that?"

"I... no. No, I guess it's not," I admitted. I had no idea why I was being so argumentative with him, when we usually got along just fine. All I knew was that the sight of him was making me feel tingly between my legs, and I decided it was Ty's fault.

Damn him, for waking up those dormant feelings in me.

Because really... it had to be just that, right? In the years since we broke up, I hadn't had *any* inclination towards rekindling the flame with Mekhi, and the smell of the pizza earlier aroused me more than the sight of him ever had.

Until tonight.

Tonight, when he was looking all manly and delicious and caramelly and smiling at me with that gorgeous smile.

Oh damn... I'm being a thought slut right now.

"So, what's up with you," Mekhi asked, breaking me from my thoughts again. "I talked to Harper a little while ago, so I know she's doing good. But what about mommy? Those BSU fools up there sniffing around behind you?"

That question brought heat to my face. Why did he suddenly care?

"No," I said, shaking my head. "No boys, just the same old, same old. Work, school, talk to Harper. Work, school, talk to Harper. Sometimes, I even mix it up a little. School, talk to Harper, work."

Mekhi chuckled at me again. "You're crazy, girl. Well I'm not gonna hold you. Like I said, I just wanted to see you. Kinda miss your face, all that."

"Umm, okay." On screen, our eyes met, and held, and the warmth that spread over me wasn't necessarily familiar, but it wasn't *un*familiar either. "I—I'll talk to you later."

He nodded. "Yeah. Hey, you're gonna be home, for lil bit's birthday right?"

"No, actually," I said, breaking our gaze. "We don't have any classes on Thursday or Friday the week after, so I was going to wait until then so I can stay longer. Four days instead of two."

"*Shit*," he mumbled, but the microphone still picked it up. "I put in leave for those days months ago, I was hoping you'd be there. You know, Harper gets mommy *and* daddy for her birthday this year…"

I resisted the urge to roll my eyes. He sounded like his momma, valid point or not.

"I didn't even think about that, sorry. I wanted to maximize the time, you know?"

He pulled his lip between his teeth, and I might have watched really hard when his tongue came out to wet his lips. "Would I be asking too much, to ask you to consider a change in plans? We can take Harper to the movies, the mall. She says she likes 'Maican food now," he laughed. "So we can take her to eat at my uncle's place, take her for ice cream. Just me, you, and her."

"Mekhi…"

"I'll pay for your plane ticket," he offered, with a teensy edge of desperation in his voice.

I shook my head. "I don't need you to pay for my ticket, I've got it. I… I'll think about it, okay?"

I really did plan to think about it, but the big, sexy smile he gave me afterward made thinking about it not really necessary. *Hell yes*, I would change my plans – but he didn't have to know that just yet.

"Cool. *Thank you*," he said, still grinning at me from the screen.

I bit my own lip this time, to keep from smiling back, and nodded at him. "I… you're welcome. I'll talk to you later."

"Aiight. Bye Lauren."

"Bye Mekhi."

We ended the call, and I sat there for what had to be several minutes, head and heart racing. Never, *ever*, in the last two years, had I had such a weird, warm, tingly feeling after communicating with Mekhi.

Never.

He'd pissed me off, made me cry, made me laugh, all of that, but what I was feeling now?

Never.

"So that was interesting," Mina said from her seat at the counter. I'd completely forgotten she was there, but when I turned around, she was wearing a goofy grin. "Ex boyfriend 'bout to be your next boyfriend, huh?"

I shook my head as I stood to return to my pizza. "Definitely not," I answered, with a confidence I didn't necessarily feel.

"Mmmhmm. Then what was that adorable flirty conversation about?" She raised an eyebrow, then pointed a pizza crust at me like a microphone.

I gently batted her hand away.

"Girl… I wish I knew."

six
...
lauren

DON'T PANIC.

I took a deep breath, and pretended to be really, *really* interested in the game of spades going on to my right. I tried – like, *really* tried – to keep my face neutral, unfazed, but I was screaming on the inside.

It felt like a damned setup.

That was the only way to account for the heart racing, stomach turning anxiety I felt over looking up from my carefully obtained, alcohol-free fruit punch at Austin's "get together", and right into Ty's eyes. He didn't exactly ignore me, but he didn't seem excited to see me either. He tipped his chin in greeting, flashed the barest hint of a smile, then turned back to the person he was talking to, some girl in combat boots and a skirt, with mosquito-bite titties and a blonde faded haircut.

So maybe it wasn't a setup, if he wasn't even glad I was here.

I downed the rest of my fruit punch in one gulp, then looked around for Mina. The idea of talking to her for an escape was quickly scrapped when I spotted her with her back against the wall and Austin in front of her, leaning closer than necessary to speak into her ear. She blushed, then shook her head at whatever he'd said. A moment later, he stepped even closer, so close that their bodies were almost touching.

Smiling, I looked away. There was no way I was going to interrupt their flirting just because my crush had walked through the door.

With a little sigh, I moved away from the main area of the apartment to use the bathroom. In there, I checked myself in the mirror.

Still good.

Twist-out banging, eyeliner and lip-gloss popping, and my ass looked *magnificent* in the skinny jeans I wore with a loose-fitting cropped top. I didn't have even a hint of abs, but my tummy was flat –mostly— and I had great boobs, so the outfit looked good. Mina had been right, when she talked me into wearing it. I didn't feel naked, I felt *sexy*.

I left the bathroom feeling a little better, and hoping to, by some miracle, just avoid Ty for the rest of the night. There were at least twenty people packed into the common area of Austin's average-sized apartment, so the hallway was crowded when I needed to get back through.

"Excuse me," I called out, to a small group of guys congregated in the middle. "Can I get through?"

They looked up, and I felt like a piece of meat as all eyes went to me.

"Of course you can come through, sexy." One of them—a tall, actually good looking one of them – stepped toward me, stretching his arm toward the tiny space between them, like he expected me to squeeze past.

I gave him a wry smile, then shook my head. "You're not going to move?"

He raked his eyes over me, then smiled. "If you tell me the password."

Here we go...

I sucked my teeth, and was ready to tear into him when someone else came through, easily parting the crowd.

"Vick, chill." Ty approached this guy, casually throwing a familiar arm over his shoulder. "I keep trying to tell you, you need to work on those fucked up flirting skills of yours. You're making her uncomfortable."

Vick sucked his teeth, tossing a disbelieving scowl in Ty's direction. "Nah, man. She knows I'm just playing with her. I mean... right?" he asked, directing his question to me.

"No, actually." I shook my head. "Shit like that isn't funny, especially not with a complete stranger. It's awkward, and unnerving."

His eyes went wide, and he raised his hands in defense. "Damn, my bad. I didn't mean any harm, sexy."

I cringed over his use of "sexy" like that was my name, but didn't say anything. One lesson at a time was probably enough. "It's fine, just remember for the next girl you approach."

Taking advantage of the opportunity, I quickly got myself through the opening Ty had made. My cheeks were hot, heart racing again, and I wanted nothing more than to crawl into my bed, but I'd ridden here with Mina, who was still in deep conversation with Austin.

Shit.

I lounged against the wall for the longest hour ever, as people began to filter out. I took another glance around the significantly less crowded room, and when I spotted Ty talking to *another* girl, I rolled my eyes.

Definitely needed to get my ass out of there.

With a deep breath, I approached Austin and Mina just as he was whispering something that made her dissolve into giggles. "Sorry to interrupt, but... can I talk to you for a second Mina?"

Biting her lip, and keeping her gaze on Austin, not me, she nodded, then slipped away from him. "I'll be right back."

"And I'll be right here," he shot back with a smile that made Mina's hands flutter to her neck before she looked away.

"Girl this better be good," Mina whispered to me as I pulled her to a quieter spot. "You told me to up the flirting, and I did, and it's working, and *now* you wanna interrupt?"

"I'm going home."

Mina scowled at me for about a second longer until my words registered meaning, and her expression shifted to concern. "Did something happen? Are you okay?"

"No, it's fine," I said, but skepticism ruled her face as she pursed her lips. "*Fine*," I grumbled. "It's just… Ty is here."

She rolled her eyes. "So talk to him." I'd told Mina everything, and her reaction had been pretty much the same as Bianca's.

"There's nothing to say! I've seen him at the library more than once this week, and nothing. He's made full eye contact with me, talked to me. If he wanted to pursue something, he would. But he hasn't, so like I said, I'm leaving. I'm tired anyway."

"Lo, don't leave because of him."

I chuckled. "I'm only here because of you. And you're occupied with Austin. You're safe with him, so there's no reason for me to stick around, other than to be a third wheel."

Mina sighed, then appeared to think about it for a minute before she shook her head. "How are you even planning to get home? Do you need my car keys?"

"Nope. We're just across the street from campus, I can walk."

"*Walk?*" Mina asked, her eyes going wide. "Hell no, you're definitely not *walking*, it's late at night!"

I groaned. "I walk home from the library at crazy hours all the time. That's what pepper spray is for."

"*Lauren…*"

"*Mina…*," I said, matching her scolding tone before I chuckled. "Seriously, stay here, have fun with Austin. The crowd is clearing out, there's only like seven or eight people left. Soon everyone will be gone, and I'm sure Austin will need someone to help him clean up. I'm *leaving.*"

"Okay, let me tell Austin, and I'll drive you to the apartment and come back."

"Mina!" I grabbed her face between my hands, forcing her to look at me. "Read my lips: *Stay your ass here and get your boo.* I will be perfectly fine, my legs work!"

"But—"

"But nothing! If you leave, it'll be pointless, cause I'm not getting in the car with you, so you may as well let it go."

She sucked her teeth, then crossed her arms over her chest as she accepted what I was saying to her. We said quick goodbyes, and I couldn't get out of there fast enough after that. I was already at the crosswalk in front of Austin's building, waiting for the signal to cross onto campus when I heard something behind me.

"Lauren, wait up!"

Shit.

The light changed, and I hurried across the street, but Ty easily caught up to me, gently catching me by the hand. "Damn, girl. Always in a hurry, huh?"

"Yeah, actually," I replied, slipping my hand from his. "I need to get home."

"Let me walk you."

His request made me do something I'd been trying hard not to do – look into his eyes. So warm, and inviting, and then he flashed me a little smile that made my insides melt. But I shook my head.

"Come on," he asked. "It's late, it's dark, you're out here by yourself…"

"I don't need you to protect me."

Again, he smiled. "I know that. I saw you in there with Vick, you were about to slice and dice his ass with words. And from the look in your eyes, maybe a blade, before I walked up," he laughed. "But still..."

"I *don't* need you to protect me," I repeated, because my brain was still stuck on his smile, and couldn't function fast enough to process a different response. I turned, and started to walk away, but he grabbed my hand again.

"Okay, you don't need protection. What if I just want to talk to you? Can I do that?"

It really wasn't fair of him to ask anything of me, when his touching my hand was making my nerve endings go haywire. If he could make me feel like this just from touching my hand, what would it be like if he touched me... *other* places?

"Yes," I heard myself say, unbidden.

"Yes?"

I nodded. "Yes."

He smiled at me again, then moved our hand-holding a step further by entwining his fingers with mine. We stood there for a moment, until he lifted his eyebrows expectantly.

"What?" I asked, confused.

"I don't know where you live, Lauren."

"Oh!" With my free hand, I covered my face as I shook my head. "I'm in McAvoy hall. You know where it is?"

"Yeah," he nodded, then gave a gentle tug to pull me in that direction. For a long time, neither of us said anything as we walked, and I tried my best to pretend that his touch wasn't driving me insane. It was a gorgeous night, sky full of stars, beautifully landscaped, nearly empty campus. It was almost romantic.

"So, you realize that this was the fourth time you've run away from me, right?" he asked, squeezing my hand. "And this time, you like, literally *ran*," he chuckled. "Shocked the hell out of me. I'm not that bad, right?"

I shrugged, then cleared my throat before I spoke, hoping I didn't sound as lusty as I felt. "I don't know. I'm surprised you followed me, or wanted to talk to me. I mean I've seen you around a few times, and you didn't seem that interested. Kind of confirmed... never mind."

"Confirmed what?"

I shook my head. "Nothing."

"Come *on*," he said, squeezing my hand as we passed the library. "What got confirmed?"

"That you weren't feeling me because of the whole "had a baby in high school thing."

Ty stopped moving, and his grip on my fingers firmed. "What?" he asked, turning me so we were face to face, instead of side by side. "Lauren, you don't really believe that do you?"

I shrugged, keeping my gaze below his face. "I don't know what to believe, Ty. Not when one minute you're in my face, acting interested, and the next you're barely acknowledging me."

"Well you can be damned sure it's not because you have a kid! I told you I think it's dope, that you're working so hard to provide for your daughter. I knew you had a kid before I sat down with you at the library last time. It's *not* about you having a child."

"Then *what is it*?" I snapped, then clamped my hand to my mouth in horror as my voice broke with emotion. I'd never, *ever* felt quite as stupid as I did now, standing in front of a guy I barely knew, who owed me nothing, near tears because he didn't like me like I liked him.

Okay... maybe the moment the pregnancy test turned positive with Harper was the one I felt *most* stupid, but this was a close second.

I yanked my hand away from him and continued toward my apartment, but it took him less than a second to catch up and stand in front of me to block my path.

"Move," I demanded, trying to sidestep him on the sidewalk, but he reached out, putting his hands at my waist. "Move!"

"Can you just let me talk to you for a second, before you run away again?"

I pushed his hands away. *"Talk."*

He let out a heavy sigh, then scrubbed a hand over his face. "It's… you're twenty years old, Lauren. You're *young*. I mean… yeah, I'm only twenty-five, so I'm still young too, but you… you're *really* damned young."

Even though I was standing there fighting juvenile tears of rejection, indignation won the argument of whether or not it made sense to argue over his completely true statement. "I'm not that young," I snapped. "I'm going to graduate with honors this year, same as I did for high school. I work, I have a car, I have investments, savings, and my daughter already has a nice little start for *her* college fund. So don't act like I'm still the same sixteen year old who messed around and got pregnant, when at twenty, I'm in a better position and doing more with my life than people twice my age."

"*I know*. I—"

"And if I'm *so damned young*, too young for you, why are you here, Ty? Huh? Why don't you leave me alone, and not keep messing with my head?"

"Because—*shit*, Lauren." He lifted a hand to massage the back of his neck as he blew out another sigh. I was upset, I'd never seen him less than completely cool. "Listen," he said, dropping his hands to shove in his pockets. "Obviously, you're an attractive woman. I'd have to be blind not to notice it, but that's not what draws me to you. You're dope as hell, for all the reasons you mentioned. And…"

I swallowed past the lump in my throat. "And…what?"

"And it's confusing the hell out of me. Usually, when I hear "twenty year old girl", I think immature, silly, party girls. But that's not you. You're smart, you're focused, you're driven, you're… *sexy*."

My mouth dried up.

Me? As in, Lauren Bailey…*Sexy*?

I walked away.

As fast as my feet could take me, I resumed my trek to my apartment, taking in huge lungfuls of air as I went. Was it the most mature, eloquent response to being called sexy? Hell no. It wasn't even logical, made no sense at all, but I kept walking anyway, because what was I supposed to say?

I couldn't make my age not be a factor for him, but I was honestly more than a little bit relieved that his reluctance wasn't because of Harper. Now, I just needed to drown myself in junk food for a week or so, and never visit the library again so I could get over my crush.

Easy-peasy.

"Lauren!"

Suddenly Ty was in front of me, gently grabbing my arms. "I'm sorry…"

"It's just a number," I blurted out, before really thinking about it. "Me being twenty, to your twenty-five, it's not that big of a deal. We're both *in* our twenties, both adults. I don't understand, but…" I pushed out a heavy sigh of my own, then moved away from his grasp. "I'm not going to make this weird. You have nothing to be sorry about, it's just how you feel. And that's your right, if you're not comfortable. So I'll see you around."

I walked away, *again*, hoping I could just get home to cry my little immature baby tears in peace, but of course that didn't happen.

"You said I could walk you home," Ty called from behind me. I didn't want to stop, but my feet did it anyway, and a few moments later, Ty was right beside me. I expected him to grab my hand again, but instead he touched my bare waist, sliding his palm to the small of my back.

"Ty, I—"

"Please?"

I looked up, meeting his gaze, and the regret I saw in his eyes did little to make me feel better. This didn't mean anything, he was just being a gentleman, trying to make me feel better about being rejected.

"Whatever," I mumbled, then began moving forward. Neither of us said anything until we were at my front door, and I was digging my keys from my purse.

Ty leaned against the wall, watching me. "Lauren," he said, as I pushed the key in the lock. "I like you. And I'd like to get to know you better."

I shrugged. "But I'm too young. Yeah, I got it."

"But *nothing*." He shook his head. "Like you said, it's just a number. If you're cool, I'm cool, so I'd like to get to know you."

Inwardly, a little spark of hope burst into a billion dancing fireworks. Outwardly – at least I hoped – I remained impassive. "Get to know me? What does that even mean?"

Ty chuckled a little then pulled my hand away from my keys, turning me so that I was facing him with my back to the door. "You know what I mean, girl. Talk to you, learn about you. Hang out, go to movies, eat together. You know what I mean? Some people call it… dating?"

"*Ohhh*," I said, allowing myself a little bit of a smile as he moved closer to me, invading my personal space with the clean, crisp scent of his cologne – must not have been in the library today. "You mean like, late night phone calls, texting, tagging me as your woman crush on Instagram?"

He laughed, and it warmed me from my fingertips to my toes. "So you *did* know what I meant."

"No comment," I replied, nervously biting my lip as I tried to keep up my coy, flirty façade. I ventured a look up at him again, and my heart skipped more than a couple of beats when I realized how close his face was to mine. Suddenly his hand was on me, and he was drawing me near, and my brain was near overload from the sensation of his fingers digging gently into my bare waist.

"So what's the verdict? You want to give it a shot, see what happens?"

I nodded, and his eyes snagged mine. "I'd like that."

He smiled, and the feeling between my legs turned from a tingle to a throb. "I'd like that too."

At this point, the wall was the only thing holding me up, because my knees were past weak. His hand that wasn't touching me was pressed to the faux exposed brick finish, and his gaze caressed my lips, then came back up to my eyes.

"Are you about to kiss me?" I asked, then swallowed hard.

"I want to." I blinked, and his face was right in front of mine, the cool freshness of his breath tickling my mouth. My chest rose and fell as I waited for him to make his next move, drawing his attention to my breasts. His eyes lingered there for a second before returning to my face, and he licked his lips. "Do you want me to?"

"Yes," I whispered, then swallowed again. "As long as you understand that it won't go further than that."

"What kind of guy do you think I am?" he murmured, his lips brushing mine. "I haven't even taken you on a first date yet, I'm not going to try to talk you into sex tonight."

"Or the night after that? Or after that?"

He drew back a little. "Lauren, what are you saying?"

"I'm saying that I don't do casual sex. So I thought maybe I should tell you that up front, before you kiss me, before you *get to know me*, that I'm not interested in that. If you are, that's fine, I have no problem with that, it's just not for me."

Ty was quiet for a moment as he studied me, then gave me a little smile. "Well, I appreciate the disclaimer, but you exercising your rights to your body isn't a problem. I'd still like to get to know you, if that's okay."

For what had to be the tenth time, relief swept over me. "Yes. It's okay with me."

"Good," he grinned. "Can I kiss you now?"

"Ye—*mmmmm.*"

My affirmative answer got lost in the moment as he covered my mouth with his, slowly, gently drawing my lip between his teeth. I hadn't been kissed in a long time, not since Wes in high school. Of course Mekhi and I had kissed, had been each other's firsts, but *this* one, the way Ty kissed me... if I didn't know better, I'd swear it was something I'd never done before.

He nibbled first, placing soft nips over my bottom lip then the top, soothing each one with an even softer brush of his lips. At the first touch of his tongue, I moaned. When he sucked my lip into his mouth, I whimpered.

I could taste him, and he tasted good. Minty, and fruity from the punch at Austin's, and something else, something I couldn't identify, so I decided it was just *him*. And just that quickly, I was drunk on the flavor. He probed the seam of my mouth his tongue, and I eagerly accepted. I did what felt natural, stroking my tongue against his, and with each movement, the throbbing between my legs grew more intense. His grip on my waist was firm but gentle as he pulled my lower body toward his. I was already embarrassingly wet, and the hard bulge at the front of his jeans only made it worse as he deepened the kiss, swallowing the moans I couldn't suppress on my own.

When he finally pulled away, we were both breathless and my nipples were hard enough to cut through my bra and shirt. He took a step away from me, his lip between his teeth as he looked me up and down, then shook his head a little.

"I'm... I'm gonna head out, now that I've got you safely home," he said, shoving his hands deep in his pockets.

I nodded. "Okay."

That was probably for the best, since I was already feeling like that "no casual sex rule" was stupid as hell. We stared at each other for a few more seconds, then I broke away, finally completing my mission of unlocking the door.

"We'll talk, soon," Ty said, still standing a few feet away.

"Okay."

"I'll see you later."

I pushed the door open. "Okay."

We exchanged nods, and then I went in, closing and locking the door behind me. I pressed the back of my head against it, closing my eyes to relive that kiss.

I flinched, jumping away when a knock sounded at the door. After a quick glance through the peephole, I took a deep breath, then unlocked and pulled it open.

"Did you forget something?"

Ty smiled. "Yeah, actually. It would probably make a lot of sense if we exchanged numbers."

seven
. . .
ty

THERE WAS no such thing as *dating* for me and Lauren, not really.

At least not in the same way that some of our peers did it.

For instance, my homeboy Austin, and his new "bae", as he called her, Mina. I knew Austin because he was frat, but we were friends beyond that brotherhood. At BSU on a sports scholarship, but he was trying to keep his academics in line too, so when I heard him mention falling behind in his classes, I stepped in to do what I could to help, and we ended up pretty tight.

He talked all the time about a girl from work who he swore was bad as hell, but I could never talk him into just *talking* to her. Somewhere along the road, that changed. They went from crushing on each other to inseparable, and always cuddled up somewhere together.

I wished it could be like that for me and Lauren.

Instead, the time when we could be alone together was hit and miss. Our lives were actually comprised of a pretty similar cycle – with the notable exception of Lauren's kid – of school, work, study, sleep, rinse, repeat. Unfortunately, those cycles didn't run on the same schedule. I could catch her at the library, but that wasn't ideal. I dropped in on her at Terrific Tech a couple of times, feigning interest in random gadgets, just to see her smile, but that wasn't ideal either.

When it came down to it, between keeping our jobs, keeping up our grades, and keeping ourselves from dying of exhaustion, there wasn't much time left for us to "date". And the time we *did* have, neither of us wanted to spend it in a dark movie theater, or crowded restaurant, or hanging around campus. I'm sure we'd eventually want to venture out, but for now, we were getting to know each other, and that was best done one on one, my place or hers.

This time, it was my place.

She'd brought her books with her, because she "was really supposed to be using this time to study", and I had mine out because she had hers. Once she got here, the books were quickly forgotten, in favor of pizza and conversation. After a while though, she'd gotten serious, and scolded me for being a distraction. She buried herself in her book and I pretended to be absorbed with mine.

It took her a grand total of ten minutes to fall asleep.

I chuckled as I draped her with a blanket, then watched the steady rise and fall of her chest for a few moments as she slept.

So damned beautiful.

No matter how many times I thought it, no matter how many times I studied her face, I was always struck by it. And she always smelled like brown sugar, even though she wasn't always sweet. I think that drew me to her even more.

Not the way she smelled – although that certainly wasn't a negative – but the fact that she wasn't so caught up in trying to impress me, or being something she wasn't, that she couldn't be herself. In the month since we'd first started "dating" she'd gotten pissy with me on occasion, nothing major, just enough to let me know she was human, and feisty, and not at all interested in portraying herself as perfect.

Which was really damned perfect.

I returned to my seat on the opposite couch to actually put my book to use. Lauren slept for almost an hour, not stirring until her cell phone rang. Even then, it didn't seem like she was too keen on waking up. I recognized Harper's smiling face on the screen.

Lauren had proudly shown me pictures of a little girl who looked just like her, with the exception of her deep golden skin. Then, she got embarrassed, because she thought she was going overboard or boring me, "coming across as some type of psycho obsessed with her kid", but really she wasn't.

It was adorable, but frustrating too, how she over-analyzed so much, but it hadn't taken me long to realize that it was just part of how she kept things in order. Everything needed a logical explanation, and she wasn't afraid to come up with those on her own.

I approached her on the couch, kneeling on the floor beside her so we were face to face. Gently, I shook her shoulder, and she frowned at first, moving away. I shook her again, and this time she opened her eyes. Recognition lit her gaze for a moment, and her lips curled into a smile, but then just as quickly, her eyelids had drifted closed, and stayed that way, again.

"Hey, Sleeping Beauty. Wake up, you missed a call."

I gently tugged her into a seated position, then cupped her face in my hands until she opened her eyes, and kept them open.

"You missed a call," I repeated to her. "From Harper."

At the sound of Harper's name, she smiled again, and nodded. "How long was I asleep?"

"Hour or so."

"*Shit*," she mumbled, shaking her head. I dropped my hands from her face as she leaned around me, reaching for her phone.

"You're not late for anything, are you? I knew you said you were off today, so I didn't think—"

Lauren shook her head, placing a hand on my arm. "No, Ty. Nothing like that, I just didn't mean to fall asleep. I could have been studying with that time, or talking to you."

"But you need rest, too."

"I get enough *rest*. What I don't get enough of is y—" She clamped her mouth closed before she finished that statement, then looked down at the phone in her hands, not meeting my eyes. "I need to call Harper back. Her attention span isn't big enough that it should take very long."

I nodded. "Go for it, pretty girl."

I moved away from her, heading into my kitchen to give her some privacy while she made her call, but I lived in a tiny studio apartment. There wasn't too far I could go.

From the kitchen, I couldn't help hearing Harper's reports that "Puppy" had gotten in trouble again, and that she would be seeing her daddy this coming weekend. It wasn't until I heard Harper ask Lauren where she was, if she'd moved to a new house, that I realized they were actually on a video call.

My first instinct was to duck, in case she could see me. I was completely disinterested in contributing to any possible confusion, but I quickly realized that from Lauren's angle, all Harper could see behind her was the window and the front door.

"Mommy is at a friend's house, baby," Lauren said, trying to mask the strain in her voice.

"But it's almost bedtime."

I almost choked on the swig of water I'd just taken. Lauren *did* choke. She broke into a fit of coughs, and I tried not to laugh in the background as she recovered enough to respond to her little girl.

"It's almost *your* bedtime, Chickadee," she said, still trying to clear her throat. "Grown-ups don't have to go to bed at eight, okay?"

"Okay!"

Harper moved on to something else, and I could feel Lauren's relief from across the room. On the counter, my own phone buzzed with a notification, so I reached for it and turned the screen on.

"Are you busy? – Jamila"

I pushed out a dry, quiet laugh as I shook my head. Why wouldn't she just leave it alone? I started to just ignore the message, but just before I tossed the phone back onto the counter, it buzzed again.

"I'm coming by. I know you're home. – Jamila"

Shit.

"Yeah, I'm busy."

"WE NEED TO TALK. Stop dodging me, and be a damned man. TALK TO ME. – Jamila"

I raised an eyebrow at the screen. Like... for real, J? Running my tongue over my teeth, I willed myself to calm down before I typed a response. I knew Jamila well enough to know that she really would just show up. I didn't feel like dealing with her, period, but especially not with Lauren around.

"Cut the bullshit, Jamila. Ain't nobody dodging you, I've already made myself perfectly clear. Stop acting like this shit is my fault."

"So you're blameless? – Jamila"

"*I* put you on ole boy's dick? Oh, my bad. Completely slipped my fucking mind."

"How many times do I have to tell you I'm sorry before we can move on from this? I'M SORRY!!!! – Jamila"

How about just one time where you actually mean it?

"None. I'm good. No hard feelings, let's move on."

"REALLY?! So... engagement back on?! – Jamila"

"Hell nah. Move on, as in leave each other the hell alone."

I shook my head. Jamila was far from stupid, so I know she didn't really believe I was going to take her back, not after the shit she pulled. I wasn't going to touch her, let alone go through with marrying her. At this point, I had to believe she was holding on purely out of desperation.

"So I guess those rumors are true then? – Jamila"

I knew better than to respond to that, but I did anyway.

"*What rumors?*"

"About you and the statistic. – Jamila"

"*??? Statistic?*"

"**THE SINGLE MOM BITCH WHOSE FACE YOU'VE BEEN GRINNING IN FOR THE LAST FUCKING MONTH. Is she over there now? Is that why I can't come by, cause this bitch is trying to pick up a new baby daddy?– Jamila**"

My eyes went wide as I read that message. I wasn't stunned, not at all, that Jamila would say something ugly about Lauren. Somewhere around the last year, after she got the ring, she'd unleashed a whole different person from the one I'd asked to marry me. What did shock me was how pissed I got.

Even though she was younger by four years, Lauren could mop the floor with Jamila in terms of responsibility and maturity, yet Jamila felt qualified to put her down, just because she had a kid? The hell was her problem?

I started typing out a response that was just as fucked up as what *she* said, but my fingers paused, hovering over the screen. This was exactly what she wanted, to get me into a back and forth with her, anything to hold my attention.

I wasn't about to give her silly ass the satisfaction.

As much as I felt compelled to defend Lauren, it would be falling on deaf ears. Jamila didn't give a shit. She was just trying to get under my skin, but what she seemed to forget was that I could get under hers, too, by doing exactly what I should have done in the first place: not falling into her bullshit.

"**Don't contact me again Jamila. I'm not doing this shit with you.**"

"Everything okay?"

I looked up to see Lauren standing in front of me at the other side of the counter, her eyes filled with concern.

"Yeah," I said, wiping the annoyance from my expression. I rounded the counter, and purely on impulse, wrapped her in my arms. It wasn't supposed to be sexual, just a hug, but she melted against me, her full breasts pressing into my chest, sending a surge of heat right to my groin.

"I should probably be heading out," she said softly, looking up into my eyes. "As Harper said… it's almost bed time."

I groaned. "And like *you* said, it's only about to be eight. Why do you need to leave so soon?"

"I've got a flight tomorrow, right after my two morning classes. I haven't even packed."

"I… didn't realize you were going anywhere."

Her eyes went wide, then darted from side to side, like she was trying to remember something. "Oh, damn. I never told you I was changing plans, I'm so sorry! This weekend is my little girl's birthday, so I'm gonna fly down and spend it with her."

And your ex, I thought, but didn't say out loud, remembering Harper's excitement about seeing her father. I'd be lying if I said I didn't wonder why Lauren wasn't mentioning *that* part, that it was going to be a happy little family reunion. Originally, she was going next weekend, the long weekend… had she changed those plans just to see him?

"Did you have plans for us or something?" she asked, in an apologetic tone that made a little twinge of guilt prick my chest.

"No, no. Nothing in particular, nothing like that. I was hoping we would get the chance to spend some time, but I understand that baby girl comes first. Okay?"

She nodded, giving me a big smile as she threaded her fingers through mine. "Okay."

Damn.

That smile of hers always hit me right in the gut. She pushed herself up on her toes, and I dipped my head to meet her. It was just a little kiss, more like a peck, but hell, *that* hit me right in the gut too. She drew back, pulling her lip into her mouth.

"I can stay for a little bit longer, since we won't see each other all weekend."

"Or you could stay here, and go back to your place early tomorrow to pack."

She lifted a scolding eyebrow, but her mouth was still turned into a smile. "Not happening, Ty."

I chuckled as she led me to the couch to sit down, and I was surprised when instead of taking the opposite end, she snuggled right up against me. She said we weren't doing the casual sex thing, and I respected that, so we typically gave each other a little space. I couldn't speak for what was going on in *her* head, but I had a hard time not touching her when we were close. She always looked good, and smelled good, and that deep brown skin of hers was velvety-soft, just begging to be touched.

It was still Spring, and warm outside, so she was wearing a soft yellow dress that made her skin glow. The top was made like a tank top, and the bottom flared out, skimming her thighs. Just looking at her in that dress was a problem. Having her pressed against me, with her breasts peeking out, and a generous view of her thighs... *fucking torture.*

But I endured it.

I draped my arm over the back of the couch, to keep my damned hands to myself, but she pulled it down, wrapping it around her waist.

"Do you ever regret the major you chose?" she asked, looking away from the TV to glance into my face.

I shook my head. "Not really. Why? You having second thoughts?"

She grimaced. "Well, I wouldn't exactly put it like that, but I'm graduating after next semester. I went into this major because it's one of the few where you're pretty much guaranteed to get a job, but I think about working in this field, and just the *thought* bores me, you know?"

"So why don't you do something different?"

Lauren pushed out a heavy sigh. "It's not really that simple for me. I have a child to take care of, so I can't really spend time "finding the career that speaks to me" and all of that. She needs food, shelter, clothing, lunch money, all of that. I'm going to need to pay rent, other bills. I just I feel stuck, and I don't even have a job yet."

I propped myself up by my elbow on the arm of the couch, scratching my head. "Well, you have to think about it like this: Yes, you're going to have bills, responsibilities that you have to take care of. That's a given, child or not. But, you also have to account for what's going to make you happy, because going to a job that makes you miserable every day isn't healthy. So, I guess think about what you're passionate about, your hobbies that mean something to you, and see if you can figure out a way to blend them. We're living in a time where with a tech degree, Lauren you can honestly pave your own way. I see the way you hustle now, putting your all into your grades. Once we get out of here, yeah, you'll have a job, but the same way you make it work now, you can put that energy into carving out your own space. Think of whatever shitty first job you're going to have as the means to get you to what you *really* want to do. Does that make sense?"

She tipped her head to the side a little as she thought about it, then slowly, she nodded. "Yeah, actually. It does, it makes a lot of sense. I guess I just it's hard for me sometimes, to see things in any way other than black and white. It's like I've trained myself to need to be able to account for every single thing, to the point that I end up paralyzed, and… maybe a little fatalistic."

"No, really?" I asked, feigning shock. My sarcasm earned me a gentle slap on the hand.

"I'm not *that* bad."

I chuckled. "Yeah, Lauren. Sure."

Her mouth dropped open like she was offended. "Seriously Ty! Give me an example."

"Uhh... let's go with you making up a whole scenario where you having a child had anything to do with me not pursuing you. You were convinced too."

She sucked her teeth. "Why can't we let the past stay in the past, huh," she giggled, sitting up so she could turn to face me. "So, you've got a point, but I've toned it down, right?"

"Uhhh..."

"Ty!"

"Yes," I laughed, tucking my arms around her waist to pull her against my chest. "You have."

"Thank you." She lifted her hand to my face, running it over my jaw. "I'm glad I was wrong... you're kind of cool."

"So are you."

She smiled at me, then moved so that she was straddling one of my legs, and pushed herself up so our mouths could touch. Her movements had pushed up my shorts, so the soft satiny fabric of her panties was the only thing separating us from being skin to skin. But we didn't even *need* to be skin to skin for me to feel the heat emanating from between her thighs, and I didn't think I was imagining the dampness of the fabric as I slipped my tongue into her mouth.

Damn, she tasted good.

Lauren always tasted good, and I couldn't keep my mind from wondering... if she tasted good *here*...

A low, sexy moan escaped her throat, and I slid my hands down to her thighs, gripping her tight as I moved her from straddling my leg to straddling my waist. I slipped a hand into her hair, gently tugging to get her as close to me as I could. When she finally pulled away, I watched the rise and fall of her breasts as she tried to catch her breath. Feeling her eyes on me, I looked up and our gazes met.

I saw it, right there, in her eyes.

She wanted me to touch her.

I *wanted* to touch her.

So why the fuck wasn't I touching her?

I slid my hands up the back of her thighs, cupping and squeezing when I reached her ass. Her eyelids fluttered closed, as I pushed up further, underneath her dress, up to her breasts. She gasped when my thumbs brushed over her nipples, then bit her lip to stifle a whimper when I began massaging them through her bra.

I moved back down, over her soft stomach, back down to the waistband of her panties, which I skipped to cup her ass again as she wrapped her arms around my shoulders and lowered her mouth for another kiss. I was beyond hot, beyond horny, beyond hard, and Lauren wasn't making it any better by pushing that heat between her thighs right up against me, gently rocking her hips against mine.

Goddamn she felt good, and she had to know what she was doing, using me to stimulate herself to the point that her breathing was getting shallow. I kissed her deeper, gripped her thighs tighter, moved with her until she pulled away, whimpering as her body tensed. I kept moving, and she dropped her head and buried it against my neck, hiding her face as she came.

Neither of us said anything. I wrapped my arms around her waist, holding her close, waiting for her heart to slow down. Her breathing leveled, but her heart kept racing, and after a few moments, she wiggled her way out of my arms and began gathering her books, shoving them into her bag.

"I need to get home," she said, yanking the bag closed and swinging it over her arm. Her hands were shaking as she picked up her phone and keys, and I quickly collected myself, jumping up to catch her before she got to the door.

"Hey," I said, turning her to face me. "Why are you running out of here like that?"

She swallowed hard, her eyes suddenly glossy with unshed tears. "I..." She shook her head, then tried to move away, but I wouldn't let her go.

"Lauren, tell me what's going on?"

"I'm *embarrassed*," she blurted, then immediately tore her gaze from mine. "What we... what *I* just did. You probably think I'm a—"

"Woman who enjoys sexual stimulation?"

Despite herself, she giggled. "You know that's not what I was about to say."

"I do," I nodded. "But that other thing you're thinking, nah, I don't think that. Not at all. We just got a little carried away."

"A little?"

I chuckled. "Yeah, just a little. I didn't get to come, *you* did that. It was just a little for me."

"*Oh my God*," she said, covering her face with her hands. "I'm mortified."

"For what?" I moved her hands away from her face, then gave her a gentle kiss on the lips. "The hell are you embarrassed for? Shit, I'm jealous. Seemed like it was good."

Lauren slapped me on the arm. "Will you stop teasing me? It's been a while, I got a little excited."

"I'm not teasing you, I swear. And it's been a while for me too, so I need *you* to stop teasing."

"Really?" she asked, her eyebrows raising damn near into her hairline.

"Damn, do you have to say it like that?"

"Sorry," she cringed. "I just... I'm surprised, I guess. Usually guys, especially handsome ones, I... I didn't think you guys took breaks."

I shrugged. "Me and my ex broke up, and I just haven't been that interested in getting involved with anyone else until now."

"Yeah," she nodded. "Me too."

In the seconds after that statement, I wondered if she was talking about Harper's father, or someone else. But, I forced myself not to dwell on it, because it didn't matter. She wasn't Jamila.

"So yeah," I said, breaking the silence. "You don't have anything to be embarrassed about, not with me. We can't do *that* again though."

Lauren put on a face of innocence. "Why not?"

I lifted an eyebrow, then pulled her close, knowing she would feel my hardness pressing into her stomach. Her eyes widened, then her lips parted as she mouthed a quiet *"Oh."*

"Yeah, *oh*," I chuckled. "I want you to always feel comfortable with me, so I'll follow your lead for us to take that next step, but we can't go *that* far again, unless we're going all the way. Unless you're trying to kill me."

"I'm *not* trying to kill you."

"You've got a funny way of showing it."

Lauren giggled, then wrapped her arms around my neck, pulling herself up for a kiss. "I'll see you next week," she whispered against my mouth, then slipped her tongue into my mouth again.

I groaned, lifting her, pushing her back against my front door as I deepened the kiss. She wrapped her legs around my waist, drawing me close, and it wasn't until I'd snaked my hands up her thighs, over her ass, and my fingers met the edges of her panties that I realized we were back in the same place.

"*Shit*," I mumbled, reluctantly lowering her back to the floor. We exchanged goodbyes, and I practically pushed her out of the door, before we ended up taking it too far, *again*. I closed and locked the door behind her, then leaned against it, scrubbing a hand over my face.

I needed to take a damn shower.

eight

...

lauren

SHE *LAUGHED* AT ME.

I waited for Bianca at the airport after my own flight, so we could get a rental and drive the thirty minutes to my father's house together. I poured my heart out to her, and my big sister, supposedly biggest supporter, sat behind the wheel of our rental and laughed until tears streamed down her face as she drove.

"What's so damned funny?!" I snapped, brows furrowed as I frowned at her from the passenger side.

She wiped tears from her face with the back of her hand, then shook her head as she switched lanes to pass a slow-moving big rig. "I'm sorry, Lo. I swear I didn't mean to laugh, but why in the hell were you and Ty hunching like damned high school kids?"

I sucked my teeth as she broke into another round of giggles. "*Hunching?*"

"You don't know what hunching is?" she asked, shooting me a look of disbelief. "I guess I have to remember you're younger than me, so your slang is different, but, dry humping, bumping uglies. You using Ty as a scratching post. That's hunching, and it's beyond me why your grown asses were doing that, instead of just getting to the real damned deal!"

"Because I don't do casual sex, B. We've talked about this."

From the other side of the car, she rolled her eyes, but didn't say anything.

"Wait a minute," I said, poking her leg. "What's with the eye rolling, what is that about?"

"You and this whole *I don't do casual sex* mess."

"Mess?" I lifted an eyebrow. "Why is it mess?"

"Well, in general, it's not. But applied to your specific situation with Ty…yeah, it kinda is. You and Ty have been "talking" – she used air quotes for emphasis – "For what, like a month now? Any free time you have, you're with him. When you don't have time, y'all are texting back and forth all day, or on the phone until you fall asleep. And, correct me if I'm wrong, but just like you're busy, he's really busy too, especially with a PhD course load. Yet, how does he choose to spend the little free time he has? Wrapped up under you. Is that accurate?"

"I guess… yes."

"Okay, so it doesn't seem that "casual" to me. Casual is "I'll catch you when I catch you", or, "I'm bored so I'll hit that person up", or, "Damn I'm horny, what was the guy from the library's name?" What you and Ty are doing, that doesn't seem casual to me."

Hmmm.

"Let's say you're right," I started, propping my elbow on the door as I turned to look at my sister. "Okay… so it's not casual. Isn't it still too early to go there?"

Bianca shot me a scowl. "Aren't you the same girl who cheered me to start screwing Rashad, no relationship in sight?"

"That was different, though. You didn't even want a relationship, I was just encouraging you to do something that was within your comfort zone."

"Exactly," she smiled. "I don't believe there's a such thing as a universal "too early". It depends on what you're comfortable with. If you need to be in a place where you and Ty are ready to exchange "I love you", or a ring, or a wedding first, that's your prerogative. For me, as big sister, I would say ask yourself a few questions. Does he treat you well, as a rule? Do you trust him to have your best interests at heart? Can you trust him to be discreet, and not have your business all over campus? Can you trust him to not sneak a fucking camera into the room?"

I cringed at that last question, knowing that her experience with a vindictive ex-boyfriend sparked it. Bianca was a well-known fashion and beauty blogger, and she was still dealing with the aftermath of him releasing videos of their private, intimate sexual encounters for public viewing.

"I'm sorry," she said, shaking her head. "I got a little off track there, but I think you get my point. Your readiness to take that next step with Ty should be based purely on your own comfort level. He should be treating you well, making you happy, not pressuring you into something you don't want to do. If all of those line up, I say go for it. Otherwise, don't do it. But if you're going to wait, it should be because *you* want to wait, not because of some arbitrary rule. Okay?"

I pushed out a heavy sigh, then nodded. "Thanks B."

"You're welcome little sister. This is one of the good things about fucking up *so* royally with my first big relationship. I already did everything wrong, so I can pass what I learned from it down to you, and hopefully save you some of the bruises I got."

With one hand still on the steering wheel, she reached for my hand and squeezed.

"I appreciate you, Bianca."

She immediately let my hand go, then pushed my leg. "Ewww, don't get mushy."

"Whatever," I laughed. "But listen, that's not all."

She groaned as she exited the highway, putting us on the road that would lead to my father's house. "What other trouble have you been getting yourself into?"

"I wasn't getting into trouble, it's about Mekhi."

Bianca dropped her head back, rolling it against the head rest. "Oh lord, a love triangle?! Really Lauren?!"

"No," I insisted. "Not a love triangle, but... I mean, he *is* looking kinda good these days."

"As opposed to when you gave him the cookies the first time?"

I tipped my head to the side. "Well, he looked good back then too, but now he's like, grown up fine now. And he has real muscles."

"Ty has muscles. I seent 'em, you showed me a picture."

I laughed. "Ty *does* have muscles, but Mekhi has tattoos."

"Ty smells like books," she countered. "What does Mekhi smell like, jet fuel?"

"Shut *up*, oh my God!" I giggled at Bianca's comment, then shook my head. "I don't know what Mekhi smells like anymore, but I *do* know that I get the feeling he's angling for us to get back together. And isn't that what the whole family wants anyway?"

Bianca shrugged. "I just want you to be happy. And I know that with Mekhi, you guys broke up because you weren't getting along, right? The relationship couldn't stand the stress of a kid then, so what makes you think it will be different now?"

"I don't know," I answered. "But I do know it would be really cool for Harper to have both of her parents."

"Harper *has* both of her parents. All over the world, people co-parent without being romantically involved all the time."

I sighed. "Yeah, I know. But he called me a couple of weeks ago, and we talked on video. He asked me to change my plans so he could see me this weekend, offered to buy the ticket. And when we talked, there was something there. I think."

"Well," Bianca said, as we turned onto dad's street, "You'll see him today, right? So maybe you'll be able to figure it out then.

You and Mekhi had something, when you were teenagers. Ty has given you a taste of *real* chemistry, grown up feelings."

I grinned at her as the house at the end of the street came into view. "You sound like you're on team Ty."

"Nope." She shook her head as she parked the car. "I'm on team Lauren. I just want whoever you're with to come correct. Ty has you glowing, more relaxed. It seems like he's been really encouraging, really uplifting, from what you've told me. Men mature slower, so I kinda think you *need* a guy his age to be a good balance for you. And he's fine. Mekhi hasn't shown me anything yet. He has some catching up to do."

On that note, we exited the car, and went inside to settle into our rooms, and of course talk to dad and see Harper. The first thing I did when I reached the door was sweep my baby into my arms, and bury my nose in her honey-scented curls. We spent the night eating and laughing, just the four of us – and Puppy, and by the time I climbed into bed that night, with Harper at my side, my heart was full and happy.

My eyes were drifting closed when my phone lit up the room, silently notifying me that I'd received a message. Sleepily, I picked it up, smiling when I saw the message on the screen.

"Hope your day has been as awesome as you anticipated, pretty girl. Tell Harper Happy Birthday. – Ty."

The end of the message included a link, and when I tapped it, it led to an e-giftcard I could redeem at a popular toy store. I blinked several times at the amount, to make sure I was seeing it right.

"It has, thank you! You know you didn't have to get Harper anything, right? Especially not this much..."

"I wasn't sure what proper protocol was, so I figured better safe than sorry. It didn't feel right not to. – Ty"

"Well, thank you, very much. I appreciate it, and I know she will too."

"What are you doing, up studying?"

"Nah. Actually got a party to work tonight, so I'm doing that, then work in the morning, then studying tomorrow night. And I've got a paper to finish. – Ty."

"Busy busy."

"Yeah. I'm leaving in the next few minutes, but I wanted you to know you were on my mind. –Ty"

That was all it took to get my heart racing. I stared at those words for a little bit, then finally tapped out a response.

"Been thinking about you too."

"Oh really now? ;) What exactly were you thinking? Give details. – Ty"

I rolled my eyes. *"Not like that, nasty. Just… thinking. About you, and us."*

"What were YOU thinking about?"

"Same. – Ty"

"*Uh huh.*"

"For real. Nothing nasty. – Ty"

"Well, there was one time, but that's your fault, for what you did yesterday – Ty"

"But other than that, yeah… looking forward to when you get back. – Ty"

"You miss me already?"

"Honestly? Yeah. – Ty"

"GTG. Talk soon. Good night.– Ty"

"Good night."

I restrained myself from ending that text with a little heart icon, but I felt tingly over the fact that he missed me. It ignited a warmth that spread all the way through my chest, and I fell asleep with a smile on my face, thinking of Ty.

∽

I WAS NERVOUS.

No, scratch that.

I was *beyond* nervous about seeing Mekhi, which was completely weird.

It didn't start until my second day back home, on Harper's birthday. We woke up, took her to have pancakes and bacon, got her dressed in her birthday outfit, and drove to the house where Mekhi had grown up.

It wasn't just me and Bianca in the car this time, so I couldn't even talk to her about it, and have her pull me back from the ledge. It was me, my dad, Harper, and Bianca doing the driving, and with each mile that passed, I felt a little sicker to my stomach.

What would he do? What would he say? How would he look?

I got all three of those answers way sooner than I was ready for them.

When would I have been ready?

Never.

As soon as we walked through the door, Harper took off in the direction of the balloons sprinkling the backyard, tossing a distracted, "Hi grammy, hi grampy!" over her shoulder as she went. The rest of the family followed her outside, with Puppy in tow, while I made a detour into the kitchen.

Mekhi's mother had always insisted we make ourselves welcome in her home, so I did exactly that, opening a cabinet to get a glass. I put it on the counter, then turned for the fridge to grab the water, and just as my hand landed on the handle, Mekhi appeared in the doorway.

He was dressed casually, in sneakers, blue plaid shorts, and a white tee shirt that stretched deliciously across his chest. It wasn't like it was the first, second, or 500th time I'd ever seen him, but today, he was in high-contrast, full HD. Smooth caramel skin, perfectly lined haircut, perfectly shaved... sexy. There was a flicker of *something* in his eyes that made my cheeks feel hot, and when he smiled, it made somewhere else feel hot.

He didn't say anything, just strode over to where I was and

pulled me into his arms. "You look good," he mumbled into my ear, and with my face against his chest, I breathed him in.

Definitely doesn't smell like jet fuel, I thought, remembering my conversation with Bianca. He smelled like leather and soap.

"I see you messed around and got a little body, huh?" he asked with a grin, biting his lip as he circled me, raking me with his eyes. "Where you get this ass from, Lo?"

I sucked my teeth and turned around to face him, pulling my face into a scowl. "I could ask you the same thing, dude. What's with the shoulders, and the arms, and the tats?"

He placed a hand over his chest, where I knew Harper's name was, thanks to that video call. "I may have been in the gym doing a 'lil something," he laughed. "I can't be in my uniforms looking all scrawny and stuff."

"Is that right?"

"That's right," he said, his arms flexing as he gripped the edge of the counter behind him and leaned back into it. "So what about you, answer the question."

"What question?"

He lifted an eyebrow. "The *ass*. Where did it come from? You didn't have that back when we were getting down."

I rolled my eyes. "It came from the exact opposite place your body changes came from. A lack of going to the gym, plenty of sitting, and horrible diet choices."

Mekhi chuckled, shaking his head. "It looks good though. You look *grown*. Grown as hell." He stared at me so intensely, not bothering to hide the lust in his eyes, that I had to look away, pushing a handful of curls out of my eyes. "You seeing somebody?" he asked, and I looked back at him.

"You asked me that a few weeks ago, and I gave you an answer then."

He shrugged. "That was a few weeks ago. Answers to that kind of question change, right?"

"Right," I nodded, pushing my hands into the back pockets of my shorts.

"So," he said, tipping his head a little. "Has the answer changed?"

I swallowed hard, then met his eyes when I nodded again. "Yes."

Why, why, *why* was it so hard for me to push that *yes* out? I was feeling Ty, liked him a lot. We had crazy chemistry, a lot in common. And he was gorgeous, in his way. Not "buff-pretty-boy" gorgeous like Mekhi, but still so, so yummy. And I wanted him, wanted him bad. Crushed on him, crushed on him hard. We'd been out together, I'd fallen asleep at his place, we'd made out.

Mekhi was basically my boyfriend.

Wait… I mean, *Ty*.

Shit shit shit shit shit sh—

"Damn," Mekhi said, interrupting my silent freak-out. "Life comes at you fast, huh?"

I just nodded, because I didn't know what else to say.

"Where's baby girl?" he asked. Something was a little different about his energy now, not like he was mad or anything, just maybe… disappointed. "I talked to her this morning, but she doesn't know I made it yet."

I pointed towards the hall, which led outside. "She ran out there."

He chuckled. "The balloons?"

"Yeah."

"Why am I not surprised?" He smiled at me, then extended his hand in my direction. "Well, come on, let's get out there so we can have some time before her little friends get here."

I looked at his hand, and he looked at *me*, waiting, keeping it out like he just *knew* I was going to take it.

And…

I did.

I waited for that feeling, the same one I'd gotten the first time I touched Ty, that warm, pleasant exchange of energy that pushed attraction past the point you could deny it.

It never came.

Not that his hand was clammy, or anything like that, but touching Mekhi... wasn't like touching Ty. I didn't feel drawn closer, the feeling of his skin didn't give me butterflies, touching him didn't make me want to take off my clothes. It made me want Ty.

Still, I let Mekhi hold my hand and lead me outside, where he was immediately ambushed by an excited Harper. Bianca raised an eyebrow at me, then tipped her head, her way of letting me know she would want to talk to me later. Mekhi's mother looked pleased with herself, my dad looked suspicious, and Mekhi's dad... had snuck back inside, probably to watch ESPN.

Harper's little birthday gathering passed uneventfully, and once she'd had her fill of cake and presents and friends, we pushed the issue of a nap, which she reluctantly took. Two hours later she was back up, so we got her bathed and dressed, and then we went to a movie.

We, meaning me, Harper, and Mekhi.

Occasionally, I could feel Mekhi watching me as I watched the movie. It was some computer animated thing about an alien and a lost little girl, and I was paying much heavier attention to it than I normally would have, to keep myself from returning his gaze.

To call me confused would have been a major understatement.

Just as I'd realized back when we were teenagers, I didn't have a spark with Mekhi. So why was he in my thoughts just as heavily as Ty? That stayed on my mind throughout the movie, into a trip to a cute little ice cream parlor where Mekhi helped Harper make her own sundae.

He and Harper were adorable times ten together, and I wasn't the only one who noticed. From our table, I watched them go from station to station in the crowded shop, and I wasn't the only one watching. More than one woman took notice of the gorgeous man with his gorgeous daughter. He was patient with her when she spilled, helped her clean it up. And he kept doing things that made her dissolve into peals of giggling that would melt *anybody's* heart. She was in complete awe as he assisted her with each step, and her eyes shone with love for her daddy, provider of ice cream, deliverer of sprinkles and marshmallows, pourer of chocolate sauce.

Mekhi looked up, catching my gaze to gift me with another smile that made me feel tingly. Why could he do that to me with his smile, but not his touch? What the hell was it? Maybe I was putting too much stock in some arbitrary thing like whether or not we had a "spark".

Or maybe I was just feeling nostalgic.

On the drive home, Harper fell asleep, and Mekhi reached over to grab my hand, threading his fingers through mine. "So," he said, with his eyes still on the road. "Lauren has a man, huh?"

"That's an interesting question to ask while you're holding my hand."

Mekhi chuckled. "What, would he get mad?"

I shrugged. "Maybe not really mad, but I doubt he'd like it very much. And I don't think your girl would like it much either."

Now, whether or not he actually *had* a girl was a complete mystery to me, but I wasn't beyond fishing for informa—

"I wouldn't exactly call her my girl."

Bingo.

"But, you're probably right," he said, releasing my hand. "Cause I'd be pissed if I found out she was holding some muthafucka's hand."

Who the *fuck* was this girl he—

Wait a minute. Pump your brakes, Lauren.

I swallowed the heavy lump of jealousy that sprang to my

throat, knowing that it had more to do with wanting to be wanted *by* Mekhi, than me actually *wanting* Mekhi.

"So it's not serious yet?" I ask, clasping my hands together in my lap.

He shook his head, his gesture illuminated by the street lights as he turned onto my dad's street. "Nah, not yet." Quiet stretched between us for a long moment, unbroken until he pulled into the drive way, and shut off the car. "Can I be for real with you?"

"It's the only way I'd like you to be."

I felt, rather than saw him nod, because I had my gaze focused outside, on the slight motions of the rose bushes in the front yard, swaying in the end.

"It was about to be serious. I was ready to make it serious. And as soon as I made that decision, suddenly all I could think about was you."

My heart stopped for a couple of beats, then I looked back in Mekhi's direction. The street lamp kicked on, bathing half of his face in light, and he was staring at me. Harper's soft snores were the only thing that punctuated the silence until I finally spoke.

"What does that mean, Mekhi?"

He ran his tongue over his lips. "It means… it's like I was ready to make Talia my girl, but then something started poking at me, like wait a minute dude, what about Lauren? What if it's different now? Like I see how hard you grind for Harper, trying to get your shit together. I see how much you love her, how much she loves you, and it makes me realize that *I* still love you too. And I feel like, if I still love you, how is that fair to Talia? And, if I still love you, maybe we should be giving this another shot."

"It's *not* fair to Talia," I replied, shaking my head. "But Mekhi, the love we share because of Harper isn't the same as the kind of love we would need to sustain a relationship. They're two different things. Like, if we didn't have Harper, if we'd just broken up in high school, like high school kids do, do you really think you'd be checking for me?"

"I get what you're saying Lo, that there wouldn't be any lingering feelings if we didn't have that connection that Harper brings. But the fact is, we *do* have that connection. We can't look at the "what if". I'm looking at the "right now", and the "right now" is that I'm torn between exploring something new with Talia, or rekindling things between me and you."

"Then we're in the same position." I unclipped my seatbelt, then turned to face him with my feet tucked under me in the seat. "But I wonder if we're putting too much importance on the past, holding on to something that should stay a memory. Like… here." – I reached forward, grabbing his hand. "Do you feel that?"

He frowned at our clasped hands for a few moments, then shook his head. "Feel what?"

"Exactly," I said, releasing his hand. "There's nothing there! And maybe that's a silly thing to use as proof, but there's no spark when we touch. When we hugged earlier, was that exciting for you?"

Mekhi tipped his head to the side, smirking. "Well…"

"*No*, fool," I laughed, slapping him on the arm. "I'm not talking about arousal, I'm talking about exhilaration. Not a physical reaction to someone, a mental reaction, that sets off a physiological one. Not because of how I looked, even though that's part of it, but because of who I *was*." I shrugged. "Like, I get what you're feeling Mekhi, because I feel it too. It's confusing, and frustrating. But I don't think we should be quick to drop the people who could be the loves of our lives for the sake of what could have been between us."

Harper murmured something in her sleep about Puppy, then snuggled closer to the huge stuffed bear clutched in her arms. We both turned, watching, waiting for her to drift back into a deep sleep, and when he turned back, our eyes met again.

"You're probably right," Mekhi murmured, giving me a lazy smile. "I really am feeling the hell out of Talia."

For some reason, that time there was no prickle of jealousy in my chest. "Is she pretty?"

Mekhi scoffed. "*Pretty*? She's fucking gorgeous. She's a nurse, on the base. Smart, big heart, she thinks I'm funny, and she has a fat ass. What more can a man ask for, you know?"

"Not much more than that I guess," I giggled. "A nurse, huh? She older than you?"

"Just by a year."

I smiled. So *he* went a little older too. "She sounds awesome."

"Yeah, she is." Mekhi reached out, nudging my leg. "You gonna tell me about this lame ass you fooling with?"

"Watch it now." I pointed a finger at his face. "I'm choosing him over you, so if he's lame, that makes you…"

"Whatever Lo," he laughed. "You wanna tell me about this dude or not?"

"Not particularly."

"Why not?"

"Because."

"Because you know I'm not gonna like him regardless?"

I nodded. "Basically. Ty is twenty-five, in a PhD program at BSU. He's tall, and has a cool haircut, and he gives me butterflies."

"I want butterflies too mommy."

Harper's sleepy, barely conscious voice traveled to us from the back of the car. That was our clue that it was time to get her in bed, before she overheard something inappropriate for her little ears.

I unlocked the front door, and Mekhi carried her upstairs, where we changed her into pajamas before depositing her in my bed, where she was asleep again before her head touched the pillow. I walked Mekhi back down to the front door.

"I'd like to come pick her up for breakfast tomorrow," he said, lingering in the open door. "And then you can have her back until it's time for your flight, since I'll be here a few days longer than you. And of course, you're welcome to join us."

I smiled. "Thank you for the invitation. I'll definitely have Harper ready, but I'll have to think about whether or not I'll tag along."

"Okay."

He lingered a few moments longer before we finally said our goodbyes, but just as I was about to close the door, he turned around, and his mouth was on mine before I knew what was happening. It was soft, no tongue, no nibbles, nothing like that. Just a sweet, lingering press of his lips, aimed perfectly not to land full-on, but more toward the corner of my mouth.

"Goodnight Lo," he said, when he pulled away, and I had to say my own goodbye to his retreating back.

I closed the door, then turned, pressing my back to it as I raised my fingers to my mouth. What had made him kiss me, I had no idea. All I knew was that when I finally moved away from the door a few minutes later… I could, just faintly, still feel the tingle of Mekhi's lips.

nine
. . .
ty

IT WAS one of those days where I wondered what I was doing.

I was really, *really* sick of school.

Beyond sick of school.

But... this was what I signed up for, and I wasn't anybody's quitter, so I sat in my tiny studio apartment and tried to focus on *Quantitative Research Methods in Business*.

I've never been so relieved for my phone to ring.

I sprang up, grabbing the phone from the table, hoping Lauren's name would be on the screen. We'd seen each other exactly once in the two weeks since she'd gone home for her daughter's birthday, and to be honest... I was missing her like crazy.

Our lack of time spent physically together wasn't either of our faults. Lauren got saddled with last minute coursework from a professor who thought the syllabus was more of a brainstorming activity than a guide, plus the stuff she already had to do. I ended up being summoned to my parent's house for a disastrous "family meeting" that took up the entire weekend I'd hoped to spend with Lauren.

The name on the screen wasn't hers.

Instead, I groaned, dropping my head into my hands before I reluctantly pressed the button to answer the call.

"Hello? *Hello?*" came a crisp voice from the other end of the line, and I grudgingly raised the phone to my ear.

"Yeah?" I grumbled.

The woman on the line huffed, repeating *yeah* with disgust dripping from her tone. "Is that how you greet your mother?"

"Sorry, mother. Hello mother," I said dryly, not to comply, but to further grate her nerves.

"You are not *sorry*," she snapped. "You are Roosevelt Tyson Sinclair, and Sinclairs are not sorry people."

Why the fuck did I answer this phone?

"Did you need something, ma?"

She sniffed. "As a matter of fact, I *do*."

Inwardly, I groaned.

"You got away from me this weekend without answering," she continued, "But I'd like you to tell me exactly what is happening between you and Jamila. She's called here crying more than once, begging me to get you to see reason. We're going to need to send these invitations out, sooner than later."

I wanted to laugh at that. "I *did* answer you, and it's the same answer I've been giving you for the last seven or eight months, however long it's been since I found out she was cheating on me. I'm not marrying that girl."

"*That girl* is the one you swore was the love of your life when I had my doubts. Once I approved, all of a sudden you can't stomach her."

I scoffed. "Ma, you only approved once you realized Jamila was a Thurston, so she had a pedigree. I can't stomach her because she fucked some dude she swore was her "friend"."

"*Language.*"

"Sorry."

"You're *not* sor—"

"Can you chill with that, please? I love you mama, but this is exhausting. Since dad passed, you've been on level ten with this bougie stuff. Can you just relax?"

She let out a haughty sniff. "Relax? Roosevelt, I have vendors calling me, caterers waiting on RSVP lists, florists ready for flower orders. No, I can't *just relax*. I'm planning a wedding!"

"For *who*?!"

"For *you*, my son! You will not embarrass me, do you understand? Can you imagine the gossip if—"

"I don't care about that, mama. I swear to you, I really don't. I'm not embarrassed by a canceled wedding or a failed engagement, not at all. But a cheating wife... now *that* would fuck with my pride."

"Language."

"Sorry."

"You—*ugh*! Listen to me, Roosevelt. You will marry Jamila Thurston this September, and you will *like* it. That girl is about to be a doctor and she is a member of one of the most prominent black families in this country. She is your wife, she is your future. You will do this, and do it with a smile, or you can kiss all of your little luxuries goodbye."

I chuckled. "Wrong kid."

"Excuse me?"

"*Wrong kid*. You forget that I already turned twenty-five – my trust fund has been disbursed. You can't threaten me with that anymore, and even if that weren't true, the answer would still be no. I'm a grown man, you can't make me do anything. Rocky might let you control her, but not me."

She was quiet for a long time before she spoke again, her voice strained. "Son, your father and his father before him, and his before him, worked very hard to build this family into a recognizable name. Historically, each generation marries into good stock, so we can continue to build that name. You're not going to find better stock than Jamila. Especially not this... unwed mother she's told me you've been cavorting with."

You've gotta be kidding me.

So Jamila ran and tattled to my mother. *Wonderful.* I was really trying hard not to be rude to my mother, but I was on the verge of just hanging up. As I'd already explained, this shit was exhausting, and I wasn't in the mood for being stern, with *anybody*.

On many levels, Jamila and my mother, Geneva Sinclair, were the same person, which was my first mistake. They both started out sweet, bubbly, and just the right amount of stuck-up. My mother's personality shifted six years ago, when my father died. He was the one who brought the "sweet and bubbly" out of her, and she lost it all when she lost him.

Coincidentally, that was also around the time when I met Jamila.

I discovered later that it wasn't coincidental at all, that the media storm about the passing of a high-level executive and part owner of Sinclair Realty had brought her to my doorstep. Before that, I was probably just another face in the crowd to her, because I was low key.

I'd gotten scholarships to cover all of my tuition, so I convinced my dad to give me the money they'd put aside for my education. I used that to cover the miniscule off-campus apartment I still lived in, because it was cheaper than the dorms. I wore regular sneakers, jeans from the mall like everybody else, no designer shit for me just because I was "a Sinclair". I kept my head down, made good grades, pledged the fraternity that all Sinclair men did, and lived my life.

And then I "met" Jamila. Beautiful girl, excelling in all of her courses except the ones that involved a computer. I was tutoring back then, and when she approached me, I thought I'd hit the jackpot. Under my tutelage, she was "suddenly" making all A's, and before long we started dating.

My mother couldn't stand her. Her hair was too "nappy", and she didn't have light enough skin, so she wouldn't even bother to learn her name. But I didn't care about that, because I'd fallen in love with a smart, beautiful girl who was just as in love with me.

I was stupid as shit.

Eventually, my mom warmed to Jamila, and I realized later that it was because she'd finally taken time to look into her, into her background, probably with the goal of removing her from the picture. Instead, she found what she considered her perfect daughter-in-law: a pretty, well-educated black girl from a good – meaning extremely wealthy – family.

A funny – meaning not fucking funny at all – thing happened once my mother and Jamila started getting along. The "sweet and bubbly"-ness started to slip away. We'd finished undergrad by that time, and she was starting medical school, so I attributed it to stress. A couple of years passed, I finished my master's, and then I proposed, because I still loved her, I think. She was starting harder classes, I was entering my PhD program. She turned into a word I don't like to call women, with sweetness sprinkled in here and there, and I was busy as hell anyway, so it was easy to just avoid her, and any talks about the wedding.

Second mistake.

I can admit that I probably wasn't the best fiancé. It was easy to get fatigued by Jamila, so it became the norm to ignore her calls, sometimes I would –honestly – forget we were supposed to be meeting somewhere. But she had my mother, her new best friend, to keep her occupied, so I didn't think much of it.

Until I started hearing little rumors about her outside activities. But, I did what I thought I was supposed to do, I went to her, asked outright if something was going on, what we could do to get things back on track. We talked about it, made up, and we were in a good place.

My third mistake was believing that.

"Are you listening to me, Roosevelt? Do you realize that this little girl doesn't fit with this family? I mean, her father is a veteran, so that's a tiny bit in her favor, but this sister of hers, with purple hair, and a sex tape scandal, and tattoos, and screwing these photographers... sweetheart, we just can't have that! And then the little girl herself... she's a smart girl, I'll give you that, but do you realize she was *sixteen* years old when she had a child? What kind of example does that set? The Sinclairs may vote blue, but we are known for upstanding family values, none of this controversy."

I let out a loud bark of laughter. "You can't be serious right now. There's all kinds of scandalous shit in the history of our family, we can start with dad being in a relationship with you, while he was still in a relationship with his first wife. I'm not judging you, and I don't mean any disrespect, but come on, mom. I don't know what's happening behind the scenes with everybody else, but our little segment of the family isn't the place to look for conservative values."

That was the honest truth, and I wasn't sure why my mother liked to pretend otherwise. My father had four children. My twenty-three year old sister, Racquel, was the baby of the family, and an environmental terrorist in the making. Roger and Roslyn were the same age, twenty-eight, but not twins, because my dad was a rolling stone. Roger – my mother's child – was one of the top-producing realtors at Sinclair. He was also gay, and planning a big-assed wedding. Roslyn – my father's child with his first wife – was making a name for herself as an exotic dancer, and raking money in teaching classes around the country. And then there was me, professional student, working at the library, and putting off joining the family business.

We weren't going on anybody's conservative family values poster, despite my mother's delusions.

"Roosevelt, I am not playing with you. That little girl is—"

"She's not a little girl," I snapped, in a harsher tone than I meant to use with my mother, but I was tired of going around this. "Her name is Lauren, and she's a grown woman. She's smart, she's beautiful, she's a good mother, and I like her, so I'm gonna be with her. Your input isn't necessary."

My mother gasped, like I'd slapped her in the face, and the only thing I could do was rub my temples.

Here we fucking go, again.

"So this little hussy already has you disrespecting your mother, choosing her over me?!"

"When did I disrespect you?"

"You're not listening to me," she hissed.

I shook my head. "So you don't want respect, you want obedience. Sorry mama, but… I'm a grown man. Obedience isn't about to happen."

"Your father," she started, her voice shaking with angry tears, "Would be so disappointed in you right now."

"I don't think he'd be disappointed in *me* at all."

A second later, the complete silence on the line told me I'd been hung up on, and my shoulders sagged in relief. I agonized for about thirty seconds over whether I'd crossed the line between firm and disrespectful with my mother, then shrugged it off. When I thought about my siblings… I was easily the one who was the most gentle with her when she got controlling and over the top, which was how I'd earned my nickname – among us— as the "good son".

Even though I knew she was probably busy, I texted Lauren anyway. After that conversation with my mother… I definitely needed some sunshine.

∼

lauren

"Hey pretty girl. You busy? – Ty"

I sighed at the message on my screen, because unfortunately, I was. I'd had no real moments of rest since Harper's birthday.

Going home that weekend had thrown off my schedule, so I was cramming to finish things that were due before the long weekend. Then, I spent the long weekend catching up on things that I'd neglected to finish other work. It was pure luck that Ty had gone out of town at the last minute, or it would have been me keeping us from being able to hang out.

Now though, mid terms were coming up, and I was a bundle of anxiety and stress yet again. I was at a point where I was seriously considering quitting my job, but the thought of having even less money than I already did killed that plan.

With a regretful sigh, I returned Ty's message, explaining that I had a paper to finish, a test to study for, and a working code snippet to deliver by Monday, and today was Saturday. He texted back that he understood, which I knew was true, but still... how was our relationship supposed to grow, when we weren't feeding it?

We'd learned a lot about each other through texting and phone calls, but to me, that wasn't the same as being close to him, feeding off the energy of physically sharing space. I wanted that, more than anything, but duty called, in the form of seemingly endless school work.

I spent the next four hours heavily into my tasks. I was able to put down a rough draft of my code snippet, and I got through the outline of my paper, which was usually the hardest part. I hadn't even touched my *Systems Outsourcing* book. It was late, my brain was fried, and no matter how hard I tried to think of something else, my thoughts kept drifting to Ty.

I picked up my phone, noting that it was after eleven at night as I tapped out a message to him.

"Hey, you awake?"

It took a little longer than usual to get a response, so I almost thought the answer was *no* until my phone buzzed with a new message.

"Yeah. What's up? – Ty"

"Nothing much... you were on my mind. What are you doing?"

"Anything except studying. Chilling. Trying to mellow out. You? – Ty"

"Still in the books, unfortunately. Gonna give it a few more hours, then go to bed."

"Sounds awful. – Ty"

"That's accurate, lol. TTYL."

I got up, drank a glass of water, ate an apple, and walked around a little, trying to give myself a boost of energy before I sat down and opened my book to study. Thirty minutes later, I gave up. I tossed my book onto the table with the rest, then took a long shower. I was rubbing my favorite brown-sugar scented body butter onto my wet skin when Ty returned to my thoughts.

He *loved* the way I smelled, and had asked me countless times where it came from, like he didn't believe it wasn't perfume. That sparked an idea in my mind, and I went to my dresser, pulling open the drawer where I kept my bras and panties.

On one side, there was a row of stuff I never touched, stuff that I'd purchased but never worn. It wasn't that I felt like I needed someone to wear them for, because I'd bought them just for the sake of feeling sexy. But I quickly realized that feeling sexy with no one to work it out on wasn't exactly fun for me.

I thought it would be fun to feel sexy when I was with Ty though. I chose a set that was the color of orange sherbet, then marveled at how pretty it looked against my skin. I'd never lacked confidence in the way I looked, but seeing myself like this, with my breasts spilling out of the sheer lace and tiny bows holding my panties together at the hips... it made my heart race.

Mina wasn't home, but I went into her room anyway, and opened her closet, because I knew she wouldn't mind. I managed to find something I could get into, a sexy black dress that molded to my body like paint, and borrowed sky-high heels too.

In my bathroom, I pulled my hair into a sexy updo, and used eyeliner and shadow to give my eyes a sensual appeal, then topped off my look with glossy red lips. Satisfied with my appearance, I grabbed my keys, phone, and purse, and left my apartment.

I didn't even make it to the elevator before I turned my ass around.

I washed my face and went for toned down makeup, then fluffed my hair into my usual fro. I took off the ultra-sexy shoes, and dress, and put on something of my own, a simple blue tank top dress. Last time I wore one around him, Ty hadn't been able to keep his eyes off me.

I left the lingerie on.

ten
. . .
lauren

FIFTEEN MINUTES LATER, I pulled up at Ty's building, suddenly nervous about just popping up on him. What if he was pissed? What if he didn't let me in?

I pushed those thoughts to the side. I was there now, so may as well see.

It took him a *long* time to come to the door. Or maybe just longer than the ten seconds I was used to it taking when he was expecting me. It was starting to rain, and getting heavier by what seemed like ten second intervals. I was under the breezeway that led to his door, but one gust of wind could leave me soaked, which would have pissed me off. A full minute passed, then two, and just when I was about to knock again, the door swung open.

Oh.

My.

Damn.

Ty was shirtless.

I'd wondered what he looked like without one, but it wasn't the type of thing a girl could just ask. My patience was rewarded, with sinewy arms, ridged abs, and shoulders that made me want

Christina C Jones

to climb him, all covered in that gorgeous dark golden-brown skin.

He was wearing basketball shorts, slung low on his hips, and I had to force my eyes back up to his face, instead of staring at his groin like I wanted. His eyes were low, lip pulled between his teeth as he looked me up and down too.

"Hey," I said, shifting nervously in my flats, waiting for his gaze to return to my face.

The corners of his lips turned up in a lazy, sexy smile that made me clench my thighs. "Hey. Thought you were studying?" He pushed his hands in the pockets of his shorts, and the waistband dipped lower.

"I… I was, but… I thought I'd come see you instead."

He stared at me for so long without responding that I dropped my gaze, and took a step back, but he suddenly grabbed me by the arm, gently pulling me inside. I didn't have a chance to say anything else before my face was in his hands and he was covering my mouth with his, pulling me into a kiss that made my knees weak. His tongue was in my mouth, hot and sweet, hypnotizing as he lowered his hands to my waist, pulling me against him.

This wasn't the first time we'd kissed in greeting, but never, *ever* like this. Since that day at his place, we'd not even made out, for fear of ending up in that position again. Ty was always cautious with me, sweet kisses, hesitant hands, both of which I knew were because of my declaration of no casual sex. He was pacing himself, not getting too hot, not taking it too far, but tonight, none of that hesitance existed.

Ty devoured me with that kiss, and I was enjoying every moment, until he pulled away, leaving me with damp panties and breasts aching to be touched as he planted a last kiss against my forehead.

"I missed you this week," he murmured, then pulled me into

his embrace. I melted against him, molding myself to the contours of his bare chest.

"I missed you too."

He led me to the couch, and as he pulled me to sit down, I caught a whiff of... *something*. As usual, he kept a little distance from me, sitting back against the arm, looking at me through heavy-lidded eyes.

"So you decided to shut the books down for the night, huh?" he asked, his words slow, deliberate, like his lips were as heavy as his eyelids seemed. A crack of thunder sounded from outside, but I was so enthralled by his eyes that I didn't even flinch. It wasn't until he raised an eyebrow and gave me that easy smile again that I realized he was waiting on an answer.

"Y-yeah," I said, swallowing hard. My lips were still tingling from that kiss earlier, and his apartment felt hot. And just, *different*. There was rap music in the background, like there always was, turned up just loud enough to hear the beat, but not the lyrics. "I got burned out, and over-stressed, and tired, and I just couldn't deal anymore."

He gave a dry chuckle. "Same here." He reached for the glass of dark, ice-filled liquid on the table in front of us and took a short sip. Bubbles fizzed in the glass when he sat it back down. "Oh, shit," he said, lazily rubbing a hand over his face. "I didn't even ask, you hungry, thirsty, anything?" His eyes were normal for a few seconds before they slipped back down to low and sexy as he waited for my response.

"Just water is fine."

He nodded, then took his time getting up going to the kitchen to get it. I could hear him pulling down a glass, filling it with ice, the normal steps to fix someone a drink, and while he did that, I thought about what I was doing here.

If I were completely honest, it wasn't about watching TV, or talking, or whatever we usually did. I wanted him to see me in the sheer lace lingerie, and then... without it.

That admission, even just to myself, made me hot.

Really hot.

I reached for his glass, since he was taking so long, and lifted it to my mouth. I smelled the liquor in it before the glass touched my lips. It took about two seconds of contemplation to decide that a little liquid courage could only help my cause, and I raised the glass, bottom up, downing it as Ty shouted my name from across the room.

"Lo, what the hell are you doing?" he asked, pushing an icy glass of water in my hands as I started choking. The liquor burned down my throat, and I regretted drinking it all in one gulp. Ty lifted the water to my mouth, helping me drink, and the cold liquid soothed some of the fire.

Embarrassed, I pulled away once I could catch my composure, and shook my head. "What the hell *was* that?"

"Crown and coke," he chuckled. "Mixed to *my* tastes, not for underage drinkers."

"Whatever." I wiped my mouth. "Shit felt like battery acid."

"That's what you get. You'd better drink the rest of this," he said, handing me the water. "I have my doubts about how well you can hold liquor."

I rolled my eyes. "It's not my first drink, Ty. How much liquor was in there?"

He shrugged. "Two shots worth, maybe. And I'd already drank about a third of it."

"Then I'll be fine," I assured him, not mentioning that Mina and I had, last year, sat around and drank half a bottle of rum, just for the hell of it. Mina passed out mid-sentence. I just got really sleepy, and really, *really* horny.

He didn't look very convinced, and shook his head. "Damn, pretty girl. You came over here trying to blow my damned high."

My eyes narrowed.

"*High?*"

Suddenly, I recognized the smell from earlier, and stepped

closer, trying to catch another whiff as he scrubbed a hand over his face, muttering *shit* under his breath.

"It's nothing to trip about," he said, reaching for my hands. "I promise you, just a little recreational use to relax every once in a while. And after the day I've had… I needed it."

I shrugged. "Ty, I'm not tripping over you smoking weed. I know what a pot head looks like, and I know that's not you."

His shoulders seemed to sink in relief.

"But," I said, stepping closer to him, "I do want you tell me what's going on."

He looked at me for a long time, his eyes a little more focused than before, then finally nodded.

We sat down together on the couch, and he told me all about his dynamic with his mom. He also vented a little about Jamila, who he'd told me about before. I doubted if he saw it, but from my view, I saw two scared women. One who was afraid to lose him, and one who already had, both trying to keep ahold of whatever pieces of control they could. But I said nothing. It wasn't my place, and it wasn't about me, it was about letting him get it out, which I suspected he didn't do often. Even though his words grew harsh sometimes, it didn't slip by me that he was always respectful, even when speaking about Jamila.

By the time he finished talking, he seemed exhausted. His shoulders were tense and his energy was just *off*. I touched his shoulder, looked him in the eyes… and asked him if he wanted to get high again.

"Lauren *hell* no," he said, adamantly shaking his head. "I see that liquor has kicked in, if you think I'm about to smoke weed with you."

I sucked my teeth. "Ugh! Why are you acting like that? I'm not a kid, Ty. You realize if it was a cigarette, it would be fine, right?"

"But it's *not* a cigarette. I'm not even technically supposed to have it, let alone be getting minors high."

My mouth dropped open. "First of all I'm not a damned minor, are you kidding me?" I laughed, longer than intended. Maybe I *was* a little tipsy. "Second, "technically"? Mmhmm, who'd you bribe to get one of those little medical need cards?"

"That's for me to know," he said, snaking his arm around my waist to pull me closer.

I gave in to his tugging, and climbed into his lap, straddling his legs. A memory flashed of the last time we'd been in this position, and from the look on his face, I knew he was thinking the same thing. "I'm gonna tell on you," I whispered, lowering my mouth to his.

"You wouldn't." He gripped my butt through the soft fabric of my dress, dragging me into him.

"You're right." Ty groaned as I rocked my hips against his, then ran my tongue along the seam of his lips. "But I want you to pretend you aren't, and introduce me to something new anyway."

Between my legs, I could feel him growing, heavy and hard. I rocked against him again, and he sucked in a breath, closing his eyes.

"You don't play fair."

He gently pushed me off of him, adjusting himself in his shorts before he stood. Alone on the couch, I squeezed my thighs together for as long as I could, then stood on slightly wobbly legs to go to the window with him.

The big window was actually a patio, but because it was raining we just opened the doors enough for the breeze. With the lights down low, Ty sat me in front of him, and I watched carefully as he assembled and lit a joint.

I'd always thought that smoking – cigarettes, at least –was kind of gross. I was never one of those kids that thought smoking was cool, by any stretch of the imagination, but when *Ty* did it... there was something unbelievably sexy about him lifting the rolled paper to his lips, taking a slow pull, then letting the smoke curl in dim light around him as he released it.

There was no bitter, acrid smell like with tobacco. The marijuana smoke was heavy and sweet, tickling my face as he blew a puff in my direction.

"You ready?" he asked, lifting his eyebrows as he held it out to me. I met his eyes, which were already getting lower again, and nodded. Pushing myself up on my knees, I moved closer, kneeling right in front of him.

Despite his own state of… relaxation, he gave me clear instructions, repeated them, then held the joint to my mouth. I closed my lips around it, and did what he said, squealing and clapping in delight when I was able to smoothly exhale the smoke.

Ty shook his head, chuckling at my reaction as I took the weed from him, and inhaled again.

"Don't go overboard," he said, taking it from me and putting it out. "We're just… relaxing, not going to the moon, right?"

I blew my smoke in his face, and he laughed, but a second later my face was in his hands again, and he was kissing me deep. The soothing effects of the marijuana began to take over, and I felt my own eyes drooping as low as his. I pressed myself closer to him, wrapping my arms around his neck, running my hands over the muscled cords of his back, wanting, still, to be closer.

But he wouldn't do it.

No matter how much I rolled my hips against his, how deep I took the kiss, he wouldn't touch me anywhere except my waist or thighs, not taking my hints that I wanted more.

Frustrated, I pulled away, mumbling something about the bathroom. Behind me, I could feel him standing as well, and when I glanced back at the bedroom just before I closed the door, I could see him stretched across the bed with his arm covering his eyes.

I pulled the door shut a little more firmly than I meant to.

What the hell are you doing, Lauren?

Only *I* could take a sexy moment — while I was high, at that — and turn it into something to stress about. If he didn't want to have sex with me, he just didn't, and I should respect that. But then... what was that arm over the eyes about? That was something you did when you were battling yourself about something, and there was no denying his body's reaction to me.

So... maybe...

I shook my head, clearing away the frustration and anxiety, latching on to the feeling of calm. I took a deep breath, closed my eyes, and let my thoughts drift away, until the only thing left was that sensation of being lifted. I pulled my dress over my head, and hung it on the towel hooks behind the door. I took one more look at myself in the mirror, and feeling satisfied with what I saw... I stepped back into the bedroom.

Ty was still draped across the bed, staring at the ceiling. When he didn't look up, I called out to him.

"Ty," I said softly, holding my head high as he slowly sat up, staring in my direction.

In those first few seconds, any concern I had about him not wanting me was stripped away. The heat of his gaze warmed my skin, and the lust in his eyes was so raw it made me tremble where I stood.

"*Goddamn,*" I heard him murmur, under his breath.

Somehow, I found the strength and courage to take one step forward, then another, then another, until I was standing right in front of him in my orange sherbet lingerie. I felt the touch of his gaze all over me, but his hands gripped the edge of the bed.

"Shit, Lauren," he said, biting his bottom lip as he looked away. "You *have* to go put that dress back on."

"Why?" I put my hands on his shoulders, running my fingers along the muscled lines of his arm.

Ty inhaled a deep breath, closing his eyes. He didn't open

them again until he'd exhaled, and turned his face up toward mine. "Because, we *can't* do this right now, not after I've had you smoking, and then the drink, and—"

"*Shhh.*" I placed a finger to Ty's lips, and he closed them, staring into my eyes as I used my other hand on his shoulder as leverage to climb onto his lap. "Ty," I started, tracing the outline of his ear with my fingers. "I understand you want to be a gentleman, and not push me, and make sure I know what I'm doing. I get it. But if I'm telling you that this is what I want to do, and you're not hearing me... that's not very gentlemanly, is it?"

Slowly, the corners of his mouth turned up into a smile, and Ty touched his forehead to mine. "No, it's not." His arms relaxed as he lessened his grip on the bed. "You wore this for me?" he asked, looking down at the lacy cups of the bra. My breasts grew hot and heavy under his gaze, and my nipples hardened to peaks as his hands touched my waist.

I nodded, my heart racing as my head bobbed up and down. "Do you like it?"

He moved, pressing the hard length of his erection against me. "You really have to ask?" I blushed, looking away, but he lifted a hand to catch my chin, turning me back to face him. "I already knew you were beautiful, Lauren. But *this*... you're perfect."

My heart leapt up into my throat at the compliment, but I didn't even get time for that to sink in before his mouth was on mine. With his hand at the back of my neck, he pulled me closer, his tongue urging my lips to part for him. I gave in, and his tongue danced against mine as his free hand drifted up to my breast.

The first brush of his thumb over my sensitive nipple, still covered by the flimsy lace, made me squirm against him, whimpering into his mouth. Then he pulled down the sheer cup, leaving me exposed to the open air for not even a second before he lowered his head, sucking my nipple into his mouth.

Pleasure shot through me like a flash of lightening, echoing the storm outside, wild and unrestrained as the rough pad of his tongue played with my nipple. I squeezed my eyes shut as his tugged my bra strap down to free the other side, then rolled and pinched my other nipple between his fingers.

An unfamiliar tightness bloomed in the pit of my stomach as he sucked harder, moving between my breasts like he was trying to decide if one tasted better than the other. He looked up at me, meeting my eyes as he edged a hand between us, slipping his fingers past my soaked panties, through my slippery folds, and then pushed two of them inside me.

Holy shit.

I gasped, then let out a shaky, ragged breath as he sank those fingers deep. My mouth hung open, helpless as he began to move, circling them as he stroked in and out. He grinned at my reaction, then used his free hand to pull my mouth to his again.

I rode his fingers with abandon, using hands behind his head to keep his mouth on my breasts as I rolled my hips. He changed our position, moving so that I was on my back on the bed, and he was over me, with my legs spread wide.

Somehow, his fingers plunged deeper, and I squirmed in pleasure underneath him. His thumb found my clit, circling and massaging until my legs began to shake, and that spring of tension in my stomach pulled tighter, and tighter until it broke, and hot electricity washed over me.

Pinpricks of light exploded behind my closed eyes, and I kept them shut as an unfamiliar sound, somewhere between a scream and a moan escaped my lips as Ty kept pushing, kept stroking, until the tremors subsided, and a cool sensation of calm flooded me.

When I opened my eyes, Ty was still balanced over me, his face hovering just inches from mine. Our eyes met, and his were filled with an intoxicating mixture of lust and awe that probably mirrored my own. But in there, somewhere, there was something else. A sort of *reverence*, which I felt in his kiss as he lowered himself onto me.

Ty was heavy, but not unpleasantly so. His kisses then were gentle, and sweet as he sprinkled them over my face, kissing my forehead, cheeks, nose, then back to my mouth to kiss me deep before he lowered his lips to my neck.

He started gentle there too, with soft kisses and teasing licks. But then, he started sucking a little harder, the kisses got a little wetter, his tongue a little more exploratory as he went. Soon, I was panting as he sought and found hot spots I didn't know I had, then made his way to my breasts. Finally, he removed my bra, then gave them the same passionate attention he'd given my neck.

A spark of anxiety accompanied my pleasure as he kissed his way over the soft flesh of my stomach, then hooked his fingers into the waistband of my panties. He didn't pull them down yet, choosing instead to press his lips to the apex of my thighs, kissing me through the sheer lace.

A low moan escaped my lips as he dragged his tongue up the center of my panties, teasing me. I bit my lip hard, willing myself not to beg him to *please, please* touch me.

I didn't have to beg.

Not even two seconds later, he'd tugged my panties down my hips, spread my legs wide, then covered me with his mouth. My upper half shot up off the bed, but he had his arms locked around my thighs, holding me in place.

He slid his tongue over my clit, firm and slow, then covered it with his mouth. He sucked hard, and my legs clenched, but then he was gentle again, shallow, pleasant, while his tongue played. And then he moved, circling his tongue, kissing me everywhere, licking me everywhere, leaving hickies on my butt cheeks and inner thighs. He devoured me, sucking, licking, kissing until the bed cover under me was wet, and my legs spasmed in pleasure.

Ty moved between my legs until his face was in line with

mine again. He buried his hands in the hair at the nape of my neck as he kissed me, then pulled back to speak against my lips. "Give me a second, pretty girl."

I nodded, only half lucid as he moved away from me. In the semi-darkness, I squeezed my legs together, simultaneously trying to calm and prolong the tingling between my thighs.

A few moments later, Ty was back, climbing on top of me to hold my face in his hands.

"Tell me again you're sure you wanna do this, Lauren. I don't want you to regret it."

I smiled at him, then lifted my hands to hold his face like he was holding mine. "I'm sure."

He ran his tongue over his lips to wet them, then smiled. "I can still taste you on my lips. You taste good."

"Oh my God," I said, trying to turn away as I blushed.

"Uh-uh, don't get shy now." Ty laughed as he turned my face back to him, then brushed my mouth with his. He moved on top of me, dropping one of his hands to nudge my knees apart. I felt him, hard and thick as it brushed against my cleft, and I scooted away from him, closing my legs.

"Wait a minute," I stammered, clutching the bedcovers. There was light, but just enough to move around and be sexy. "What about protection?! Ty, we can't—"

"That's what I was doing," he quickly explained, putting a soothing hand on my leg. "When I told you to give me a second, I was putting on a condom."

"I need to see it."

There was no hesitation from him. I heard him fumbling with the lamp on his bedside table, and a second later, the room was flooded in soft light. Sure enough he was sheathed in a condom, and the torn wrapper lay beside two unopened ones on the table.

"Lauren…"

I lifted my gaze from his erection to his face, meeting his eyes. "Yeah?"

"I know this is still really new, but I need you to understand that I care about you. And part of that is protecting you. I'm not sleeping with anybody else, or anything like that, but still. I wouldn't have put either of us at risk like that."

I nodded, then smiled at him. "I... I can see that. But, I need *you* to understand that I had to make sure, and that's nothing against you. I just... I can't risk an STD *or* a kid, so... I just had to be sure."

He smiled back. "No offense taken. I think we're on the same page."

"Yeah. So... are we gonna..."

"*Hell yes*," he said, giving me a look like I'd lost my mind. "Can we... do you mind if I leave this on?" He gestured toward the lamp. "I wanna *see* you."

I chewed nervously at my lip as my eyes skirted over Ty, standing completely naked at the side of the bed, tall and gorgeous and hard and thick. I was confident, but not *that* confident, but he was looking at me like I was the most beautiful thing he'd ever seen, so I nodded.

"Yes."

He was on me before the word completely left my lips, spreading my legs to settle between them. Despite his enthusiasm, he didn't immediately shove himself in me. Instead, he gave me more of those lazy, intoxicating kisses, then pushed his fingers between my legs again. He had me dripping wet again, at the brink of another orgasm, when he moved his fingers, spread my legs wide, and looked me right in the face as he sank inside of me with a groan.

He felt incredible.

I was so wet that there was barely any resistance, but my body held him tight as he burrowed into me. We shared a smile, and he kissed me again as he began to move, with deep, slow strokes that made me whimper. He watched my face, gauging my reactions as he moved, probing deeper, stroking faster, pushing harder in response to my changing expressions and increasingly frantic purrs and moans.

I sank my fingers into his back, and he seemed to get harder. Propping my legs around his waist, I held tight as he stroked, over, and over, and over, and *over* until that tightness in my stomach was back for the third time. He buried his face in my neck, biting and kissing, pressing so close that his body created a delicious, wet friction against my clit.

I was on fire, about to explode, with so many foreign sensations attacking me. Him between my legs, his mouth on my neck, him, *period*, moving inside me, it was *magnificent*. I bit into his shoulder as he propped up my leg, pushing deeper, and even the saltiness of his sweat on my lips was good.

My nerve endings were going wild, and sweaty tendrils of my hair stuck to my face and his as he stroked me harder, faster, and *ohhh myyy Goddd*, it was so good.

"Is it good?" he asked, breathless, as if he were reading my mind.

"*Yes*, it's good," I told him, over and over, *yes yes yes yes yes yes yes yes hell yes, yes yes yes yes yes*. He moved, so our bodies were no longer pressed together, pulling my legs tight around his waist as he ground into me, pressing against a spot that I knew was going to make my heart stop, but all I could say was *yes yes yes yes yes*.

And then, out of nowhere, my entire body went hot. I tensed, and then I melted. The same electricity from both times before washed over me again, but this time it went on, and on, and on. I barely heard the guttural groan from Ty as he came, because my own heartbeat roared in my ears.

He collapsed beside me, then pulled me against his chest, panting just as hard as I was. I barely found the energy to snuggle closer as he pulled the covers over us, holding me tight.

When I finally caught my breath, I looked up to find him

staring at me. I smiled, and he smiled back, brushing a handful of curls back from my face.

"That was..." I let my sentence trail off, unsure of what word to use.

Ty chuckled. "Yeah, pretty much. I am *completely* sober now."

"Me too," I giggled, moving so that I was propped on my elbow. He stared at me for a moment, then reached for me, running a finger down my neck, then along my shoulder.

"Any regrets?"

I tipped my head to the side for a moment, thinking about it, then leaned forward, planting a kiss right on his lips.

"No. Not at all."

eleven
. . .
ty

I WOKE up after our late night together to an empty bed, and in my still-groggy state, decided it must have been a dream.

I got up, used the bathroom, brushed my teeth, and tried to think about what I was gonna have for breakfast. Then I decided fuck it, it was the weekend, I was getting back in the bed.

But when I climbed in, and stuck my face back into the pillows, I realized her warm, familiar scent of brown sugar was embedded in my sheets. I inhaled deep, then caught a glimpse of the pretty orange panties I'd taken off of her hanging from the foot board.

I smiled.

Definitely not a dream.

"Hey."

I looked up to see Lauren peeking around the single wall that separated my bedroom area from the rest of the apartment. She was fresh faced, and glowing, with her hair pulled into a thick ponytail on top of her head. She stepped around the divider, and inwardly, I groaned.

She was wearing my shirt.

It wasn't like it was the first time I'd seen a girl in one of my tee shirts, but this wasn't just a "girl", this was *Lauren*, looking sexy as hell in one of my shirts. It skimmed the tops of her thighs, and just that little glimpse of skin was enough to bring last night back to mind in clear focus, full color, and vivid imagery. Her legs around my waist, my fingers inside her, her breasts in my hands and mouth, the feel of that silky brown skin… *damn.*

"Good morning," she said, smiling as she padded over to the bed in bare feet. For a quick moment, the thought that I'd be happy to wake up to this sight every morning crossed my mind. I quickly shook it away, because thoughts like that were how I'd gotten mixed up with Jamila.

"Good morning to you too."

I smiled as she crawled onto the bed, sitting up on her knees in front of me. "I've been awake for like an hour, so I grabbed my books from my car to study a little. That's why I wasn't in bed. You had a pack of new toothbrushes under your cabinet, I hope you don't mind that I used one. I didn't bring an overnight bag. I wasn't snooping or anything, it's just that brushing is always the *first* thing I do in the morning, so I—"

"Lauren," I chuckled, sliding a hand over her thighs. *Damn her skin feels good.* "It's fine. I don't have anything to hide, you can use whatever you need to use around here. Make yourself comfortable."

She nodded, and then bit her lip as her eyes traveled over my bare chest, and then down to where the covers were pulled up to my waist. There was uncertainty in the way she had her hands clenched at her sides, but still… there was a look I'd never seen from the sweet Lauren I'd been getting to know, as she moved closer to me.

I'd be lying if I said I was completely comfortable with the way things went down last night. It wasn't that I had regrets, or wanted to take it back, but if I had my choice, we would have both been completely sober when taking that kind of step.

She'd made it clear that she didn't want what we were doing to be solely about sex, and I wanted to be respectful of that. Let her have control of that aspect of the relationship. The problem was, I wasn't sure *either* of us were in control last night.

Lauren was strong, and feisty, but she was also easy to read. Her mouth was twitching, trying not to grin, so I knew she was happy. She kept biting her lip, so I knew she was nervous. Her nipples were hard, poking against the thin fabric of my white BSU shirt, so I knew she was horny. What I *didn't* know was what was going to happen next.

But, Lauren showed me.

Her face took on a sudden, focused determination, like she was talking herself into something, and the next moment she was on top of me, straddling my lap. When she brought her lips to mine, she was hesitant at first, but then I pushed my tongue into her mouth, and it was on.

It wasn't until my hands were halfway up her thighs that I remembered her panties were hanging off the end of my bed, and therefore not on *her*. I palmed her ass, gripping a cheek in each hand to pull her closer, knowing she could feel how hard I was between her legs. She broke the kiss, roughly pushing me away as she moved back.

Shit.

"Lau—"

She snatched the covers back, and my breath caught in my throat when her soft, velvety hands covered my dick. Her gaze traveled up to my face, locking with mine. Her eyes were clear and focused, and she was *completely* aware of what she was doing.

"Ty... condom?"

I moved away from her just long enough to grab a condom from the drawer beside the bed, and she watched with interest as I put it on. I let her push me back on the bed again, and she seemed eager as she climbed on top of me, but then she hesitated.

"What's wrong?" I asked, cupping her chin in my hand to pull her lips against mine.

She shook her head, not meeting my eyes. "I... maybe we should do a different position."

I narrowed my eyes. "Why?"

"Because..." she sighed, then finally looked at me. "I don't know what the hell I'm doing, Ty. I'm trying to be sexy, but I don't have any experience."

"*Relax*, Lauren." I kissed her again, then gripped her by the thighs, pulling her forward. "You think I'm looking for you do tricks and splits or something?"

She shrugged. "I don't know. That's my point, though. I was thinkin—"

"*Stop thinking*," I said, then immediately shook my head. "Wait, that's not what I mean. I love the fact that you like to think things through, but you have to stop *over*thinking every little thing, pretty girl. Okay?"

She opened her mouth like she wanted to argue the point, but I lifted an eyebrow, then pulled her onto me. Her argument turned into a gasp and she bit her lip, moaning as I drew her body tight against my chest, burying myself deep inside her.

"Okay," she whimpered, balancing her hands on my shoulders as she raised up, then closed her eyes as she sank onto me again. I couldn't help watching her face as she moved, lips parted, brows furrowed, rolling her hips as she went. She felt like heaven, tight, and wet, and slippery. I dipped my head, trapping a juicy chocolate nipple in my mouth as it bobbed in front me.

She dug her fingers into my hair, and I felt the beginning of tremors in her legs as her movements grew more frantic. Her head fell back, and she gripped my shoulder tight as she sank against me, trading the up and down for a slow, intense grind. We traded kisses as she wound her body in deep, gratifying circles, and I pushed a hand between us, finding her clit with my thumb. A shudder ran through her body as soon as I touched it, and she dropped her head to my shoulder.

"*Ty,*" she whimpered, then whispered, over and over, right in my ear, and it took every bit of self-control I had not to come. *Not until she did first.*

I moved my thumb in circles, matching the movements of her hips. I groaned as her nails sank into my back, teeth sank into my shoulders, as *she* sank onto my dick, deeper, and deeper, until I felt her tense in my arms.

She cried out as she came, her face buried against my neck. Her body clenched around me, drowning me in tightness and wetness, riding me hard until I came, with her pulled tight in my arms.

We stayed like that, not even bothering to pull ourselves apart, until both of our hearts had stopped racing. Lauren pulled back first, pressing her forehead against mine as she grinned.

"Why you smiling so hard?" I asked, giving her a peck on the lips.

"Cause." She kissed me back, harder, then smiled again. "I think I know *exactly* how I want to spend the rest of the day."

∼

UNFORTUNATELY, WE DIDN'T REALLY GET TO SPEND THE DAY that way.

It was a great fantasy, but in reality, we both had things that had to get done. We showered, and Lauren washed her lingerie, then hung it in front of my window to dry while we ate cereal and studied for a few hours. She'd put on a different tee shirt, another one of mine, and I could see her nipples through the thin white fabric.

Her phone buzzed, and she picked it up, reading the screen for a second before she burst into laughter. After a few seconds, she glanced up at me, and seeing the book in front of me made her eyes go wide.

"Sorry I'm being all loud," she said, tucking her phone away. "Harper's dad just texted me something."

I smiled. "Harper did something funny?"

Lauren looked away, down at her own book. "No, it was just a picture he saw online, something he knew I would laugh at."

Oh. Okay.

It was nothing to get up in arms about, but something made the moment awkward enough that it didn't sit right. But then Lauren asked me a question about what she was working on, and that little interruption was forgotten in favor of enjoying my time with her.

She got up to use the bathroom, and I was plotting on ways to convince her we needed to have sex again when someone knocked on the door.

Shit.

I prayed it wasn't Jamila – or worse, my mother – as I crossed the room. My shoulders sank in relief as I looked through the peephole. I unlocked the door, pulled it open just a crack, then peeked out.

"Austin, what's up, man?"

Oblivious to my hesitance to let him in, Austin shrugged. "Not shit."

I wasn't expecting him to just walk in, so I didn't have a real grip on the door. He pushed right past me, strolling inside and looking around.

"What the fuck, Austin?" I moved around him, pushing him back toward the door.

He narrowed his eyes, holding up his hands to keep me back. "I should ask you the same thing. I left that complicated ass calculator over here the other day when I asked you to help me with my Linear Algebra… I texted you yesterday, told you I was coming to get it. This is the time you told me to come by, fool."

"Ah, shit," I said, scrubbing a hand over my face. "My bad, I completely forgot. Here." I grabbed his calculator from my desk, handing it to him.

"Thank you. You've gotta stop forgetting shit, messing up plans, dude. You've signed up to volunteer for more than one frat event, and never bothered to show up because you were buried in your books. You always get like this around mid-terms, what's up?"

I groaned. "I'm *good*," I insisted. "Can we talk about this later?" I was trying to get him out before Lauren came back, but when his eyes went wide, looking at something over my shoulder, I knew it was too late.

It wasn't a secret or anything that Lauren and I were seeing each other. We'd actually kicked it with Austin and Mina before. Mina knew Lauren wasn't having sex, which meant Mina told Austin, which meant Austin knew I wasn't getting any. But, when I turned around, to see what Austin saw, Lauren's appearance told a different story.

She was still wearing my tee shirt, but she was in the middle of a combination between a yawn and a stretch, with her eyes closed as she stopped just at the edge of the living area. Her arms were high over her head, so the shirt was riding up over her bare legs. An inch higher, and Austin would get a show.

"Lauren!"

Her eyes popped open, and after a half-second of confusion, she noticed Austin behind me. She clamped a hand over her mouth, and disappeared into the bedroom area.

"Now I see why you forgot about the calculator," Austin said, barely keeping his composure before he broke into a laugh.

I struggled to keep a smile off my face as I turned back to him. "Shut up, dude."

"Why I gotta shut up? Did y'all…"

"Not your business."

"So you *did*." Austin chuckled, clapping me on the shoulder. "I see you, taking it to next level. When you buying the ring?"

"Austin..."

"I'm fucking with you, Ty. Lauren!" he called out.

"What?!" she yelled back.

Austin laughed again. "I'm not about to tease you, I swear. Mina is out in the car, I was gonna say do y'all want to grab some lunch with us, like a double date."

I sucked my teeth, then shot Austin a scowl. Hell no I didn't want to go on a double date, I wanted him to move along, so I could do what I was about to try to do before he showed up at my door.

"I'd like that," Lauren said, popping her head into the living area. "We have to get dressed though."

Austin shrugged. "That's cool. We'll meet y'all at the sushi spot up the street. I mean... unless we're interrupting your plans or something?"

"Hell yeah."

"Not at all." Lauren shot me a scowl, then smiled at Austin. "We'll be there."

As soon as Lauren was back in the bedroom, I opened my front door. "Get your ass out of my apartment man, coming along, fucking up the program."

"See you in a minute," he laughed, ducking through the door. I slammed it behind him, then hurriedly fixed the scowl on my face as Lauren stepped into the room, with her dress back in place.

"Why don't you want to go?" she asked, pulled her hair down from her ponytail.

I sighed, then walked up to her, drawing her into my arms. "I was just hoping to have you to myself pretty girl."

"And by that, you mean now that I've given you some, that's all you want to do?"

I lifted an eyebrow. "You say that like it's a bad thing…"

"Ty!"

I dodged her playfully aimed swat to my arm, then grabbed her around the waist, pulling her close. "Ay, don't get mad. *You* said that was how you wanted to spend the day, I'm just trying to facilitate your plans."

"Oh." She bit her lip, then grinned. "I did say that, didn't I?"

"You did. Why'd you change your mind?"

She cut her eyes away from me, then wrinkled her nose, but didn't say anything.

"What is it?" I asked, lowering my hands to squeeze her butt. She giggled, then dropped her head against my chest with a little sigh.

"I think we may have gone a little too hard. I'm sore."

"*We* didn't go too hard. That last time was all you. You were the one doing all the deep grinding and—"

"Ty!" She seemed so embarrassed that I willed myself not to laugh. Instead, I cleared my throat.

"Okay, okay. I'm really sorry you're hurting."

She turned her face up to me, eyes shining with happiness as she shook her head. "I'm not. I've had an amazing time with you. No regrets."

"You're sure?"

Lauren nodded, then pushed herself up on her toes for a kiss. "Positive."

I pulled her into an embrace, just breathing her in as she nuzzled her face against my chest.

We never did go meet with Austin and Mina. Instead, we ended up back in my bed, no sex, just our laptops, and pizza between us while we both did our thing for school.

Well… she did hers.

While her fingers flew over the keys, I was too busy watching her to be productive. This thing between us was still, *really*, really new, but I couldn't help my mind from drifting, over and over, to one conclusion.

I was going fall in love with this girl… but I wasn't sure I wanted that to happen.

twelve

. . .

lauren

"*I'D LIKE A... CAT... pleeeease, it's my favorite animal!*
I'd like it to be ... YELLOW... pleeeeease, that's my favorite color!
I'd like it to eat ... BACON ... pleeeeeease, that's my favorite food!
And I'll call it... HARPER... juuuuust like youuuu!"

It was all eyes on me as I frantically dug into my backpack, trying to shut off the singing toy in the middle of class. I'd opened my bag to get a fresh pad to take notes, and instead I'd set off the stuffed purple dog Harper had apparently packed for me.

My professor and all of my classmates were giving me the stink-eye by the time I managed to shut it off, long after it had finished the song. I stuffed the dog back into my bag, retrieved the notebook I'd gone for, and pretended I didn't realize anything had happened.

First damned class of the day, on a Monday, and it was already going wrong. I'd spent the weekend entertaining my dad and Harper, then taken them to the airport only to find out that their flight was delayed. They didn't end up on a plane until nearly midnight, and I didn't sleep until my dad let me know they were safely home, at almost four in the morning. I'd almost overslept, and didn't check my bag before my left, which was apparently how Harper snuck a toy in on me.

Awesome.

When class was over, I got out of there as fast as I could, ignoring the looks from my classmates. I fumbled through my other two classes for the day, and the fact that I was meeting up with Ty for lunch was the only thing that kept me from doing something I never did – skipping classes – so I could go back to my apartment and sleep.

We were supposed to meet at Blakewood Bistro, a little coffee shop, slash bookstore, slash restaurant on campus. I didn't see him around, so I grabbed a table and ordered myself an iced latte while I waited.

Minutes rolled by, and I checked my phone to make sure I hadn't missed a text or call. I even went into our text message history, to check the time we were supposed to meet. At this point, he was almost twenty minutes late.

I blew out a heavy sigh, then drained the rest of my latte, willing the caffeine to kick in at any point. I was already cranky from lack of sleep, and now Ty's lateness was moving me into the territory of *pissed*.

We'd been dating for almost three months now, and while things had mostly been wonderful, his bad habit of forgetting when we were supposed to meet somewhere was starting to get to me. He was double-booking himself sometimes, setting up dates for times he was supposed to be at work, or getting so absorbed in studying or research that the hours rolled away while I sat somewhere waiting for him.

Like now.

This was the fourth time it had happened, and while I knew he would be deeply apologetic, and it wouldn't happen again for a while, I was pissed. When it reached the point where he was thirty minutes later, I sent him a text asking where the heck he was, then tossed the phone back onto the table.

"Ooooh, I know *that* look. Waiting around for Ty, huh?"

She can't be serious.

I narrowed my eyes at Jamila as she sat down at my table, looking annoyingly regal in a teal maxi dress and gold jewelry, with her locs pulled into an intricate updo. Ty hadn't said too much about her, just like I hadn't told him too much about Mekhi. Only the pertinent things, such as why the relationship ended, whether it was on good terms, things like that.

According to him, she hadn't taken the break up well.

Ty had never, ever bad-mouthed her to me, but he was very to-the-point about the fact that she'd cheated. He'd also made it clear that she thought they were getting back together, which was never a good sign. So honestly, I was surprised it had taken her this long to approach me. But today, I wasn't in the mood for any bullshit.

"Can I help you Jamila?"

She seemed surprised that I knew who she was, then quickly covered it with a smirk. "Oh, so my fiancée thought it appropriate for you to know who I was?"

I tipped my head to the side, just looking at her for a few moments, confused. "Okay. I see you're crazy. You're not his fiancé anymore."

"This ring says different," Jamila snapped, giving me a wicked smile as she sat up a little straighter, sliding her ringed hand across the table in my direction.

I rolled my eyes. "You're still wearing the ring, when it's been what, nine months since you broke up? Aren't you almost 26? Your ass is too old to be this pitiful."

"I'm pitiful? Honey, you're the one sitting here stood up for a date. What's his excuse this time? Frat duties? Work? Studying? You should know that this is just how he operates, he'll never really make you a priority. Not to mention that he's engaged."

"Hmmm, if he really is a cheater, and never made time for you, why do you still want him? Why on earth would you wear a man like that's ring?"

Jamila looked dazed for a moment, then began sputtering. "I... well—"

"Well nothing," I said, waving a hand like I was shooing her away. "Look, I'm not in the mood, for whatever bullshit you're trying to start with me. Let me straighten it out for you. Fact – Ty isn't your fiancé, he's my boyfriend. Fact – I'm not about to sit here and argue with you. Have a good day."

She sharply drew her head back, like she was stunned over my dismissal, but I was serious. I was tired, hungry, and pissed off at Ty. Today was *not* the day.

"No let me straighten it out for *you*," she snapped, pointing her finger across the table. "I know you think you hit a gold mine because Ty has money, but you need to move along. He's mine. You're going to have to find somebody else to play desperately-needed daddy for that little girl of yours."

"*Listen to me, bitch.*" I was out of my chair in a flash, hands planted on the table as I leaned over. The restaurant was mostly empty, because it was an odd time of day, but I still kept my voice low as I spoke, because causing a scene wasn't my thing. "I don't know who the fuck you think you are, or who the fuck you think *I* am. Yes, I'm young, and I walk around here with my books, and I don't bother anybody, and I go to class, and I make my good grades. But don't you think for *one second* that any of that means I won't snatch you up and mop every fucking floor on this campus with your face if you *ever* bring up my child again. As a matter of fact, don't talk to me at all. I don't know you, you don't know me. If you've got an issue, take that shit to Ty, and do not fuck with me again. Okay?"

By this time, I was right in her face, and with the way I felt at that moment, the fear in her eyes was justified. Only divine intervention kept my hands planted on that table, instead of grabbing her by the hair and swinging her around like a doll.

"Get away from my table, bitch." I said, when she still hadn't done anything to respond for a full minute.

She blinked hard, then slid her chair away with a huff. "I've got better things to do anyway!"

"Then go do them!"

I rolled my eyes at her as she left, *beyond* annoyed. It didn't even take five minutes for me to realize that I'd maybe overreacted, but that was okay. At least it was unlikely that she'd bother me again.

When I checked my phone – forty minutes late – there was no response from Ty, still. I gathered up my things, paid for my coffee, and I was still pissed when he finally called me back three hours later, while I was at work. I hit the ignore button, and went back to what I was doing.

I hadn't let *her* see that it bothered me, but her statement about not being a priority to Ty rang a little too true. I understood that he was busy, because I was too, but to me that meant he should understand the value of my time even more. I barely had spare moments in my schedule before Ty came into the picture. Now that he was here, I was moving stuff around, taking time away from studying and sleep so we could be together. And what did I get in return?

Nothing.

Wait.

Okay... so that was an exaggeration. It really wasn't fair to act like Ty wasn't making sacrifices of time for me, because I knew for a fact that he was. But still... it wasn't okay to stand me up.

"I see you're still in that same sour mood, huh?"

I forced a smile to my face as Mina walked up to me, with a thick stack of shelf tags in her hands.

"Nope, I'm happy," I said, pointing to my fake smile. "See?"

"You look like a serial killer. Come help me switch out these tags, and tell me what Ty did."

I sucked my teeth, but followed her to wall of printer ink, easily the least busy section of the store. "Why do you assume Ty did something?"

"I don't *assume*, I know. We've been friends and roommates for two years, and I don't think I've ever seen you this pissed. Wait... no, maybe when that photographer guy leaked those videos of your sister. But you were ready to kill that day, so I don't think that counts. But *this*," she waved a finger in front of my face, "you're giving me pissed off girlfriend right now. So spill it, what did he do?"

Taking several tags from her hands, I began the tedious work of matching the new, more minimally designed tag to the current product on the shelf, replacing the old tag with new. "Girl, he blew me off again today."

"Sounds kinky."

"... Mina."

She playfully rolled her eyes as she pulled down one of the old tags. "I'm *kidding*, come on. What do you mean, he's like... been out of touch, not answering texts?"

"*No*. We had a lunch date today, and his ass didn't show up!"

"...*oh*." Mina cringed, then turned back to the shelf.

"Yeah, exactly," I said, shaking my head. "And to make it worse, that crazy ass Jamila popped trying to antagonize me."

I got an odd sense of satisfaction from the way Mina's mouth dropped open, face pulled into a deep scowl. "Wait, run that by me again. She did *what now*?"

Okay so maybe I *didn't* overreact.

"That's the same damned thing I thought! Like, I almost couldn't believe it was actually happening. Like this girl is seriously just going to walk up to me and say some reckless crap like I wouldn't... *ugh!*" I crushed a handful of old tags in my hand, then tossed them into the trash can we'd brought along.

When I glanced back at Mina, her eyes were glossy, and she was stifling a laugh. "What's funny?"

"*You*," she shot back. "I can just imagine you sitting there, looking all cute with your hair in a puff, and that baby face, and a cute little dress, and your cute little Converse on. And Jamila is thinking, *oh this girl is an easy target.*"

"And then finding out that, uh, *no bitch*, I'm *not*."

We gave each other the *hell yeah* nod, and then our gazes locked for a few seconds before we both burst into laughter.

"What did you say to that girl, Lo?"

I sucked my teeth. "What did *I* say? She approached me! And she brought up Harper, and you *know* I don't play that shit."

Mina lifted an eyebrow. "She mentioned baby girl, and you didn't have to call me for bail money?"

"*Only* by the grace of God, because I swear, I wante—"

Putting a hand on my arm, Mina cleared her throat, then subtly tipped her head, gesturing behind me, and when I turned around, I was greeted by the sight of Ty.

Despite my anger, he looked good.

He was wearing a blue BSU hat, white tee, and sweats. Dressed down, and I could see in his eyes that he was tired, but even like that... Why the hell did he have to be so fine?

I reminded myself that I was at work so I wouldn't cross my arms, but I still gave him the evil eye as I ground the standard Terrific Tech greeting through my teeth. "Thanks for visiting Terrific Tech today, how can I service your tech, communication, or entertainment needs today?"

"Lo... babe, listen, I—"

"*Not* at my job Ty," I said, just above a whisper.

"Can you take a break?"

I ran my tongue over my teeth. "Sure, go wait for me outside. I'll meet you out there, really. Definitely won't forget, and then not call until four hours later."

"Lauren..."

"Go wait for me, for real."

Ty ran a hand over his face, then shoved his hands deep in his pockets. "Please, Lo? Can we talk?"

"No." My answer was immediate, and the disappointment on his face almost made me feel bad for being angry. But… still. "I can't talk about this with you right now. Don't *want* to talk about it."

"Okay, so what time do you get off?"

I shook my head. "I get off at midnight Ty, but I'm not talking about it then, either. I'm going home and going to bed. It's been a long day."

"I'll call, when you get off. We can talk on your way home."

"Sure. I'll be waiting."

I said that with just enough sarcasm that he understood I would *not* be waiting, then walked off, heading to the back where he couldn't follow. Mina came to find me a few minutes later, but I ignored her scolding insistence that I should have let him explain. The rest of my shift was spent in a pissy mood, and the drive home was even worse. As soon as I pulled into the parking lot of my building, I pulled my phone from my purse to check what I already knew.

Ringer on.

No missed calls.

Of course he hadn't called.

I shook my head as I trudged up the stairs. My thoughts probably should have been devoted to whether or not this was a deal breaker, whether I should accept any calls from Ty again, *ever*, but instead I was thinking about the pint of cookies and cream in the freezer. It was Mina's but she was staying over with Austin – surprise, surprise – so I could just replace it for her. A hot shower, my bed, and more ice cream than I should probably eat sounded like the perfect end to a shitty day.

But Ty was at my door.

From my distance he appeared to be asleep, his back against

my door, legs sprawled across the hall. I rolled my eyes, then approached quietly, fully intending to just unlock the door and slip in without saying anything. I was just that pissed, but I couldn't make myself do it.

Pushing out a heavy sigh, I kneeled in front of him and nudged his shoulder. A few nudges later, he opened his eyes, and gave me a sleepy smile that made it hard to be mad.

I looked away from him.

"Why are you sleeping in front of my door like a stalker?" I asked, looking down the hall instead of at him. In front of me, he lumbered to his feet, then leaned back against my door.

"Needed to talk to you, pretty girl."

Crossing my arms, I turned to him, tilting my head back to look into his face. "Needed to talk so bad that you didn't even bother calling on my way home, like you said you would?"

"I came to talk in person instead. I've been here, waiting on you."

"But you *said* you would call. This is the problem, Ty! You setting up a time for us, and not following through. Can you move from in front of my door? I need to sleep."

"Lauren, *damn*, can—"

"*Move*, before I—"

I tried, for maybe half a second, to fight it. Ty grabbed me at the arms, his grip gentle, but firm, dragging me close to him. He brushed his lips over mine, softly at first, then more insistent as he pressed against me. When his tongue touched my lips, I opened for him, and he dropped his hold on my arms, moving his hands to my face.

I was... confused. Hurt, and angry, and turned on. Eager to move past this hiccup, but reluctant to let it go. After leaving an emotionally abusive relationship that went on for many years longer than it should have, my sister had drilled many things into me. Leaving when it was time. Knowing your worth, accepting nothing less than you deserve. *Not* falling for bullshit. All important lessons, which I took to heart, but the problem was... I had no threshold by which to measure.

Ty was my first relationship as an adult, and this was our first argument. Being pissed off at my boyfriend was a phenomenon I didn't know how to handle. But I *did* know his lips felt good. He moved his hands from my face, wrapping me in his arms, and that felt good too... which probably meant I was doing this whole "I'm mad at you" thing all wrong.

"I'm *sorry*," he said, when he pulled away. He looked me right in my eyes, which pained me, because he looked exhausted too. "You're mad, and I get that. You have every right to be, because I fucked up. I'm not about to hold you hostage, or make you talk to me. I just want you to give me a chance to explain. Can I have that?"

I held his gaze for a few seconds longer before I looked away, then twisted out of his arms. "Whatever, Ty. What was it this time? Frat troubles? Meeting with your advisor? Forgot about a shift at work today?"

"My mother."

Oh.

A little of my anger slipped away, but I crossed my arms so it wouldn't show. "Is she okay?"

Ty lifted his eyebrows, letting out a dry laugh. "Depends on your definition. Is she physically ill or injured? No. Did she call me early this morning, with a doctor at her bedside like she was dying? Yes."

"What?!"

"Right." He shook his head, then scrubbed a hand over his face. "So, I drove up there – a two hour drive – and she's in bed with her full queen regalia, with ice packs, and smelling salts, and her psychiatrist, psychologist, hairdresser, doctor, everybody trying to figure out what the damned problem is."

I narrowed my eyes. "I thought you said she wasn't ill or injured."

"She's *not*. Unless being dramatic as hell is a disease." He paused, tipping his head to the side as if he were really considering it, then gave a subtle shake of his head. "Anyway, apparently she was bugging Roslyn about grandkids, and Ros finally told her she just wasn't interested in having kids. They argued, and now my mother is bedridden for a few days, due to "emotional distress". And it took all day to find this shit out, talking to the house staff, her, my siblings, the doctors, piecing it all together because she's being cryptic. So basically a waste of a damned day. And with so much going on, our date completely slipped my mind. And I'm *so* sorry for not reaching out to let you know what was happening."

Keeping my arms crossed, I scowled. "Do you think I'm stupid or something, Ty? What's with the elaborate ass story?"

He frowned, in what appeared to be honest confusion. "What are you... do you think I'm lying to you?"

"I don't know what to think! I just know that this is the fourth time you've asked me to meet you somewhere, and you never show up. It's not just about this time, it's about *all* the times. I'm over it. If seeing me isn't important to you, and valuing my time isn't a priority, there's nothing more to say here."

"Lauren, you are absolutely a priority to me."

"Prove it."

He threw his hands up. "I have been! Any time I'm not in class or at work, I'm trying to figure out when *you're* not in class or at work, so we can be together. I've put off responsibilities to my frat, switched work schedules, put off homework or studying, so I can take you out for ice cream, or meet you for your lunch break, or just to kick it. Because I *want* to be around you. I'm disorganized, Lauren. Not disinterested."

Right when I was about to respond, footsteps on the stairs reminded me that we were having a private conversation in the non-existent privacy of the hall. I unlocked the door and dragged him inside, where I rounded on him.

"Look, Ty... I'm not trying to monopolize your time, or take you away from the other responsibilities you have. You're busy, I'm busy, we're busy, I get it. I understand. The problem is when we make plans, and then you break them, without even the courtesy of a text or phone call, until you're apologizing afterwards. That makes me feel like it's not important to you, and honestly, it makes me wonder if somebody else is getting that time."

His scowl sank even deeper. "Somebody like *who*?"

I shrugged, then shoved my hands into the back pockets of my khakis. "Maybe your fiancé."

I'd been avoiding that line of thinking all day, but in some deep part of me, I was honestly perturbed by Jamila walking around, unchecked, claiming Ty as hers. The last thing I planned to do was get into a rivalry about any man, but... it bothered me.

"I don't *have* a fiancé, Lauren."

I rolled my eyes. "Maybe you should pass that along to Jamila. She came to see me today, while I was waiting at Blakewood's for you. Showed me her ring, explained that I was in the way, and insisted that I find another daddy for Harper."

"*Shit.*" Ty scrubbed a hand over his face, then pinched his fingers against the bridge of his nose. "I will talk to her. Make sure she doesn't bother you again."

I scoffed. "Oh, *that's* not what you need to talk to her about. How do you think it makes me feel to have that ring shoved in my face, have her telling me I'm basically a placeholder?! Is that what's happening here? I'm just something to play with until you're ready to go back to her?"

Those words barely crossed my lips before he was on me again, pulling me against his chest as he held me in his arms. "*No.* Absolutely not." He put a hand under my chin, tipping it up, then used his thumbs to wipe away the unchecked tears on my face. "I promise you, Jamila is not, nor will she ever be someone that you need to be concerned about. That is over and done. I want you, only you, and I'm sorry. I'm so, so sorry for making you feel like this, and you have my word that I will do better."

God, this would be so much easier with a phone-a-friend option.

I really needed Bianca or Mina around, somebody to tell me "go ahead and believe him girl", or "girl please, he lying". Something, from someone who knew more about this than me, who'd done it before. At the moment, I was feeling a little too easily swayed by his handsome face and soft lips, and words that were exactly what I wanted to hear.

I didn't even know if that was fair though, to assume that because he was saying the "right" things, they had to be lies. Maybe... he was just telling his truth.

"One more time, Ty." I licked my dry lips, then made sure to meet his eyes, so he would know that I meant this. "If you stand me up, ever again, that's it. If something comes up, we can reschedule, that's fine. But don't you ever leave me waiting on you again."

He nodded, then brushed his mouth over mine. "Okay pretty girl. You've got my word. Are we good?"

"Yeah."

I wanted to be harsh with him, push him away, kick him out. But... the weight of his hands at my waist felt like home, and I hadn't seen him all weekend. Before that, I was battling with my cycle, so we were honestly overdue for some intimacy. Now that we'd made peace, the possibility of feeling his skin on mine blew anger out of the water.

But... *still.*

"I know you're probably still mad," he murmured against my lips. "Now that we've talked about it, do you want me to leave?"

I shook my head, then snaked my arms around his waist. "Uh uh. I want you to let me help you get organized."

thirteen
. . .
ty

"SO WHAT'S YOUR BUDGET?"

I heard Bianca's question, saw her sit back, tablet in hand, poised to take notes, but I couldn't seem to find any words. I'd looked around her blog, watched a few of her vlogs, just to get a feel for her personality before I reached out, but Bianca in person was much different than Bianca on screen. Lauren had told me they looked just alike, and showed me pictures. Hell, I'd seen it on screen myself, but face to face, sitting in the same room… the only reason I *knew* it wasn't Lauren with blue hair and tats and piercings was because Bianca didn't make my heart race the way her sister did.

"Hello?" she said, snapping her fingers in front of my face. "We don't have a ton of time, so let's do this."

Two weeks had gone by since I fucked up so bad she almost kicked me to the curb, and I'd been doing well with my time management, mostly due to her help. She even found extra time, and organized things in a way that allowed me to get more sleep – one of many ways she enriched my life.

Lauren was smart, funny, beautiful, and the way she was

going after success, pursuing a successful future... that shit was sexy. Even when she was going a little off the deep end with the overthinking and the stress, she had a bubbly, sweet energy that I'd begun to crave. And *damn*, before we took it to that level, I never would have expected her to be such an intensely sexual person. She was always ready, and eager, and *she* initiated sex more often than I did.

So, hell nah, there weren't going to be anymore missed dates, and I was going above and beyond for her birthday, which was coming up in just under two weeks, to drive home the point that I fully intended to be kept around. That's where Bianca came in.

I knew she and Lauren were close, so who better to ask for advice?

My brother, Roger, was being featured in Sugar&Spice magazine. The magazine's head photographer and videographer was Bianca's boyfriend, Rashad. Rashad's sister, Raisa, was a DIY home improvement and design blogger, and Roger, a realtor, would be filming a segment with her on inexpensive ways to stage a home for sale. So when he flew up to film his segment for the website in their workspace, I met him there so I could have a sit down with Bianca.

We made ourselves comfortable in a seating area across the room while they worked, and Bianca didn't waste any time getting right into it.

"Ty! Budget?"

Shit.

"Sorry," I said, scrubbing a hand over my face. "Just a little distracted."

She scrunched her face, just like Lauren did sometimes. "You're not like, thinking about that sex tape thing are you?"

Well, I wasn't, *but...*

"Nah."

Bianca visibly relaxed. "Good, cause that would just be

awkward. But now that we've established that, seriously, I need you to tell me your budget."

"I don't have one."

She lifted an eyebrow as she drew her head back a little. "No budget because you haven't really thought about it yet, or no budget because you've just got it like that?"

I chuckled, then dropped my head, scratching my freshly lined hair. "Um… no budget because I need it to be special for her."

"Wow." Bianca lowered the tablet to her lap, and looked at me for a long moment, her expression pulled into a look I could only describe as impressed. My heart fell a little, because the last thing I needed was a focus on money. But then she spoke. "So, you're pretty serious about her then, huh? You *need* it to be special?"

I relaxed. She *was* impressed, but not about the money. "Yeah," I said, nodding. "I do. I'm sure she told you—"

"That you fucked up?" Bianca chuckled. "Yeah, she did. I was about ready to choke you too, because you had her head messed up. But I'll tell you straight up… *this*," – she motioned between me and her – "means a lot to me. I've been through a bullshit relationship before, and I've seen and endured a lot. I won't stand idle and watch it happen to Lauren. But you coming here to see me in person, really putting in some effort… you've got me. I'm on Team Ty unless you fuck up again."

I laughed because it was funny, but I didn't doubt for a second that she was serious. "I appreciate that, Bianca. I'll have to do this with your dad eventually too, so I'm glad to have you on my side."

"Oh, my dad is laid back. *Harper* is the one you might have a problem with. Cause if she doesn't like you… whew. Everybody will know, and she'll hurt your feelings too," she laughed. "Anyway, so, if budget isn't a factor, I think you can really go over the top and blow her mind. But she likes you enough that she'll be happy with pretty much anything you do. So my thinking is that we should probably go somewhere in the middle. Tell me what you were thinking."

"Well, a nice dinner, suite at a nice hotel with a view of–"

"So you're just going to *tell* her you're fucking her baby sister?" I looked up as my brother, Roger approached us, taking a seat beside Bianca. "Bold move baby brother."

My eyes went wide as I turned my attention back to Bianca, who was glaring at me. "I, um, I didn't mean…"

They burst out laughing at the same time.

"He really got shook for a second there, didn't he?" Bianca asked Roger, dabbing tears from the corners of her eyes as she laughed.

Roger chuckled as he shook his head. "He *did*. I didn't even expect that. Does he think it was a secret?"

I cleared my throat, unamused, and they both turned back to me, bursting into laughs again.

"Okay, okay," Bianca said, wiping her face. "Dinner and a hotel is really nice, but you need gifts too."

"Plural," Roger added, and Bianca nodded.

"Right. And speaking of birthday sex, one of those gifts should be bomb ass lingerie."

"Really?" I raised an eyebrow. "That's not too intimate? We haven't even been together four months yet."

Bianca sucked her teeth. "No. My sister loves cute panties. Lingerie is the sexy best friend of cute panties. Pick something nice, that you want to see her in. Something *really* nice, do not take your ass to target, or Cupid's, or some local seedy sex shop. Don't you dare."

"Go to La Perla," Roger chimed in. "Or better yet, Agent Provocateur."

"Do *not* go to Agent Provocateur, that shit is overpriced!"

"But the name looks good on the gift box."

Bianca's eyes went wide. "This is true…" She sat back, fingers intertwined, looking up at the ceiling as she considered it. "Your brother makes a compelling argument for the luxury brand, *but*... I still think something little less extravagant is more appropriate for a four month old relationship, especially for Lauren's tastes. There's a little place here in town, you can go before you leave, called *Scantilily*. They have beautiful, quality stuff, and if Lauren wants to purchase more for herself, if she splurges a little, she can afford it."

"I like that," Roger agreed. "This girl is smart, you should listen."

Bianca blushed, and picked up her tablet. "I'm gonna write this down for you."

Roger nodded. "What else does he need? Shoes?"

"Nah, Lauren isn't a shoe girl, and she only carries a bag out of necessity."

"Is she into fashion at all?"

"She is, but she usually just raids my closet. She keeps it simple because she's more focused on saving for Harper than buying clothes, so she doesn't shop much."

"Well there you go," Roger clapped. "He can take her on a shopping spree."

Bianca frantically shook her head. "She'd never go for that. She'd buy one cheap thing, and refuse to get anything else."

Roger dropped his chin into his hands, joining Bianca in deep thought. I said nothing, just watched, because apparently no input was needed from me. Suddenly, Roger sat up, snapping his fingers. "I've got it! You can buy mall-specific gift cards, and you can't refund those. Give her a gift card, don't say the amount on it, don't ask her if she's used it for anything. She'll be able to get whatever she wants."

"That is *brilliant*! I think I love you."

Roger smiled. "And I, *you*."

They shared a laugh, then high –fived, and Bianca began pecking away again at her tablet, taking notes. "Okay that's two gifts. We need at least one more thing. Something with personal meaning for you two."

"Or jewelry," Roger suggested.

"Can they be the same thing?" I asked, speaking up.

"Sure," Bianca and Roger chimed, together.

I nodded. "In that case, I've already got that covered."

∼

D*AMN I'M LUCKY.*

That was the thought that kept running through my mind at the sight of Lauren across from me, her eyes sparkling with happiness and restrained excitement.

We were out of the suburbs where BSU was located, into the city, where the real nightlife went down. I hadn't told her where we were going beforehand, but when we walked up, she'd squeezed my hand, whispering to me that she'd been wanting to come to this place for a while. So that was at least one point in my favor.

"I think I'm going to order a drink," she said, unable to keep her mouth from spreading into a big smile. "I mean, I'm legal now... I kinda *have* to, right?"

I shrugged, then laughed at how hyped up she seemed at the prospect. "Well, you have your own personal designated driver, so drink up, pretty girl."

Damn she looked beautiful, in a short black dress that fit perfectly over her curves. She'd been to the spa and hair dresser earlier – her gift from Mina – and I was initially shocked to see her hair straightened, floating around her face and down her back in soft waves. I loved her kinky curls, loved burying my hands and face in them. This was different, but still sexy as hell.

I reached across the small table for her hand, bringing it up to my mouth to kiss her fingers. "Happy birthday, babe." She smiled again, one of those secret sexy smiles she gave to let me know she was horny, but then it shifted into flat and polite as the waiter approached the table. I eyed her for a second longer, then looked up at our server myself, and…

What the fuck?!

He looked just as shocked by my presence as I felt by his, and he muttered something unintelligible before hurrying away from the table. My blood was already boiling by the time I looked back at Lauren, who'd covered my hand with hers.

"Ty… what was that about?" she asked, her eyes filled with concern.

I shook my head, blowing out a heavy sigh as I slipped my hand away from hers to sit back. "Nothing, Lo. I'm not trying to mess up your birthday night, let's just—"

"*Ty.*" She looked so confused that I immediately felt guilty. "Just tell me, or thinking about it, wondering what the hell that was will be all I can do, and I'm *not* going to have a good time."

"I…" I started to protest, but I knew it was pointless before I even opened my mouth. I sighed again, then sat forward. "Jamila. That's the guy she…"

Lauren narrowed her eyes for a second, then they widened in understanding and she sat straight up. "Oh. *Oh,*" she said, pressing her lips together for a moment. "I'm sorry, I—"

"No. You haven't done anything to be sorry for. Let's just enjoy our night."

She nodded, and a different waiter came to serve us, but the sight of Elijah's bitch ass had killed my vibe. We'd actually been cool, until I found out he was fucking my fiancé behind my back. I was able to put on a good front for Lauren, and keep her laughing so she had a good time, but my mood was shot. Almost ten months had gone by since I discovered that little betrayal, but every time I saw one of their faces, I got pissed like it hadn't been any time at all.

When we were getting ready to leave, I excused myself to the bathroom. On the way out, I told myself I was going to squash it, and leave that shit behind me. I had a beautiful, sweet girlfriend, who was nothing like that leech Jamila. I had no reason to still be hung up about it.

But then, on my trip back to the table, Elijah just had to stop me.

"Yo, Ty. Hold up man."

I took a deep breath, then shoved my hands in my pockets before I turned around, so I wouldn't give this dude a well-deserved right hook to the jaw. "What the fuck do you want, Eli?"

He swallowed hard, then shrugged. "I'm saying, at some point we've gotta get over this shit. We were cool, man. We're frat."

"I don't have to do shit. Is this why you stopped me? Cause it's my girl's birthday, and I'm trying to do something nice for her. We have somewhere else to be."

Elijah scoffed. "Oh, so you're doing right by this one."

"Muthafuck—is your ass *crazy*?" I asked, snatching him up by the collar and pushing him into the wall. "You've got a lot of fucking nerve, commenting on my business. I'm not above still handing out that ass whooping I should have given you about Jamila."

"Oh *now* you care?" he shook his head, then struggled against my hold on him, and I let him go, shoving him away. "You didn't care enough to fight about it back then."

"Because I knew her ass was a gold-digger, figured you deserved each other."

His eyes narrowed. "If you knew that girl at all you'd know it wasn't even like that. *She's* not like that."

"Well she did a good fucking impersonation. I found more information about *my* finances on her computer than I had my damned self. Explain that shit."

"It's not for me to explain."

I sucked my teeth. "Then why the hell are you talking about it? Get outta here, man."

"Look, Ty, I don't want any trouble. I just think you should give her a chance to explain herself. All of it."

"Whatever, Elijah. Get the fuck outta my way before I change my mind about kicking your ass."

I shoved past him, harder than necessary, then took the long way back to our table so I would have time to train my expression into something less pissed off. Lauren was finishing off the cake and ice cream dessert she'd ordered, and I couldn't pay the check and get us out of there quick enough.

She'd had two drinks at dinner, those fruity things that mask the liquor and get you messed up before you realize it. Lauren hadn't lied about having a high tolerance for liquor though, so she wasn't drunk, just good and tipsy as we drove to the next stop. She sang along with the radio at the top of her lungs, paying me next to no attention on the twenty minute drive to the hotel.

I used that time wisely, to work myself out of my fucked up mood.

I could admit that I'd messed up with Jamila. She'd tolerated my mixing up times, missing dates, forgetting important things much longer than Lauren. Even once I started doing it on purpose, because I wanted to see how long it would take her to get fed up. If she *ever* got fed up, which I highly suspected she wouldn't have, because she had a higher goal in mind.

She'd been complaining about the sluggishness of her laptop, talking about wanting to get another one. I figured fixing her computer was something simple I could do to say I was sorry about the time management issues, so one day while she was asleep in my bed, I started it up. I intended to clean it and run some diagnostics, change a few settings, do whatever I could to improve the performance. I was checking her folders for unnecessary files, viruses, etc, when I ran across a password protected folder with my full name, *Roosevelt Tyson Sinclair.*

Now, my first thought was that it was pictures or old emails between us, something like that. It probably wasn't right to hack into it, but curiosity got the best of me. I got that folder open, and… it wasn't old pictures and emails chronicling our love.

There *were* pictures, and emails between us, but there were articles too, about my family, and our net worth. Bank statements that had to come from online accounts, which she had access to, but still. What the fuck did she need all of that for? She even had statements from my trust fund accounts, which had nothing to do with anything, especially when she'd already agreed to signing a prenuptial agreement. Her parents were both doctors, and she was going to be one soon. They didn't need *my* money.

I maybe could have written it off, if it wasn't for the message that popped up from her email program. I just glanced at it, not really intending to read, but one of the words made it catch my eyes.

"*Get money girl. Good luck.*"

I clicked on it, and immediately read through the email thread between her and a friend, which chronicled in vague terms, the fact that she was basically only with me for the money. Things about moving the wedding up, so she could start moving money from the account without me saying anything, and a bunch of other shit that made me sick to my stomach. *That's* when it dawned on me that the download date for some of those articles and pictures were from before we'd even met.

Jamila had *chosen* me, as a mark.

Still, my stupid ass believed that maybe it had started out like that, but at some point her feelings had changed. There was no way she could fake the way we made love, the feelings we shared, the dreams and future we'd planned together, that shit was *real*.

And then I found out about Eli, because I dropped by her place, back in town two days early from summer break, and found them… nah. I couldn't let my mind go there if I was trying not to be pissed off.

Anyway.

Yeah, it was shitty of me to not make sure I was respecting her time. And it was even shittier to deliberately miss dates and such. But to act like that trumped targeting somebody to con them out of money, lying to them, making a fool of them, screwing their friend, and whatever other shit she'd done that I didn't even know about yet.

They were fucking crazy – not *me*.

By the time we pulled up at the hotel, I actually did feel better. I helped her out of the car, handed the keys off to the valet, and led her inside.

"Ty, what is this?" she asked, as I pulled her into the elevator. She was a little wobbly on her heels, but her eyes were alert, and clear.

"Part of your birthday surprise, beautiful."

She shook her head. "You didn't have to bring me to a hotel. I mean, this is a really nice one, but still. If we're having birthday sex, I mean… I have a room, you have a room…"

"But this isn't just *any* room," I said, grinning as the elevator chimed to let us know we'd reached our floor.

There were only two rooms on the top floor, and ours was on the left, facing the lake. I led her inside, and she went straight to the full length window like she was drawn by a magnet, looking out on the lights of the city shining over the water.

"*Wow.*" She turned to me, with a big smile on her face. "This is *beautiful*, Ty! This is… this is too much, but it's beautiful."

"I'm glad you like it. Come 'ere."

I grabbed her hand, leading her to the huge bed, and the two boxes she hadn't noticed sitting on top.

"You didn't have to—"

I shook my head, quieting her protest. "I know I didn't have to. I wanted to."

I would slip the gift card into her bag or something later, since it didn't really have a nice presentation, and I wanted that to be another surprise anyway. I picked up the larger of the two boxes and put it in her lap, but she just looked at it, making no moves to open it.

"What is this, Ty?" she asked, almost sounding nervous.

"I guess you need to open it to find out."

Lauren shot me a scowl, then chewed anxiously at her bottom lip. "I always get worried when people give me gifts, you know everything I feel shows up right on my face."

I laughed. "Yeah, I do. But if you don't like it, that's okay. We can switch it for something different. Okay?"

She let out a breathy sigh. "Okay."

Lauren stared at the box for a few more seconds before lifting the lid. I held my breath until I heard a quiet gasp as she peeled back the layers of tissue paper to see the lingerie inside.

"This is *gorgeous*," she said, pulling out both pieces and fingering the soft blue and silver lace of the bra and panty set. "I can't accept something like this Ty, this had to be so expens—"

"Mind your business," I interrupted, chuckling as I pressed a kiss to her cheek. "You like it?"

"I *love* this." She turned to me, pushing her body against mine to kiss me. I savored the lingering flavor of those fruity drinks on her lips and tongue, then groaned when she pulled away. "I can't wait to wear this for you."

I grinned. "Hell, me either."

She scrunched her nose at me as I pulled the lacy underwear from her hands and pushed it back into the box, which I tossed behind us on the bed. I slipped the second, smaller box into her hands, suddenly feeling nervous.

I could tell she wanted to protest again, but I lifted an eyebrow at her and shook my head. "Open the box, Lauren."

She took a deep breath, and pulled the lid away quickly this time. Her eyes got *big*.

"Ty," she said, her voice already cracking with emotion. When she looked up, her eyes were glossy with tears, and she gave me a sweet smile that turned into a laugh as she looked down at the contents of the box again. "I can't—" she stopped to giggle again, then shook her head at me. "You are... a damned fool. But this is beautiful."

"Can I put it on you?"

She nodded, quickly, pulling her gift from the box. "Please."

We stood and went to the mirror, where I pushed her hair to one side and fastened the chain around her neck. The chain was so long that the pendant hung almost between her breasts, but it was an inside joke anyway. Nobody else had to see it.

"A glass slipper," she whispered, turning the tiny, diamond-studded platinum pendant between her fingers as she caught my gaze in the mirror. "If I'm Cinderella, does that mean you consider yourself Prince Charming?"

"Your words, not mine."

Lauren giggled, then turned to face me, her expression suddenly more serious, even though her eyes shone with happiness. "Ty... I've had a wonderful time with you tonight, and I appreciate *everything*. But I want you to understand that you didn't have to get me any gifts, or the hotel room, none of that. I don't want you to feel like you have to buy me stuff to impress me."

I smiled, because she looked so honestly concerned that it made a strange tightness fill my chest. "Lauren, it's fine. The money isn't a concern, trust me."

"I..." she faltered, then took a deep breath, looking away from me as she spoke the next words. "I need to confess something..."

My heart shot up to my throat, then dropped down into my stomach a second later, as all kinds of scenarios shot through my mind.

"I googled you."

Whew.

"That's it?" I asked, chuckling. "That's normal these days."

She shrugged. "I know, but still. It felt *icky*, because I only did it seriously because of something Jamila said to me. Like, I googled you early on, to make sure you weren't in the news for spreading herpes or anything like that, but..." – she sighed. – "that day she and I had that run in at Blakewood's, she implied I was after you for money. And I was like what *money*? Ty drives a Honda!"

"Hey! Hondas are good cars."

Lauren giggled, then lifted a hand to my chest in a soothing gesture. "I know that. There isn't anything wrong with a Honda, I'm just saying it doesn't scream multi-generational real-estate wealth money. And you just don't look or act or live like a spoiled rich kid."

"Because I don't consider myself one."

"I just want it to be clear that I don't care about that. I'm not looking for a meal ticket, or a sugar daddy, or a baby daddy, none of that."

I grinned, then pulled her into a kiss. "I know that, little Miss Independent. Being taken care of, accepting that kind of help... I think it goes against your nature, like your head would implode or something."

"Shut up," she murmured against my lips, then kissed me again.

"Did you know about my family when you got into my ass that night after I showed up at your job?"

"Yep. I was ready to send your rich ass packing," she said, rolling her neck.

She yelped when I grabbed two handfuls of her ass, dragging her closer. "I'm glad you gave me another chance."

"I'm glad you haven't made me regret it."

I lowered my mouth, capturing her lips in another kiss before I pulled away. "Happy birthday, gorgeous girl."

"Thank you." She smiled against my mouth, then drew away, turning back to face the mirror. "I have a surprise for you."

I lifted an eyebrow. "For *me*?"

She nodded, then reached under her arm to unhook her dress,

then slowly unzipped it. She shrugged the straps away from her shoulders and let the dress drop to her feet, where she kicked it away.

Goddamn.

She stood in front of me in the vibrant, hot pink version of the lingerie she'd worn for our first time. Knowing that she'd had that on all night under her dress made me harder than could possibly be healthy, in less than two seconds.

Lauren turned to face me, hand on her hips, feet clad in four inch heels, with that glass slipper tucked between her breasts. She smiled, and I reached for her, picking her up to carry her back to the bed.

Happy Birthday to *me.*

fourteen

. . .

Lauren

"WELCOME TO TERRIFIC TECH, can I help you with something today?"

I knew for a fact I was giving excellent customer service today.

I was chipper as hell, practically bouncing off the walls, because I was still high off the way I'd spent my birthday. Three days had gone by, and my body was still humming with pleasure, even though I'd not had the opportunity to physically be with Ty since then. As easy as it would have been to just stay the night with each other anyway, it usually led to neglected schoolwork and studying, or someone waking up late.

So we were good.

It wouldn't be long until we were able to go on break, and I'd already cleared it with both sets of grandparents that out of my seven days of upcoming spring break, I would be using two to spend with Ty. It had taken a lot of self-reflection, and a long talk with Bianca to convince me that it was okay to use two of those precious days to have uninhibited fun with my boyfriend, and honestly... I still wasn't convinced. The talk with Mrs. Tanya, Mekhi's mother, hadn't helped my uncertainty one bit.

She was already a little pissy that I had a boyfriend in the first place, particularly since it wasn't Mekhi. She hadn't said anything outright, probably since *I* wasn't the one who told her, but I caught her little hints, and she was going strong with the sales pitch on Mekhi. When she called on my birthday and asked about my plans, she'd gotten extremely short with me when I told her I would be with Ty. So taking time from my spring break, which I always spent with Harper, to be with the boyfriend who wasn't her son... whew. Mama wasn't happy.

But *I* was happy. And even Mrs. Tanya's lack of sunny disposition when I told her about the trip that morning couldn't kill *mine*. I fingered the "glass" slipper on the chain around my neck, then gave the older woman in front of me a huge smile, waiting for her to tell me what she needed.

"Well, I believe I've found myself in need of a new phone," she said, glancing disdainfully at the smart phone in her hand. I glanced over her shoulder at the meaty-looking bodyguard five feet away, and wondered if she were some kind of celebrity. She looked vaguely familiar, but I chalked that up to her being a Vanessa Williams lookalike, and took the phone from her hands.

"Can you tell me what it's doing?"

She shook her head, giving me a look of confusion. "Well... that's the problem, dear. It's not *doing* anything. It's just stuck on this front screen."

"Hmm. Well, let me take a look at it, and if I can't do anything, maybe, Nerd Troop can help. They can fix just about anything if it can power on."

A perfectly groomed brow lifted over the dark frames of her sunglasses. "Nerd Troop?"

I nodded. "Yeah. Our company repair team." She still looked at me like I was speaking a foreign language, so I decided against trying to further explain. "Let's sit down, so I can look at this, okay?"

"Please do."

She took the seat I offered at the communications center desk, once her bodyguard had brushed it free of enough imaginary filth that it met her standards.

"Has this happened before?" I asked, as I keyed in my information to access the product manual and troubleshooting database.

"No. And my son usually does this type of thing for me, but he's at work. I'm here to see *him*, so one would think he would make himself available to me, but apparently not. I had my security call my daughter in law to meet me for assistance."

I nodded. "Okay. Well, we can go ahead and at least look at some things while you wait for her."

"Yes, let's."

She stared at me as I removed the protective case from her phone, checking the screen for responsiveness, but I kept my eyes on what I was doing, not wanting to make things any more awkward than they already were.

"You know you're a really beautiful young woman," she said, and I looked up, giving her an embarrassed smile.

"Thank you."

As soon I looked back down at the phone, to remove the back battery cover, my eyes widened in alarm. Was she about to hit on me? Was she like… a sugar mama?

"Is this all you do?"

I lifted my eyes in response to her question. "This? As in… fix cell phones?"

The same eyebrow from before slowly hiked up again. "No, child. This, as in, work at this little store. Is this *all* you do?"

"Oh!" I pulled the battery out, placing it down on the counter while I checked for any water damage in the phone. "No, I'm in school. A senior at BSU."

"How *wonderful*," she said, giving a gracious little clap of her hands. "BSU is one of our most honored HBCUs, and not at all an easy school to get into. Smart, beautiful, and obviously not lazy if you're spending time at this menial job. You remind me of myself at this age. Boys must be just nipping at your heels."

I blushed. "Umm, I wouldn't say that, but I have a pretty serious boyfriend."

"Who is just as focused and responsible as you, I hope."

Feeling proud, I nodded. "Yes ma'am." I put the battery and cover back with the phone, and turned it on, waiting for it to fully load.

"Good for you, young lady. I'm sure he's a lucky man."

"I like to think so."

Her mouth turned up into a smile of open delight, and she put a hand on my arm. "And that little sassiness, oh my goodness! If my sons weren't both already betrothed, I would have you at the next family dinner. Maybe a pretty girl would convince them to come. Well, one of them, at least."

She was about to say something else, but then her body guard tapped her shoulder, leaning forward to tell her something. "My daughter in law is arriving," she relayed to me, once she gave me her attention back.

"Perfect timing," I said, then held up the perfectly working phone. "Sometimes it just needs that hard reset, so next time try that first. Just take your battery out, let everything sit a few minutes, then put it back in. Good as new, and you can just have lunch with your daughter in law instead of hanging around here."

She smiled at me again. "I think I'll do that. Thank you dear," – she pointed her face toward my name tag – "Lauren."

And then she didn't move again, just left her mouth parted like something had shocked her. I couldn't puzzle over that for very long before the front door chimed, and I glanced toward them and saw the devil – I mean, Jamila – step in.

She must have felt my eyes on her, because they immediately locked with mine, then went to the person beside me. Jamila smirked so hard she had to have been saving that one up for years, and *then*... it clicked for me why this woman seemed so familiar.

Geneva Sinclair.

If she took off those big fancy sunglasses that hid half of her face, I'd be looking right at Ty's mother. Jamila walked right up to us, looking extra smug, and muttered something low into Mrs. Sinclair's ear. The older woman's expression had already gone from pleasant to shocked, and now she looked at me with open disdain as she practically snatched her phone from my hands.

"So *you're* the little hussy going around breaking up perfectly happy relationships, are you?" Instead of the nice cadence she'd used with me before, her tone was suddenly clipped, and distinctly snotty.

"I've done no such thing," I quipped back, being careful to measure the amount of attitude I gave, because this was Ty's mother, and I was at work.

She gave a haughty sniff. "Then what do you call cavorting around with a man who is betrothed to another? Where is your mother? Does she know you're conducting yourself as a mistress?"

"*Excuse you.*" My fragile hold on composure slipped at the mention of my mother. Why did these women keep bringing up my family? "First of all, my mother is resting peacefully, let's leave her that way. Secondly, my boyfriend is only involved with one woman – me. Ty and Jamila broke up almost a year ago, and it's really creepy that neither of you will let this go."

"You little harlot, how dare you—"

I interrupted her with a laugh. "How dare *I*? Before you call me out of my name, you should know it's widely available information on the internet that you were your husband's girlfriend while he had a wife."

Mrs. Sinclair snatched off her sunglasses, showing off a beautiful face that was twisted into an ugly scowl. Over her shoulder, Jamila was practically bubbling with glee. "Listen to me, little girl," she snapped, jabbing a finger in my face. *Too* close to my face. I was about two seconds from batting her hand away when a tall figure in an avocado-colored shirt that matched mine stepped between us.

"Looks like you ladies could use some assistance over here," Austin said, with a bright smile on his face even though I heard the strain in his voice. He put a hand on my arm, and bent low to speak into my ear. "Lauren, take your ass to the break room, *now*."

"But I—"

"*Now*, Lo." He lifted his eyebrows. "I'm trying to keep you out of trouble, go."

I shot a glare around him at Bitch 1 and Bitch 2, then stomped my way into the break room, where I paced back and forth for ten minutes, waiting on Austin to come and get me. He'd taken on additional duties as part of one of his classes, and had thus been promoted to assistant manager. He had a tiny bit of pull, and if this silliness got reported to my boss… I hoped he would vouch for me.

When he finally came to the door, he shot me a smile. "You're good," he said, and my shoulders sank in relief.

"They didn't report me?"

He scoffed. "Oh hell yeah, they reported you. As soon as you left, they insisted on seeing the boss man. Mrs. Geneva swears you were a couple of seconds away from attacking her with a razor blade under your tongue. You know, because you're *that type of girl*, according to her."

Austin was laughing – laughing hard – about this, but it wasn't funny to me.

"So what happened?!"

"I told Steve her ass was lying, that's not even like you. And he knew that already, but you see how dramatic Mrs. Geneva can be. I explained that too. I've known Ty for a few years, so I've met her before, and seen her brand of craziness. Plus you had a nosy ass customer filming, so don't be surprised if you end up on YouTube. But, he did show Steve the little video, and he kicked them out."

I pinched between my eyes, pushing out a heavy sigh. "Oh *God*. How wonderful."

Austin chuckled. "Don't sweat it Lo. You're good."

"But what is Ty gonna say about me getting into it with his *mother*?"

"Ty knows that woman is crazy!"

I massaged the back of my neck, remembering the story he'd told me about her reaction to his sister's lack of desire for a child. Maybe he was so used to this that it would be okay.

I took a few more minutes to compose myself, then headed back out to the floor to finish my shift. When I left, I was super tired, and needed to study for a test I had at the end of the week, but I *really* needed to see Ty. Talking to him would be fine, but I needed to see him, touch him, to know that things were okay between us after the altercation with his mother.

But... hadn't she said she was there to see him?

I didn't think she would be staying with him in his tiny apartment, but maybe they were together. I was sure she'd gotten to him first, probably even popped up at the library while he was working. Feeling defeated, I drug myself home and buried my face in my book, watching the time for eleven o'clock, when the library closed and Ty would be off.

At around nine my phone chimed, and my heart almost stopped when I saw it was him.

"Hey... just heard a very interesting story about you and my mother. Are you okay? – Ty"

Shit. What did she tell him?

"Yeah... I'm okay. What did you hear?"

"Well, according to my mother, who came in about thirty minutes ago limping and moaning like she was a war victim, you verbally attacked her and threw a huge tantrum in the middle of a crowded store, and messed up her phone. – Ty"

I rolled my eyes, because *really*? I verbally attacked her? Threw a tantrum? Broke her phone?

"But then Austin called while I was on my break, and told me what actually happened. I'm so sorry you got ambushed like that. I'm going to talk to her about that shit, it's not cool. – Ty"

"Are you gonna be with her tonight?"

"My mom? Nah. I didn't even know she was in town until she popped up at the library. She loves showing up unannounced. – Ty"

"Can you come by?"

"You sure? I know how you are about your study time… – Ty"

"Yes, I'm sure. I need to see you."

"I'll be there as soon as I get off. – Ty"

"Thank you."

When we'd finished making our plans, I tossed my phone on the bed and made myself get back into my schoolwork for about another hour. After that, I took a long shower, and put on a tank top and soft cotton shorts, with no underwear. If things went by *my* plan, I wouldn't need them.

Ty knocked on my door at 11:14, and I flung myself into him as soon as I opened it. He chuckled, then pulled me into his arms, squeezing me against his chest.

"You're not mad at me?" I asked, wrapping my arms around his waist as he stepped inside, closing the door behind him.

"Mad at *you*? Not at all."

He locked my door and then took me by the hand, leading me into my room.

"I'm off tomorrow, so I'm going to have a sit down with my

mother about what happened today. I've been dealing with her and Jamila's craziness for so long that I can just ignore it. But, I can't do that anymore, not when it's affecting you. I'm going to handle it, okay?"

I nodded. "Okay."

Sitting down on my bed, Ty pulled me into his lap, with me straddling him. He grabbed my chin, drawing me into a kiss.

"*Mmmm,*" I moaned, draping my arms over his shoulders. "I've needed that today."

"Just today?"

I grinned. "*Every* day. All day."

"That's more like it," Ty said, playfully smacking my butt.

My phone buzzed, and though I didn't want to interrupt the moment, I had to grab it in case it was about Harper.

"Hello?"

"Hey sexy."

Shit.

I cringed at the greeting Mekhi had chosen, particularly because I was sitting in Mekhi's lap, and there was a chance he'd heard it.

"Hey Mekhi, is everything okay? Is Harper okay?"

"Huh?" he asked, sounding confused. "Yeah, Harper is fine. I just called to talk, if that's okay?"

Ugh. It hadn't gotten past me that since Harper's birthday – since finding out I was seeing someone – Mekhi was calling and texting "just to talk" more often than he ever had.

"Actually," I said, looking at Ty, who was looking at me, his expression blank. "I'm with Ty right now, so…"

"Oh, my bad. I didn't mean to interrupt. I'll holla at you later."

"Okay. Bye."

"Bye."

I didn't believe for a second that he "didn't mean to interrupt". Why else was he calling me at nearly midnight? I hung up the phone and tossed it across the bed before cautiously turning my attention back to Ty. Was he going to be mad? He'd never brought it up before, but this wasn't exactly the first time a text or call from Mekhi had interrupted us.

Instead of commenting on it, he grinned, the stuck his fingers down my shirt, pulling out my pendant. "Did you put this on because I was coming by?"

I frowned. "What? No, I've worn it every day since you gave it to me."

"Really?" he asked, eyes wide.

"*Yes*, really. Why wouldn't I? It's special to me."

He looked at me for a long moment, not exactly smiling, but his eyes were happy.

"What?" I prodded his shoulder. "Why are you looking at me like that?"

Ty shook his head, looking down for a second before he returned his gaze to mine. "Nothing. So, what's up? You said you *needed* to see me tonight. What do you need?"

I smiled, then climbed down from his lap to stand in front of him.

"I need you to take off your clothes."

∼

"Wake up."

I nudged Ty's shoulder again, trying to rouse him so he could go to class, with no luck.

His alarm had woken me up, and after listening to it go off for a full minute without him stirring at all, I turned it off. I settled on top of him, studying his sleeping face, running my fingers over his stubbled chin. This moment felt so completely perfect that I shook my head, pushing *that* thought away.

I moved myself up, pressing my lips to his, and finally, he moved. He groaned a little, then lifted his arm, wrapping it around my waist before he drifted right back into sleep. I giggled, then pulled away, sliding my nude body against his as I went. By the time I made it to my destination, he was waking up again, and I took his morning hardness in my hands.

"You awake?" I asked quietly, waiting for a response. His eyes were still closed, but he nodded. I was already wet and ready, so I sank onto him with ease.

"*Shit*, Lauren," he groaned, roughly grabbing and squeezing handfuls of my ass. I opened my legs a little more so he could go deeper, and suddenly he grabbed me around the waist, pulling me down against his chest. "No condom this morning?"

I shook my head, burying my face against his neck as he gripped my hips, moving me up and down. This wasn't the first time we'd not used protection. We'd gotten tested together, and I was on birth control, so there was really no reason not to other than personal paranoia about getting pregnant. Sometimes I insisted on protection – usually when my menstrual cycle app warned me that I was entering a fertile time – and sometimes not. This morning... *not*.

I just wanted to feel him, nothing between us, his skin against mine. I knew Ty preferred it like this too, from the way his body reacted, getting harder and bigger. He rolled us over, putting himself on top, and I wrapped my legs around his waist as he drove deeper.

"Good morning," he muttered against my ear, then drew it between his teeth. "You're going to have me skipping class, waking me up like this."

I giggled, because as much as he *wanted* to do such a thing, I knew it wasn't going to happen. This was Ty's last year of formal coursework before he started his dissertation, and he had to knock it out of the park to maintain his GPA. Sure enough, thirty minutes later I was kissing him goodbye at the door so he could rush home and change.

When he was gone, I took a shower and got dressed. I didn't

have class for another hour, but I could use the extra time to look over my notes from last session, and be well prepared. I was sitting at my desk when I realized that I hadn't checked my phone that morning, or even seen it since the night before.

Laughing at myself, I checked all around the room, then remembered tossing it on the bed. Sure enough I found it dead, wedged between the mattress and the wall. I put it on the charger and grabbed an apple and a granola bar, peeling open the wrapper as I sat down at my desk. Twenty minutes later, I packed up, grabbed my phone, and headed across campus to get to class.

As soon as the phone powered on, it began chiming with missed call notifications. My heart nearly stopped when I realized they were from Mekhi's mother. Was something wrong with my baby? I hit the button to call her back, and took a seat on a nearby bench, because I didn't trust my legs not to give out.

"Hello?!" As soon as I heard the attitude filling Mrs. Tanya's tone, I knew I was in trouble.

Shit.

"Good morning Mrs. Tanya!" I said, trying to be cheerful even though dread was creeping up my back. "I saw I missed some calls from you, is everything okay?"

She sucked her teeth. "Where have you been?! I was calling you all night!"

"I was *home*. Is Harper okay?"

"I had to take her to the emergency room last night."

My heart leapt up into my throat. *"Emergency room?!* What happened, is she okay? Do I need to come?!"

"She had an extremely high fever, and she was asking for her mother, who claims she was home, but was more likely laid up somewhere."

What?

I checked my anger, and pushed for more information about what was important at the moment : Harper. "Is she still at the hospital? What did they say was wrong with her?"

"They sent us home, and she's at school now. You would know this if you'd kept your ass at home and answered the phone."

I frowned. "Wait a minute now, I'm – respectfully – going to have to ask that you not speak to me like that. I *was* home, my battery died and I didn't realize it."

"And I'm sure it was because you were laid up with your little boyfriend. Pawning the baby off on the grandparents so you can run the streets and whore around."

I reeled back like someone had slapped me. "*Pawning the grandbaby off*?! Mrs. Tanya, you were the main one insisting that Mekhi and I pursue whatever opportunities we could to make a good life for Harper. He chose the military, I chose school. No one is "running the streets", unless you count the sidewalks I take to get to class, and the route I use to get to work and back. My entire life for the last three years has revolved around taking care of my responsibilities. I see Harper whenever I can, save for her future, send you guys money to make sure she has whatever she needs. You can't say that I haven't!"

"But you can't deny whoring around, can you? My son offered you a perfectly good life, a chance to have your family together, and you passed him over for some little boy up there at that school. I'll tell you this, Ms. *Lauren*. If – *when* – you get pregnant again, don't you think for a second you can drop that one off here. I'm already raising one of your babies. *No more.*"

A second later, the complete quiet on the other end of the line told me she'd hung up, but I didn't move the phone from my ear. I could only sit there, stunned that she'd gone off and said those things to me. And I *still* didn't know what was going on with my baby!

I called my dad and got no answer, and I knew the same would be true for Mekhi. They were both at work at this time, at jobs where they couldn't just answer the phone at any time.

Shit.

Was *I* pawning off my responsibility? I thought I was doing everything the right way, accepting the help that I'd been offered, but if she felt like *this*, like I was taking advantage of her…I could remedy that.

Chest heaving, I lowered my phone to my lap and pulled up my internet browser, looking for a last-minute plane ticket. I almost threw up looking at the price, but I took my still pristine, never used credit card from my wallet and paid for it. I rushed back to my room to pack a quick bag, and I pushed the *"girl, what the hell are you doing?"* thoughts from my mind. In my room, I took just a few moments before heading to the airport to send out an email.

I had to let my professors know I wouldn't be making it to class.

∼

THIS WAS HOW PEOPLE ENDED UP IN JAIL.

I was sure that at any moment, a SWAT team was going to dive off the roof, from behind cars, or out of the street drains to hold me down for daring what I was about to do.

Of course, none of that happened.

After my flight, I parked my rental in the lot at Harper's daycare/preschool hybrid, went inside, and walked right up to the front desk. I could see the kids in her class behind one of the glassed wall, and spotted Harper sitting between another little girl and boy, intensely focused as they colored on a big sheet of poster paper. I smiled at that, then turned my attention to a woman I recognized as one of the teacher's assistants.

"Hi, you're Claire, right?" I asked.

She gave me a big smile. "Sure am! Can I help you?"

"Yes," I nodded. "I'm Lauren Bailey, Harper's mom. I want to pick her up."

Claire clasped her hands in front of her. "Oh, I thought you looked familiar! Her grandmother, Tanya, usually picks her up, right?"

I swallowed hard.

"Right. But, I just got off a plane to come and see my baby, so I thought it would be a nice surprise."

She bobbed her head up and down, still beaming. "Of course, of course! Especially after that little scare her grandmother told me about when she dropped her off this morning. Is that why you came down?"

"Um… yes, actually, in a roundabout way."

"Oh, I can just imagine how scary that had to be," she said as she turned to the computer and keyed something in. "To check that beautiful little girl's fever, see *105* come up on that little screen. Bless her heart." She gave a heavy sigh, then moved the mouse around to click something before she visibly brightened. "But then," she laughed, "to get all the way to the emergency room, and when they check the temperature it's perfectly normal. What a way to find out you've got a busted thermometer right?! That's the problem with this new technology, it goes wrong and you can't…"

Claire kept talking, but I stopped listening, because *oh-my-God-you've-gotta-be-fucking-kidding-me*. All of that going off about irresponsibility and "whoring around", but she couldn't even tell me nothing had been wrong with Harper in the first place? That she'd simply made a mistake?

Okay.

Any little guilt I felt over what I was doing immediately slipped away.

"Can I see some ID?" Claire asked, holding out her hand.

I handed her my driver's license, and she keyed something in, then handed it back to me. "Okay, you are good to go!"

I narrowed my eyes. "Wait… that's it?"

She nodded. "Of course. You're Harper's mother, you're on the list of people who can check her out. I'll go get her for you."

I stood there, stunned as she left to go get Harper. Stunned in a *good* way, because I'd honestly been a little worried that there would be more to it, that they would have to call and get Tanya's approval, which would have been a whole other ordeal.

When Harper came bouncing out, wearing her backpack, the sight of her warmed my heart. I felt infinitely better when I had my girl in my arms, pulling her into a big hug.

We said goodbye to her teachers, and I strapped her into the car seat they'd given at the rental agency. My first stop was at my dad's house, to pack a suitcase for her from the clothes she had there. Instead of calling, I sent him an email, explaining how and why Harper was with me. I didn't want her to overhear *that* drama.

Pretty much everything I'd done in my life, since I found out I was pregnant, was for the benefit of my child. If wanting to step outside a *little* bit, by having a boyfriend who was arguably just as "responsible" as me qualified as running the streets or being a slut... what could I say that would convince anyone otherwise, if they'd made up their minds?

"Pawning" Harper off on someone was the last thing I wanted to do. She was *my* responsibility, mine and Mekhi's no one elses. So maybe it was time to stop relying on help that apparently came with judgment and strings, and just make it work for myself. Thousands and thousands of amazing single mothers made it happen. I'd seen it myself, interacted with the women, heard the stories in the support groups I frequented online. If they could make it work... so could I.

I waited until we were on the plane to text Mrs. Tanya to let her know she didn't need to pick Harper up from school, and then turned the phone off. Mostly because I didn't feel like entertaining her response, but we were supposed to turn our devices off anyway. Part of me wanted to say nothing at all, but I knew that was just being ugly. As mean as she'd been to me, she didn't deserve the fear of not knowing where Harper was, when I knew she loved her dearly. I was still pissed about what she'd said, but who knows... her words had sparked something, and maybe it was time.

I was bringing my little girl to live with her mommy, where she belonged.

fifteen

. . .

lauren

I... didn't think this through.

Not even a little bit.

This wasn't the first time I'd made an impulsive decision that didn't turn out well. In fact, my impulsive decisions rarely turned out well, which is why I planned, and thought out, and over thought everything.

Except this.

One of the decisions that needed my tendency to think through every possible scenario, I'd thought through none, except the one where everything ended neatly, happily ever after. I'd reacted in hurt and anger, which was never a good idea, and now...this wasn't happy. Not at all.

I was lucky that Mina, who I hadn't considered at all when I made the decision to bring a four year old to live with me, was basically living with Austin now anyway. We still saw each other because we worked together, and occasionally had lunch, but she did 95% of her sleeping, studying, and living at Austin's place. So that was one hurdle avoided.

I set Harper up at the kitchen table with paper and crayons, praying that she would stay occupied long enough for me to do the much needed studying I hadn't been able to do on the plane. But I couldn't focus. I kept looking at my phone, knowing that at some point, I was going to have to talk to somebody about what I'd done.

Using my laptop, and the convenience of online ordering, I got a pizza for Harper and me, then powered on my phone.

Twelve voice mails.

Eighteen texts.

I pushed out a heavy sigh.

Two of the voicemails and four of the texts were from Ty. One voicemail was just saying hey, another sounding a little worried that he hadn't been able to get in touch with me. The texts were the normal randomness he always sent me throughout the day.

One voicemail, three texts from Bianca, all asking if I was okay. My dad had probably reached out to her. He didn't do texting, but there were two voicemail messages from him, both wanting to know, again, if I was okay, asking me to call him back.

Three voicemails, *five* texts from Mekhi. Was I crazy, did he need to take emergency leave, would I quit playing and take Harper back? They were all along the same vein, and all made me roll my eyes. It was pretty safe to guess his mother hadn't shared her little tirade with him, but I didn't care. As far as I was concerned, he was part of the problem, because nobody told his ass to share *my* business with his mother, for her to use it against me.

Four voicemail messages, six texts from Tanya. In the voice messages, there was a clear range. First, she was livid, and I was everything except a child of God. The next one was calm, and extremely fake. In the third, she threatened legal action, which didn't scare me. There had never been a shift in legal custody of Harper, and even if she sued for visitation rights, it would be a waste of her time. I didn't mind her seeing Harper, so there was no argument there.

In the last voice message, she sounded heartbreakingly sad, and I felt a tiny bit of guilt crop up again. It was not, and never had been, my intention to make her feel like "her baby had been snatched from her", but what had she really expected?

It struck me very clearly that none of her voicemails or texts held a single note of apology. I certainly wasn't holding out for that, but it was clear, at least to me, that she'd meant what she said. So since she claimed I wasn't handling my responsibility, *fine*. Harper would *live* with me. Problem solved.

Well, not really.

Because here I was with my phone ringing again – Mekhi – with a test in the morning that I desperately needed to study for, with a four year old drawing at the table. Excuse me – drawing *on* the table. And then the wall.

Father, help me.

It was after ten at night, and Harper was wide awake after sleeping for the entire flight, and the phone was ringing again.

Tanya.

Then my dad.

I sat down at the computer again, emailing my professor to beg to take my test another time. If I could move it, I could get Mina to watch Harper, and figure everything else out from there.

Someone knocked on the door, and Harper ran around screaming, excited about the pizza. I put her at the table with two slices and a cup of milk, but my stomach was in knots. I knew I should probably answer the phone, but what was there to say? It was done, and I wasn't changing my mind.

Harper knocked over her milk, and I felt like a zombie cleaning it up, then pouring her another, which she promptly spilled. The phone rang again, and I snatched it up, not bothering to look at the screen before I answered.

"*What?*" I snapped, nearly wiping a hole in the table as I cleaned up the spill.

"So you *are* alive then, I see."

I pushed out a heavy sigh at the sound of my dad's kind, deep voice, then leaned against the kitchen wall to watch Harper dance in her chair as she ate her pizza. "Yes, I'm alive. And so is Harper. We're both alive and well, so if you could pass that along to Mekhi and his mother, I'd be grateful. Really not interested in speaking to either of them."

There was silence for a moment on the other end of the line, and I could just imagine him settling back into his recliner. "I'll call and let Tanya know, but you should talk to Harper's father, let him know what's going on."

"Why?" I shrugged. "He's already gotten his mother's version, I'm sure."

"Lauren."

There was no inflection in his voice, just a simple statement of my name, but it said everything. My father was a man of very few words, and very slow to anger, unless someone wronged me or Bianca, both of whom he called his favorite child. But *just that little word*, him saying my name, carried the weight of the world, and I immediately felt badly.

"Fine. I'll text him back."

"You should call."

I sighed. "I will. Just… not tonight. I can't."

"I understand. It's late, so I won't hold you. Just wanted to hear your voice, have you tell me yourself that you're okay."

I gave my shoes a wry smile. "Thanks dad. I'm fine."

"Okay. I love you."

"I love you too."

"And Lauren?"

"Yeah?"

"I read that email you sent me. You're nobody's failure, or deadbeat mother. Not in the wildest stretch of imagination. It was good sense to accept mine and Mekhi's parents' offer of help with my grandbaby. You don't *have* to do it on your own. My home is always open. And that invitation extends to Harper *and* you, and even that little knucklehead boy you haven't introduced me to, because I know you're nobody's fool. You understand?"

I scrubbed a hand over my face, wiping away stray tears before Harper saw them. "I do."

"Good night."

"Good night dad."

I dried my face when I hung up, then listened to Harper sing a song comprised fully of the lyrics *"was that my graaaampaaaa?"* over and over while I drafted a text to Mekhi.

"Harper is fine. I'm fine. We're fine. You can stop calling. I'll let you talk to her tomorrow, let me know what time."

It didn't even take a full minute to get his response back.

"Lo, what the fuck is going on? My mom says you snatched Harper from school? – Mekhi."

I rolled my eyes.

"I didn't "snatch" MY daughter, I picked her up and brought her to my apartment. Since she's so sick of Harper being "pawned off" on her while I "whore around", I brought my daughter to live with me."

He took a little longer to respond to *that*.

"She said that to you? – Mekhi."

"What reason do I have to lie about it?"

"None, I guess. But you know she didn't mean that shit right? She's just... you know she wanted me and you to be together, so she's wilding I guess. – Mekhi."

"Not my problem. She was saying how she felt, it only came out because she got angry."

"I'm telling you, she only feels that way BECAUSE she's angry. – Mekhi."

"Whatever. I don't have time for the bullshit. I don't want my child living with someone who thinks of me in such a negative way, at ANY time."

"Goddamn it, Lo. Y'all women... I'm gonna see if I can get some leave time, and try to straighten this out, talk some sense

into somebody. You need to be able to focus on school. – Mekhi."

"*Again, whatever. You do what you want to do, my decision is made.*"

I powered the phone off and put it on the charger, not caring to see his response. As if he was going to fly down here like superman and fix something. *Please*. If he wanted to talk sense into somebody, he could start with his damned mama.

I knew I was already starting out wrong when I put the TV on Disney junior for Harper. I wasn't into parenting by cartoons, but I needed to study for this test. Even with grapes, juice, and her favorite show, Harper was still bouncing all over the place, and I cursed my lack of permanent childproofing for the apartment.

Dropping my head into my hands, I tried to focus on the words I was studying, but every time I got into the tiniest bit of a groove, my beautiful daughter would scream, yell, or knock something over with a loud gasp. I know she was just excited about being in the apartment, about the plane ride, about being with mommy, about the pizza, and any number of other things, but it was shredding my nerves.

My laptop chimed, notifying me of a new email. For about ten seconds, I was hopeful, seeing my professor's name as the sender. I clicked the message, crossed my fingers, and… "*No, Ms. Bailey. You may not reschedule the test unless you have a note from a doctor, and I mean a real note, not for any made-up ailments. You're a good student, probably the best in class, but I can't make this type of exception. If you miss the test, you will receive a zero, but you've done so good that it won't fail you for the entire class. Hope to see you. – Dr. Brian Wade.*"

SHIT!

I screamed it in my head because I couldn't in front of Harper. No, it wouldn't mean a fail, but it would drag my grade from an "A" to a "C" with the way the test was weighted. I would have to ace my final, just to get a "B", which added extra pressure to my tight schedule. I hadn't even planned to *take* the final for this class, because students with an "A" average going into the last week of school didn't have to, per his syllabus.

This is why you think things through. This. Exactly this.

I dropped my head into my hands, again, because it was the only thing I could think to do. If I'd just waited another day, or a week, *planned this*... I was so stupid.

So, *so* stupid.

"MOMMY!"

"Yes baby?"

"COME LOOK AT THIS!"

"I can't right now baby. Can you use your inside voice?"

The headache building at my temples blossomed and spread to the point that my head was pounding, and still, Harper yelled and screamed and bounced around the room. She tripped over the charger cord to my laptop, nearly dragging it off the table, and I bit my lip to check my anger.

I searched my mind, for any possible solution. Mina had class at the same time as me, Bianca lived a five hour plane ride away... what the hell could I do?

"MOOOOMMMYYYY!"

That wail came about two seconds before a loud crash, and I looked up just in time to see a lamp – in an out of the way corner of the room that Harper had no reason to be near – go toppling to the floor with a loud crash.

"Harper!" I yelled, standing up from my seat. "Get your ass somewhere and sit down! Stop hopping and jumping around and be quiet!"

The moment of silence after that seemed to stretch forever. The TV was on, volume up, but I heard nothing, as if we were in a vacuum. Right in front of me, I watched as Harper's face crumpled, her mouth opened, and she began to sob.

My heart broke a little more with every fat tear that rolled down her chubby cheeks, and I couldn't get to her fast enough, sweeping her up into my arms. "Mommy is so, so, *so* sorry," I soothed, rubbing her back as I rocked her back and forth."

"I want my grandma!" she sniffled, looked around, and then broke into louder sobs that rattled in my chest, making me feel even emptier. I'd brought her here, but she'd been with other people so long that she didn't even want me.

So I sobbed too.

We sobbed together, for I don't know how long, until a knock brought me to my front door. I glanced through the peephole, and sighed when I saw who was on the other side. I dried my face as best I could with one hand, then slowly opened the door.

At first, Ty smiled at the sight of me, but then he took in my disheveled appearance, lack of energy, and the four year old in my arms, and his expression dropped into concern.

"Hey... what happened?" he asked, stepping inside.

I closed the door behind him, and shook my head. "I don't even know where to begin. But, this is Harper. Not really how I imagined the first meeting, but Harper, can you say hello to mommy's friend Ty?"

Harper pulled her face away from my neck just long enough to glare at him, then wiggle out of my arms. She ran to swipe a slice of pizza from the table, then went back into the living room with the TV.

I shook my head. "I'm sorry about that, and I've been too messed up in the head all day to even think about correcting her little attitude," I whispered, pulling Ty into the kitchen, where Harper couldn't hear. "Just before you came, I yelled and cursed at her. I've never spoken to her like that before. I hate seeing people scream at their kids, but I... Ty, I can't deal right now." Out of nowhere, I burst into sobs again, and Ty immediately pulled me into his arms. He swayed back and forth, rocking me, saying nothing.

When my tears finally calmed, I drew back, wiping my face with my hands. "I'm sor—"

"*Stop* apologizing," he said, using his thumbs to push new tears away from my cheeks. "Tell me what's going on."

I gave a heavy sigh, then quietly told him the whole story, from the harsh phone call to the email from my professor. I was looking over his shoulder the whole time, watching for Harper, but she was – *finally* – too enthralled with the TV to move.

"So, that's what Harper is doing here, and why I'm falling the fuck apart," I finished, shaking my head. "I don't even know what to do at this point."

Ty lifted an eyebrow. "Uh, I don't know, maybe ask for help?"

"From *who*? Mina has her own stuff, Bianca is hours away, and has her own stuff. Same thing with my dad, and I'm not asking her grandmother for *shit*."

Ty's eyebrow lifted even higher, and then he started touching his arms and legs like he was checking for something.

"Ty, what are you doing?" I asked, taking a step back.

"Oh, nothing. Just making sure I'm still here, not invisible or anything like that."

It took a couple more seconds to register, but I sucked my teeth when I realized what he was implying. "Ty, I can't ask you to—"

"Why the hell not?"

"*Because*," I sighed, then glanced over at Harper again. "First of all, Harper doesn't know you, and you don't know her. Because I don't want to be introducing my child to all kinds of strange men, or *leaving her* with strange men. And you have your own stuff to do. We have class at the same time tomorrow Ty!"

His eyebrow remained cocked. "So I'm a strange man? Not your boyfriend of the last four months? You don't trust me around your kid?"

"I don't mean it like that. I'm just saying that I have to be careful who I have around my daughter. Can't you understand that?"

"Of course I understand that, but Lauren, why are you with

me if you think I'm not worthy of being around her? And I'm not saying that in a pissy way, I'm just being up front. If I had a child, I wouldn't seriously date anyone that I wouldn't be comfortable allowing them to interact with. Is that how you feel about me?"

"*No*," I insisted, because I didn't. I'd never gotten any creepy kind of vibes from Ty, and he'd done nothing to make me think he would harm me *or* Harper, but… wasn't four months a little early to have a man around her?

"Lauren, listen to me, pretty girl. You need to study. You need to go take this test tomorrow. I have class, but my professor is using tomorrow's session like office hours anyway, for people to ask about their grades. I can sit here in your living room, make sure she safe and cared for while you study. I can watch her for you while you go to class. Hell, we can walk with you, wait in the hall so you can see us through the door. There are ways to accommodate your concerns, but you have to be willing to accept the help. Maybe it's not ideal, but what are your other options right now?"

I sighed.

None.

I had exactly *no* other options.

"She doesn't even like you," I said, crossing my arms.

He sucked his teeth. "Man, whatever. Where's your tablet?"

I was skeptical, but I gave him the tablet from the end of the counter, and watched as he went into the living room and sat on the couch beside Harper. I didn't follow, but I moved to where I could see them, and stayed tucked away to listen.

"Okay lil' mini-Lauren."

"My name is Harper."

"Okay then Carpet."

"*Harper!*"

"…Marker?"

"No, *Harper!*"

She turned to Ty with a little scowl, but I could hear a giggle building in her voice.

"*Ohhhh*! My bad, *Harper*. Got it. Harper, I'm Ty, and I'm a friend of your mom's. She needs to do some grown up stuff, so I'm going to chill out here with you, and we're going to try not to be loud. Now... I'm not asking, aiight? I'm telling you we're about to chill and have a good time, because I'm cool, so why would you *not* have a good time? And you seem cool too, so I think we can just sit out here, be cool together, and let mom do what she needs to do. Right?"

I could only see their profiles, but I could tell Harper was still scowling. She stared at him for so long I almost thought it wouldn't work, but then her face softened into a smile, and she nodded.

"Okay then!" Ty lifted a hand for a high-five, and Harper gave it standing up, then bounced back onto her seat. He glanced over his shoulder to wink at me, then grabbed the remote to turn off the TV. "So you know what a library is, right?" he asked Harper, and she nodded again. "Excellent. So this thing," – he held up the tablet – "if we go to the library website, it can help us have a lot of fun. Let me show you."

I let out a little sigh of relief.

Ty and Harper seemed to be doing just fine together, so I quietly gathered my things and went into my bedroom to make an attempt at studying, leaving the door partially open so I could hear them. My mind was far from free, but at least I had a plan for averting a disaster that could ruin one of my grades.

I buckled down and focused on my book, and finally got into a flow. Even with the occasional round of deep laughs from Ty, and giggles from Harper, I was able to settle in and actually absorb some information to a point that I felt prepared for the test.

Just when I was about to get up, Ty appeared at my door.

"Hey," he said, peeking in. "Sorry to interrupt, but Harper is knocked out. Does she always just pass out mid-sentence like that?"

I laughed. "Yeah, she does that a lot. And you're not interrupting, I'm done. As ready as I'm going to be, and I need to get some sleep."

"You want me to bring her in here for you?"

"In a minute."

I stood, and like he was reading my mind, Ty stepped into the room, closing the door behind him. I settled into his arms, basking in the clean smell of his cologne as he held me tight.

"It'll be fine," he said, pressing a kiss to my forehead. "You'll knock this test tomorrow out of the park, and I know the assistant director of the daycare. We went to high school together, did undergrad together, and she's my soror. We can see about getting Harper a spot."

My lips parted in surprise. I'd totally forgotten about the "unofficial" BSU daycare, located across the street from the buildings on the south side of campus. That was the side of campus that housed the art and theater buildings, so I rarely, if ever, had occasion to go there. It wasn't BSU affiliated, but if I remembered correctly, most of the kids were those of BSU students and staff, and the students in early childhood development often did internships there.

"That would be incredible," I said, nodding. "And... maybe I can talk to my boss, see about adjusting my hours. I can use the money I usually send her grandparents to cover the tuition costs."

Ty smiled. "Exactly. See, not so bad right?" He pressed his lips to mine, in what he intended to be a sweet, simple kiss. But when he tried to pull back, I draped my arms over his shoulders and pressed a hand to the back of his head, keeping him close.

His hands slipped under my tee shirt, but he kept them at my waist, pressing his fingers into my skin. I moaned against his mouth, craving his touch, even though we'd just had each other, over and over, the night before.

"Life has been kicking your ass this week pretty girl," he said, then dropped his mouth to my neck, trailing kisses along my throat. "My mother, Harper's grandmother, this test… I want you to be okay. How can I help?"

He looked up, and when I met his gaze, the concern I saw in his eyes took my breath away. I swallowed the lump that built suddenly in my throat.

"You can make love to me."

I closed my eyes, holding on to this shoulders as he lifted me onto my desk, propping my legs around his waist. He was *so* right I could scream. I was drained, mentally, emotionally, and physically exhausted, but I needed Ty to do exactly what he was doing. He tugged my shorts and panties down my legs, then freed himself from his clothes, and a moment later, he was inside me, buried deep. Helping me be okay.

sixteen
. . .
ty

"STILL A SLEEPY HEAD, I SEE."

Lauren's eyelids fluttered open, and after looking around the study room, she gave me an embarrassed smile as she sat up. This was the first time I'd seen her in the library since Harper arrived – the first time I'd seen her, period, in a few days. She'd been constantly moving, rearranging her schedule to accommodate having her little girl with her.

"What time is it?" she asked, her voice still groggy as she lifted her hands high over her head to stretch.

I slipped my phone out of my pocket for a glance. "A little after eight."

"*Crap.*" She cut her stretching motion short and stood, packing her things. "I have to pick Harper up from the daycare center by eight-thirty, so I need to head out. Thank you for waking me up."

"You're welcome pretty girl." I pulled her into my arms for a hug, and she allowed me a few seconds before she moved away to pull her bag onto her shoulder. "Maybe when I get off, I can come by, and—"

"No." Lauren seemed just as surprised as I felt by her quick refusal, and she stepped forward to place her hand against my chest. "I'm sorry, Ty. I know we haven't had much time together, but... I don't know how good of an idea it is to have you around Harper so much, when it's still so early in our relationship. I just feel iffy still about having a man who isn't her dad around her."

I frowned. "Lauren, Harper knows who I am. The daycare brings the kids to the library every day. I've actually seen *her* more than I've seen you in the last few days."

"I know," she said, taking a deep breath. "And I'm not trying to be weird, I promise. Can you just give me a little time to work this out? I'm still trying to get settled into this new schedule, but once I am, we can figure out how to make sure we get time together, alone. Okay?"

It wasn't like I had much of a choice, so I nodded in agreement, even though I didn't really understand her hesitation. I knew it wasn't about me – she had to work through her own stuff, and come to terms with her current situation.

At the door, she pushed herself up on her toes to give me a kiss. "I got my test results back today. Made a ninety-six. It would have been a zero if you hadn't watched Harper for me, so thank you. I appreciate you."

"You're welcome Lo." I tamped down my agitation and kissed her, knowing that it could very well be another week before I got the opportunity to do so again. In the meantime, the only thing I could do was try not to miss her too much.

∼

I MISSED LAUREN.

Yeah, yeah, maybe that's sappy, but whatever.

I missed my girl, and it was the craziest feeling to have when we were right in the same city.

I tried – like *really* tried – not to be salty about the fact that I was seeing Lauren even less than usual now, because I knew baby girl Harper came first. I applauded her for making her child her priority, because it went against the stereotype of young black mothers that got constantly shoved down our throats. I admired her for it. I was proud as hell that she was doing her thing.

But... I missed her.

When Lauren wasn't in class, she was at work, six days a week to accommodate Harper's daycare schedule. The school closed at eight-thirty, so in order to get in the hours she normally would have by staying until midnight, she was going in earlier, immediately after classes.

In the evenings, she spent time with Harper until she fell asleep, and then she had to study and do her coursework, which had her up until two and three in the morning. And at *some* point, she had to sleep herself. The only time I could catch her was the suddenly rare occasion that she popped up at library – like a few days ago – dragging herself into a study room for an hour before she had to move on to the next thing in her schedule.

But I didn't dare complain.

Lauren had enough on her plate without adding my complaints to the mix. I knew where she was, what all of this was for, so I was good – for the moment – with giving her some room. Not too much though, because I wasn't stupid.

Her daughter's father had a little habit of texting and calling about things that weren't related to Harper. Lauren was a grown woman, and could talk to whoever she pleased, but I'd be lying if I said it didn't make my jaw twitch when I saw his name and face light up her phone. It wasn't that I didn't trust Lauren, but I couldn't help that shit with Elijah and Jamila from popping into my head.

Speaking of Jamila.

I was in Blakewood's having lunch, in a seat that was tucked away out of sight. I saw Jamila come through the door, but she didn't see me, which meant I had the perfect opportunity to sneak up on her.

As bold as she usually was, as eager as she'd always been to be seen, in the week since that little altercation between her and Lauren, and then Lauren and my mom at Terrific Tech, she'd been conspicuously unavailable. I'd texted her and left voicemail messages that we needed to talk, because I was ready to move past this shit, and have her out of my life. *Of course* she was avoiding that.

I waited until she was seated with her little coffee and pastry, then I moved, taking the seat across from her at the table she'd chosen by the window.

"Hi Jamila."

She jumped, nearly choking on a mouthful of food before she regained her composure enough to say anything back. "T-Ty! Heeey, what's up?" Her eyes were big, and darting around like she wanted nothing more than to get up and run out of there.

"I've got the same damned question. You've been ghost."

"Oh," she shrugged, noncommittal. "I've just been around, you know. Just busy."

I raised my eyebrows. "Busy? Busy lying about being my fiancé still? Bothering my girl with lies? Yeah, I can imagine."

"I don't have to sit here for this shit."

"Oh, but you do. Cause see, my next step is going to be talking to the police about restraining orders and harassment charges, and I bet that wouldn't reflect kindly on you when you start your residency, would it Dr. Thurston?"

She narrowed her eyes. "You *wouldn't*."

"Why the fuck not, Jamila? This shit has gone on for too long, and you don't seem to get it. I tried ignoring you, tried being an asshole, and neither approach got the message across to leave me alone so we could get on with our lives. You fucked up, and you're *still* fucking up. You're not leaving me with any options here."

"You're still pretending to be a goddamned saint! I put up with plenty of shit from you Ty. And you have the nerve to break up with me without even talking about it, and flaunting this new chick in my face, all over campus, after we were planning a wedding."

I scrubbed a hand over my face, then let out a dry chuckle. "Because you cheated, Jamila. Not only did you cheat, but you were a fucking con artist in the first place. Did I make mistakes in our relationship? Sure, I'll own that. But I *loved* you, J. While you were deciding exactly how to get in with me, I was crushing on you. I was excited that you were feeling me too, while you were just happy that I fell for your bullshit. I was falling in love, you were calculating how much Gucci you could buy."

"It was never about any fucking *Gucci*!" she hissed, then glanced around like she was just remembering we were in public. She sat back, crossing her arms over her chest. "I know you'd love to make it seem like I was just some money-grubbing parasite, but it wasn't like that."

I scoffed. "Then tell me what it was like."

"Does it matter anymore? Like you said, you've moved on. Giving somebody the best of you. Making this big huge effort to be available for her, when you never did for me."

"You're going to lie on me right to my face?"

She sucked her teeth. "So you weren't standing me up left and right? Not speaking to me for days at a time?"

"*After* I found the emails about you using me for money, hell yeah I stopped making an effort. I wanted to see exactly how committed you were to my bank accounts."

Jamila glared at me through narrowed eyes as she shook her head, then gave a dry laugh. "So you *knew*? Before you found out about me and Eli, you already knew about the money?"

I smiled. "Surprise! It was petty, I can admit that. But that's *all* I did. I never mistreated you, never cheated, never spoke ill of you, to anybody."

"The idea that you never mistreated me is a joke. Ignoring me, abandoning me, was *absolutely* mistreatment. And then you have the nerve to wonder why I cheated. Your vindictiveness drove me into his arms."

"Whatever you have to tell yourself to sleep at night. Bottom line: it's over. There's no going back for us, and I'm tired of saying it. We're done."

Jamila shrugged, then pushed a handful of locs over her shoulder. "*Fine*. I was already done anyway, Ty. I've said my goodbyes to your mother, and she's quite upset about it."

Even though the conversation was essentially over, I just sat there. Something was keeping me rooted to the chair, and I was positive that it was the little cryptic suggestions from Eli *and* Jamila that there was something I was missing.

"Why, Jamila?" I asked, slouching back in my chair. "You say it wasn't about Gucci... why else?"

She shook her head, but the angry fire was gone from her eyes. "It doesn't matter anymore. I had my reasons, it didn't work out, move on. That's what you wanted, right?"

"Want I want is the closure I never got. You tried to *con* me, Jamila, and I didn't hand your ass to the police, or report you to the school admins. You don't think I deserve to know the full story?"

Elbows propped on the table, Jamila dropped her face into her hands. When she looked up, her eyes were glossy, and I could tell she was fighting not to cry. "It... it was for my parents, Ty."

I frowned. "*What*? Your parents are both well-respected private practice doctors, and they came from money in the first place. Don't lie to me anymore, please. Your family has money."

"My family *seems* like they have money," she said, shaking her head. "It's all gone. Bad investments, the hospital bills from the accident... it's gone, and they're drowning in debt. Dad's hands were messed up, so he can't really work anymore, and my mother is working herself to death trying to keep up. They took on even more debt to pay for this wedding, and now...we're over, so that money is basically down the drain. I haven't even told them yet. I don't know *how* to. *Yeah, you were already broke, but wanted to give your oldest daughter a nice wedding, so you spent money you didn't have, but... surprise! No wedding! More debt for nothing!"* She shook her head again, then lifted her mug to swallow the rest of her coffee, though she looked like she needed something stronger.

Shit.

Was she telling the truth? I knew her father and younger sister had been in a bad car accident a few months before we got together. They were both in the hospital, in critical condition for a while, so I knew she was telling the truth about the bills adding up, even with health insurance. Long stays in critical care, even if insurance covered 80% of the cost, could easily bankrupt someone. Multiply that by two people, factor in a *major* loss of income... it made sense. And they weren't the only people to lose huge amounts of money when the economy went south. Maybe they'd never recovered?

I liked Jamila's parents, a lot. They'd treated me like their own, and I'd never once felt uncomfortable with them. They would have been good in laws, and I honestly felt bad knowing they were struggling. But Jamila was a liar. A *proven* liar. And I wouldn't put it past her to lie about this.

"Did it ever occur to you to just tell me about this? Ask for help?"

She nodded, using the backs of her hands to wipe sudden tears from her eyes. "Many times. But it was like, why would you help me, after what I did, you know? I knew you loved me, but that was... I couldn't imagine it going over well. As sweet as you are, I knew you would put me out on my ass, and not want anything to do with me."

"Give me the ring back."

Her eyes went wide for a second, then she looked down at the diamonds sparkling on her hand. She pressed her lips into a straight line, and for a long moment, I thought she would refuse, again. But then she gently twisted the ring off her finger, and slid it across the smooth surface of the table.

I didn't immediately reach for it.

"Leave Lauren alone. She has enough bullshit going on without you adding to it. Don't talk to her, don't annoy her, don't talk about her. Leave her alone. Stop saying you're my fiancé, talking about a wedding. Don't talk about *me*, not even to my mother, since you two seem to be best friends. Are we clear?"

She closed her eyes, for just a second, then nodded. "Yes. I'll leave you alone. Moving on, right?"

I nodded, then reached across the table for the ring.

"Send me something verifiable," I said, turning the ring in my hands. It was crazy how something that once meant so much was now just a worthless piece of metal to me. "Send me something that I can have independently verified, showing the debt. Show me what your parents need, and… I'll buy your engagement ring back from you."

Jamila just sat there, staring, until the meaning of my words snapped in place in her head. "Ty, wait a second. You don't have to—"

"I know I don't *have* to. It was wrong of me, to keep stringing it along after I found out you were in it for the money. I should have ended it then, before your parents spent more money on a wedding that wasn't going to happen, because that trust was already destroyed. And even before I found out, I was fucking up. That was *my* bad. So this is where we end it. We both get something we need. You get your parents in a good place, I get left alone, we're both happy, right?"

She shook her head. "I'm not going to bother you *or* Lauren anymore. You don't have to pay me off. I was talking to Eli, and he wants to see if we could really have something, and I want that too. This went too far, because I wouldn't let it go. I'm going to be a doctor! I'll finish my residency, then go work at the practice with my mom. It'll be a struggle, but it'll be fine. You don't have to do this for me."

I laughed. "If it was for you, I wouldn't. It's for your parents. And it's so we clear the air. The money doesn't mean shit to me, but good energy does. I'm just trying to keep my karma right."

"Silly ass," Jamila replied, laughing. She chewed at her bottom lip for a second, then leaned forward. "Seriously though, thank you. If you're offering for real, I'm not going to turn you down, because their finances are pretty dire. They have this great façade built up, but they've got some big cracks. Anything you do would mean a lot, and I'm really grateful."

I shrugged. "Just get the paperwork to me, and I'll talk to the family lawyer about verifying everything."

She nodded, giving me a tight smile. I stood up, intending to leave, but she called out to me just as I turned away from the table.

"Ty!"

"Yeah?" I asked, eyeing her warily. What now?

"I don't know if this matters at all," she started, playing absently with one of her locs. "But it wasn't all about the money. It started that way, but you're a really great guy, so it wasn't hard to fall in love. I wasn't going to rob you and leave. I'd already decided that, right before you really started showing out, which I guess is when you found out about the money. I cheated because I was hurting, and then you broke up with me, and I just got so angry. I decided you couldn't take the marriage, and the wedding, all of that from me, because you promised. I know it's crazy. I know it doesn't make any of it right, but you broke my heart too. I'm just sorry things ended up the way they did."

I pushed out a heavy sigh, then shoved my hands, ring included, into my pockets. "I don't know if it matters either, J, but I appreciate you telling me. I can't say I'm sorry how it turned out though. I did love you, thought I wanted you to be my wife, but getting to know Lauren, and being with her shows me that marrying you would have been a mistake. I wouldn't have *her* in my life. You and Eli are about to see what happens, and there had to already be something there, cause that's who you turned to for comfort instead of me. So don't be sorry. Consider it course correction."

She smiled, nodded.

I smiled back.

And then I turned and walked away, finally feeling like that chapter was really behind me, and I was fully free to give Lauren everything I had.

~

I LEFT BLAKEWOOD'S IN A GREAT MOOD, AND DECIDED I WAS GOING to go see Lauren. Yeah, it was outside of schedule, but it seemed like lately I couldn't *get* on her schedule, so may as well just make it happen.

It was a Saturday, so no classes, and I knew it was the one day she had off work. I could go, say hi to Harper, maybe get a few kisses from my girl, then let her do whatever she had planned for her day – probably studying and catching up on her coursework.

My car was still in the library parking lot, and it was shorter to walk to her place from Blakewood's than to go and get it. It took me less than five minutes to get to the door of her building, and I took the stairs two at a time, instead of waiting on the elevator.

I knocked on her door, then waited.

And waited.

And waited.

I knocked again, making sure not to be too loud with it, in case Harper was taking a nap. When I still got no answer, I pulled out my phone to just call her. It would ruin the surprise factor, but oh well. I was happy as hell to be done with Jamila – the money meant next to nothing to me if it got her off my back – and I wanted to see Lauren's pretty face.

Just as I was about to hit send on the call, I heard a hand on the doorknob and smiled. That smile dropped when the door opened, landing me face to face with Mekhi.

What the fuck is he doing here?

When the fuck did he get here?

Why doesn't this motherfucker have a shirt on?

Neither of us said anything for a long time. I don't know what was happening in his head, but I was talking myself down from putting my fist through his face.

"Can I help you my man?" he asked finally, leaning against the door frame. "You got a delivery or something?"

I gave a dry chuckle. "Nah, bruh. I'm here to see Lauren."

He narrowed his eyes. "See Lauren for what?"

"None of your business. She's my girl, I'm here to see her. Is she here?"

"Your *girl*? As in… you're supposed to be her boyfriend? Oh." he gave me a sly smile that multiplied my urge to smack the shit out of him. "Lauren didn't anything about somebody coming by to see her."

"What's your point? I'm here, go to tell her."

His smile widened. "Um… actually, she's a little indisposed right now. In the shower getting cleaned up."

He winked at me.

What the fuck was he…?

This motherfucker *winked* at me, implying…

Fuck this, I'm knocking his bitch ass out —

"MR. TYYYYY!"

Harper came flying toward the door, shoving past her father's legs to wrap her arms around mine in a hug. I swallowed my rage so I could smile at her as she beamed up at me.

"Hey Barley."

"*Harper*," she giggled. "You wanna read some books with me again?!"

I glanced up at Mekhi, who honestly looked sick to his stomach about my easy interaction with his daughter.

Punk ass.

"Not today, sweetie." I knelt so that I was at eye level with her. "But I'll see you at the library, and you'll be at the book garden event with your class, right?"

She smiled at me, and nodded fast.

"Okay, I'll see you then."

"Okay! Bye!"

She threw her arms around my neck for a hug, and she was back in the apartment as quickly as she'd come out. I didn't bother saying shit else to Mekhi, just stood and started down the hall.

"I'll tell Lo you stopped by," he yelled down the hall, and only sheer force of will kept me moving. If things went further with Lauren, kicking Mekhi's ass was bound to have some residual damages, not to mention what Harper would think if she saw it.

When I stepped back out into the sunniness of outside, I was pissed. I wasn't a dummy, I knew there was a chance ole boy was just trying to get under my skin by implying shit about him and Lauren. Hell, he was *probably* lying. What bothered me was the fact that Lauren hadn't said anything about the fact that he was here, and apparently comfortable enough to be chilling without all his clothes on.

What the fuck was *that*?

I'd gone from happy as hell to feeling like shit in the course of less than thirty minutes. I trusted Lauren – wanted to trust Lauren – but behind what happened with Jamila, and the phone calls and texts… it honestly made me uneasy.

seventeen

. . .

Lauren

"MOMMY, IS MR. TY YOUR BOYFRIEND?"

I yanked my tee shirt over my head as quickly as I could, covering myself since Harper left my bedroom door wide open when she burst in to ask that random question.

Usually, I wouldn't care, because it was just me and Harper around. But last night, Mekhi had popped up with a duffel bag of his things, proclaiming that he'd taken emergency leave to see if we could "figure things out".

I'd been too exhausted when he showed up at my door to protest. I simply pointed at the couch before I crawled back into bed. When I woke up this morning, he was already cooking breakfast for Harper, and had promised a trip to the park, which I was apparently signed up for as well. It was a hot day, and by the time we left I was sweaty, sticky, and pissed because I was sweaty and sticky and tired. As soon as we were back in the apartment, the first place I headed was the shower.

But now, it was time to have a talk.

I was honestly still stressed, and feeling even more worn out than before. I'd hoped the trip to the park would be a daddy/daughter thing, while mommy caught up on sleep. Or studied. Or picked up some extra hours at work, since daddy was here. But that wasn't what happened, so here we were.

And it wasn't just that I was stressed, I was pissed, at his lack of consideration for what I may have planned to do. Yes, he'd taken emergency leave time, but it wasn't so last minute that he couldn't have sent a simple text to warn me he was coming. So, yeah, there was stuff to "figure out". We would feed Harper lunch, put her down in my room for a nap, and then he and I would sit down and discuss exactly what the hell there was to "figure out".

"Mommy, my question!" Harper stood in front of me as I sat down on the edge of the bed to run a brush through my wet hair. "Is Mr. Ty your boyfriend?"

I pulled the ponytail holder from my wrist to create a messy bun in my hair. "Why are you asking me that question baby?"

"Cause I heard daddy say it when he was talking to Mr. Ty."

I frowned. "Wait, what? What are you talking about?"

"*Mommy*. Mr. Ty was at the door, and daddy wouldn't let him in, and Mr. Ty said he couldn't read with me today, and then he left."

"Ty was *here*? Today? While mommy was in the shower?"

Harper gave me an exaggerated nod, then ran out of the room, with me close behind.

I found Mekhi kicked back on my couch, with the TV on ESPN.

"Hey," I called from the kitchen as I opened the fridge. I was careful to keep my tone light, even though between annoyance and exhaustion, I was about ready to snap. "Did I miss anything interesting?"

"Not at all." Was the quick reply.

Too quick.

"Oh, so Ty didn't come by here to see me?" I flipped the

refrigerator door closed and stalked over to where he was. "Why didn't you come and tell me?"

He shrugged, then gave me a smile that failed miserably at being innocent. "You asked about anything *interesting*."

I filled my cheeks with air, then pushed it out, slowly. "Mekhi... how long ago?"

"Minute or two."

Shoving his feet down from Mina's coffee table, I shot him a scowl. "Thank you so much for letting me know I had a visitor. Can you feed your child please? When I get back, we need to talk."

I quickly pushed my bare feet into tennis shoes and sprinted out the door, not bothering with keys or phone since Mekhi was there. I knew Ty had a short library shift on Saturday mornings, so I was betting on him having walked to my apartment from there. Why hadn't he just waited for me to get out of the shower?

Sure enough, right around the time my chest started burning from my lungs struggling for air, I caught sight of his familiar, confident stride as he headed away from my direction.

"Ty!" I yelled out, twice before I was close enough that he heard me. He stopped, and I jogged the rest of the way, dropping my head in exhaustion when I reached him. "Hey," I said, bending over to catch my breath. "Harper said she saw Mr. Ty today. Why didn't yo—is everything okay?"

When I finally looked up, and *really* saw his face, Ty looked distinctly pissed, but I had no idea what about.

"No, actually." He shoved his hands in his pockets, looking right at me. "It's not. When were you planning to mention that your Ex was here, chilling in your place half-dressed?"

I lifted an eyebrow. "*What*? Half-dressed? He had clothes on when I just saw him."

"Yeah, well, he was missing a shirt when *I* saw him. You weren't going to tell me he was here?"

"He just got here, late last night!"

Ty laughed, the dry, sardonic type you gave when there wasn't anything funny, and it grated on my already frayed nerves. "It's almost two in the afternoon, Lauren. You haven't had an opportunity to call, send a text, nothing?"

"I wasn't even thinking about that!" I shook my head, wondering why it was such a big deal in the first place. "He's Harper's father, and she lives with me now. He's going to be around. I hope that's not a problem for you, because…"

"Him being around for things involving the child you have together *isn't* a problem. The problem is him being here without you saying shit about it, like you're hiding it from me. Why not be up front, so there's no chance for a misunderstanding?"

I rolled my eyes. "I didn't realize I needed your permission to have guests."

He drew his head back, eyes wide in response to my last statement, and I immediately regretted my unnecessary sarcasm. "You don't need my permission, but it's basic respect for the person you're dating to be transparent about shit like this."

"Ty, come on. Why are you making a big deal about this? He's Harper's father, that's it!"

"That's it?" That time, Ty's laugh was real, a deep, throaty chuckle that pissed me off. "Lauren, does *he* know that? Cause the little shitty attitude he had with me at your door? Had nothing to do with Harper. Implying that you were in the shower because he'd just fucked you? Had nothing to do with Harper. Seems more like jealousy or sabotage to me."

I sucked my teeth. "Seriously, Ty? You want to talk about jealousy and sabotage, let's start with Jamila, and why we've been dating for months, and yet she was still walking around wearing your engagement ring. Let's talk about her poisoning your mother against me, and bringing up my child!"

"It's not the same thing." He shook his head. "If you dropped by my house and Jamila answered the door in her bra, and then said some shit to you, it would be the same thing. And besides that, I've checked Jamila about messing with you, and you don't see me giggling and shit with her on the phone, in text messages like you do with old boy."

My cheeks grew hot about that. Not because I'd done anything wrong, but because I suspected Mekhi's motives weren't innocent. "You're turning it into something it's not!"

"No, I'm trying to prevent it from turning it into what it *could* be. Being open and honest, telling you I don't like this shit now, instead of letting it fester and fuck things up between us."

"So *I'm* fucking things up between us?" *I* laughed then, a long peal of giggles that would have seemed crazy to anyone walking by. Luckily, the campus grounds were relatively empty. "Ty, you act like I'm the one who was forgetting dates, and standing people up. Like I'm the one with the crazy ex fiancé picking fights in the middle of restaurants. Like *I'm* the one whose mother shows up at the job, with split personalities, trying to get folks fired. Newsflash, that's *you*! *Not me*. I've never, *ever* dealt with this kind of drama and bullshit, not when I was by myself. Everything was normal, and quiet, and I was perfectly fucking fine! Maybe this," – I gestured between us – "Wasn't a good idea. The stress, and the arguing…I can't do this."

Ty narrowed his eyes, but not before I caught the flash of hurt that he quickly hid. "So you feel like your life was better before we met. Seems like you're having problem after problem from dealing with me."

I shrugged. "Seems like."

"Okay." Ty rubbed at his bottom lip with his thumb, then nodded, at nothing in particular. "Okay," he repeated. "How about I solve that problem for you?"

Wait… what?

Ty said nothing else, didn't even look in my direction again before he turned to walk away. Somewhere, under the overwhelming exhaustion and defeat, if I pushed aside the stress, anxiety, and fear that had been piling on me in the last few weeks,

I knew I should catch him. I should call his name, and apologize, but I couldn't make my feet move, and I couldn't open my mouth. I just watched him walk away, long enough to know that he didn't look back before he got too far away to see him.

In a deep, *deep* place, my chest hurt, but the rest of me was numb. I wasn't even sure when I started moving again, but the next thing I knew, I was trudging up the stairs in my apartment building, and then in front of my door. I turned the knob, and Mekhi was there, drying freshly washed dishes.

"Hey," he called over his shoulder, not turning around. "Lil' bit fell asleep eating, so I put her in your room. I figured me and you could sit down and discuss some things." He put a hot pink plate down on the counter, and finally turned around.

Whatever my face looked like, it must have been bad, cause his pleasant expression dropped into one of apprehension, and he swallowed hard. I got right in his face, not caring that I had to crane my neck to look at him, or that he could probably snap me in half if he wanted.

"What did you say to him, Mekhi?" I asked. Never mind that *I* had probably made it infinitely worse – his ass had been the catalyst.

"Who?" He tried his best not to sound guilty, but that twitching at the corner of his mouth, attempting not to smile, told me everything.

My nostrils flared as I balled my hands into fists at my sides. "Don't play with me, Mekhi. It's not funny. Did you make him think something was going on between me and you?!"

"I mean…" his face spread into a smile. "… maybe, I guess. I was just playing around with him though, I didn't mean shit by it."

I shook my head, disgusted. "You didn't mean shit by it? You didn't have to *mean shit by it* for it to be a fucked up thing to do!"

Especially when infidelity was a major factor in his last relationship.

"Come on, Lo. Call his ass back, I doubt he's that pissed."

"Yeah, he *is*. And I made it worse by defending your ass, because even though I knew your little texts and phone calls had a motive, I didn't think you'd do something like *this*. And for *what*, Mekhi?"

"To get his ass out of the way!" He tried to grab my hand, but I immediately snatched it away. "Lauren, if he's not serious about you, which he can't be if that little minimal shit sent him packing, then he needs to step aside. I was chilling, trying to be respectful of your relationship, but if I'm perfectly honest, I want my family back. You, me, and Harper. That's what makes sense."

"To *who?!* Who does it make sense to, Mekhi? We established months ago, that yeah, we can get along with each other, but the chemistry wasn't there. There wasn't any *spark!*"

Mekhi sucked his teeth. "Fuck a *spark*, Lauren. I'm talking about logic. Compatibility. The fact that we have a child! I was talking to my mom, and—"

"And *there* it is," I interrupted, tossing my hands up. "You were talking to your mother, who doesn't want you to have a girlfriend *and* a baby momma. Grow up, Mekhi! Your mother's word isn't the way, the truth, and the light. Us having a child together because of a reckless decision we made as teenagers is not enough for me! We will *not* sit here and say "fuck a spark", when I think that spark means everything!"

He scoffed. "So you're telling me you didn't feel anything when I kissed you?"

I scowled. "When you kissed me, I felt a little something, a little flicker. Ty sets off *fireworks*. Sparklers, pinwheels, bottle rockets, a damned pyrotechnic extravaganza. And you… gave me a little prickle."

"You didn't even have to say all of that," he responded with a scowl. "You're fine and all, but it's not like our chemistry is causing any fires."

"That's exactly my point. Just because it looks good on paper doesn't make it right for us. I understand you want to follow your mother's advice, because she raised you. But we're grown-ups, Mekhi, and what you're doing isn't fair. Not to me *or* Talia."

As soon as I said her name, Mekhi's phone began ringing across the room.

"I'd bet money that that's her," I said, standing between him and the exit to the living room. "Maybe I should go answer it, sounding all breathless like we just finished fucking. Do you want me to—"

"You made your point, Lo." Mekhi expression was pained, and he seemed properly embarrassed about the nonsense he'd pulled with Ty.

"I feel like I need to be explicitly clear though… you and I aren't going to be together in that way Mekhi, not if we have to force it. I could tell by how desperate you looked when you thought I was about to answer your phone, you *like* Talia. Don't let your mother get in your head and mess that up."

He chuckled. "I came down here to tell you the same thing. Don't let my mother get in your head and mess shit up. You're up here tired, stressed, and irritable, because you can't focus on what you need to do with Harper around. Do you think you were able to be a better mother before, or now?"

It raised the hairs on the back of my neck for him to imply that I wasn't being a good mother, but I bit my lip, holding back an immediate response. I *was* stressed. I *was* tired. I *was* irritable. It *wasn't* the best environment for a child, and on some level, I already knew that.

"It's done now," I shrugged, shaking my head. "And I don't want anybody doing anything for me if they feel like they're being taken advantage of."

"Nobody feels taken advantage of, Lauren."

I scoffed. "So your mother didn't spout all of that bullshit?"

"You've never said anything out of anger and frustration that you didn't mean?"

My mind went immediately to telling Ty that his presence had brought me nothing but problems, and I looked away, swallowing hard. I couldn't even claim that the difference between me and Tanya was that I had a *reason* to be angry. Because really… I didn't.

"Anyway," Mekhi said, edging past me. "Just think about it. You're overwhelmed. Our parents miss their granddaughter. It seems pretty obvious to me what you should do."

I rolled my eyes. "It's obvious to me I can't stand you right now."

"Sorry." He shrugged, then shot me a grin before pointing in the direction of his phone. "I'm gonna call Talia back."

"Are you going to tell her about all of this, about you trying to get back with me?"

He hesitated as he reached for his cell, then looked back at me. "I don't know… should I?"

"What?! Are you crazy? *Hell no*." I shook my head, and tried to pull my face out of a scowl. *This man really is an idiot.* "No, you shouldn't tell her about this, because *this* isn't anything. Focus on making her happy."

"Really?"

I nodded. "Really. I'm going to go lay down and get some sleep."

I left him in the living room to make his phone call, while I went and climbed into my bed beside Harper. Her little face was peaceful as she slept – pretty much the exact opposite of the turmoil I felt inside. My anger at Ty had been misplaced… completely pointless, and I wished I could go back in time and muzzle myself.

It was funny to me now, that I'd considered boys "trouble". And hell maybe they were, when they were flaky and confusing, like Mekhi. But if boys – well, men – were trouble… it really seemed like Ty was exactly the right kind. He'd brought love, and laughter, and much needed fun and energy to my life. Even when he'd messed up, there was no denying the effort he put in to correct it, and show that he was serious about me. Even in the course of today's disagreement, he'd been the one to approach it like an adult, trying to address it before it festered and turned into something else. And what had I done?

I'd stomped on it. Thrown the past, along with things he couldn't control, in his face. Told him he was ruining my life. Hell, if anybody was trouble, it was me.

Way to be mature and responsible, Lauren.

I rolled onto my back, twirling my glass slipper pendant between my fingers. Remembering the night he put that beautiful gift around my neck, and the way he'd looked at me, the way he'd *kissed* me, brought tightness to my chest.

"So, so *stupid*," I whispered to myself, squeezing my eyes shut as tears came. I didn't even know where I could possibly begin to try to make things right.

eighteen
. . .
ty

"*MR. SINCLAIR.*"

My eyes were open, and I was awake, but that was pretty much all I could say about my current state. I heard my professor talking to me, but it wasn't until she was right in my face, lips pressed into a disapproving scowl that I sat up and actually focused on what she was saying.

"Class has been over for almost ten minutes, Mr. Sinclair. Is there a reason you're still occupying my classroom?"

I suppressed a heavy sigh as I looked around the classroom, and sure enough, it was empty. My mind was so gone that I didn't even remember *coming* to class, so it didn't shock me that I'd spent the time when I should have been listening to the lecture zoned out.

"Sorry Dr. Jackson. I've got some personal things going on. Won't happen again."

I could feel her concerned eyes on me as I gathered my stuff, but ignored her. The last thing I needed was her expecting a heart to heart, or even further explanation than what I'd already given.

When I stood, hoisting my backpack over my shoulder, she

moved to block my path, and cleared her throat. "Would these *personal things* have anything to do with why you turned in the absolute sloppiest work I've ever seen from you last night?"

"I turned in an assignment?"

She narrowed her eyes, and crossed her arms over her chest. "A jumbled mess, masquerading as a completed assignment came to me via the student portal last night, from your login, Mr. Sinclair. You've always turned in impeccable work, but that assignment was worth ten percent of your grade, and the only thing you earned were the forty points I gave everyone for simply turning it in."

I scratched at my scalp, then shook my head. This was one of the last classes I would ever take, and a less than perfect grade could ruin my hard-earned near-perfect GPA. Even with that knowledge, the fact remained that I'd turned in a horribly executed assignment and zombied my way through class, because I couldn't get my mind off of Lauren.

"I don't know what to say." I shrugged, then adjusted the strap of my backpack on my shoulder.

She tipped her head to the side, sighing. "I don't need you to say anything, I need you to do better. Remember that from here until the end of the semester, everything you do is playing catch-up to balance this grade." She moved aside, then motioned for me to move along.

I was already so late for the next class that I didn't bother. I took my ass back to my apartment, and tried not to think about Lauren. But the effort that went into not thinking about her wouldn't allow anything else to occupy my mind.

Did she *really* feel like I'd done nothing except bring problems into her life? I thought we were good, thought we were enjoying each other, having fun, but apparently her thought process was different.

Still though, the bullshit with Jamila, my mom, and not to mention my early fuckups with time… I could see how all of that could wear on her. But it seemed to me like the good times we'd shared over the last four months outweighed the bad, by far. I almost wondered if there was something else to it. Like maybe there *was* something going on with her and Mekhi. Not that I was an expert in discernment, but Lauren didn't seem like the type to cheat.

More like the type to breakup over a bullshit argument, so she wouldn't have to.

I ordered a pizza, ate the pizza, finished off a bottle of crown even though it was the middle of the day, and then I took my ass to sleep. The next day, I dragged myself to class, with marginally better results than the day before. I was getting ready for my afternoon shift at the library when somebody knocked on my door.

I couldn't decide if I was surprised or not that it was my mother.

Since that incident with the person I wasn't supposed to be thinking about, my mother had been surprisingly quiet. Avoiding me, because she knew she'd gone too far. But, if nothing else, my mother was a creature of habit, and she couldn't go too long without some type of interaction – or attention – from her children.

"Hello Roosevelt," she said, her voice somber as she stood at my door, dressed in all white. "May I come inside please?"

I lifted an eyebrow. "Ummm… yeah. What are you wearing?" I asked, following her inside and closing the door behind her. Her neck, fingers, ears, and wrists were dripping with diamonds, which was normal, but the huge, puffy white skirt, tee shirt, and white heeled sandals were *not*.

"You don't like my outfit?"

"You look like you're going to a fifties soda shop in heaven."

She scowled. "Roosevelt…"

"I'm playing, mom. You look beautiful, as always."

That brought a big smile, and she pulled me into a tight hug, then squeezed my face between her hands. "Thank you, my dear sweet boy. Now tell me, are you still upset with your mother?"

"Hell yes," I said, twisting out of her grasp. "What you did wasn't cool at all. You have to chill with that. As a matter of fact, I've been meaning to talk to you for a while about something."

She sniffed. "You aren't about to call yourself doing some type of intervention, are you?"

Yes.

"Nah. I just want to know how you're doing?"

My mother lifted an eyebrow, then lowered herself into one of the barstools at my kitchen counter, and crossed her legs. "What do you mean, how am I doing?"

"You know… how are you dealing with dad being gone?"

I caught a flicker of panic in her eyes before she buried it behind a lifted chin and a scowl. "Your father has been gone for six years now, Roosevelt. I would like to think I'm *dealing* just fine."

"Oh, you think so?" I made sure my tone carried just enough skepticism to seem like I was trying to hide it, then scratched my head.

"And what in the hell do you mean by *that*?"

I shrugged. "Nothing. I'm just saying, you've been like a whole different person since he passed away, and we all thought it was just a phase you were going through, so we were letting you cook. But I guess this person we've been seeing is just the new you."

"This person we've been seeing? Phase? What phase? Roosevelt Tyson Sinclair, I am delightful, you can ask any of the women in my lunch group, they love me! By *we*, I'm going to presume you're speaking about yourself and your siblings, so pray tell, what exactly is "wrong" with *me*?" She tossed her hair over her shoulder, hands clasped in her lap as she waited for me to give what she obviously thought was going to be a weak response.

"Well, if I had to throw out just a few words, they would be... judgmental. Overbearing. Meddlesome. Melodramatic. Uh, let's see... pompous. Did I already say intrusive and unpleasant?"

My mother gasped after every one of those words, living up to that *melodramatic* descriptor as she clutched a hand to her chest, lowering her head as if she were growing physically weaker with each gasp. "I *cannot* believe you would speak to me this way. This must be the influence of that little harlot co-ed you've been—"

"This is exactly what I'm talking about," I said, chuckling. "Harlot? That's judgmental, pompous, and mean, you hit three notes with that one. And it's not even true. If anything, your homegirl Jamila..."

She sucked her teeth. "Will you stop speaking ill of my future daugh—"

"*Stop that.*" I shook my head, then clasped my mother's hands between mine. "Listen, you *have* to stop it with this Jamila thing. It's overbearing, meddlesome, intrusive, and just *crazy*. I'm not marrying her, because she cheated on me. I know you think she was your dream daughter in law, but she isn't. I need you to hear me on this."

"But—"

"But *nothing*, mom. Seriously. You have to stop this. I don't understand why this is so important to you?"

My mother pulled her hands from mine and took a deep breath, pulling a white handkerchief from her bag and dabbing at her eyes. "Why *isn't* it important to you? Your father was a great man, who did a wonderful job with you and your siblings. It baffles me that preserving his legacy, and passing down his name, means nothing to any of you. Roslyn won't get off the pole long enough to have a baby. Roger *prefers* poles, so no babies there either, unless he adopts, which he seems to have no interest in doing. Racquel... that girl is off saving the trees so she can smoke them later. Who knows if she'll still have baby-making capabilities by the time she's done blowing up bulldozers to save the rainforests of Timbuktu? But *you*," – she reached up to clasp my face again – "You are the one who can do this for me. Marry a good girl, from a good family, and make me some little good-haired grandbabies to carry your father's name for at least one more generation. Well… between you and Jamila, the good hair thing may not happen, but they'll be *beautiful* little brown angels!"

I shook my head. "You realize that "good hair" stuff is offensive, right?"

She cocked her head to the side, confused. "Why on earth would—"

"Nevermind," I said, chuckling. "Anyway, you have nothing to worry about. I want a family someday. It just won't be with Jamila. It will be with a woman of *my* choosing, for *my* reasons. I know you want to keep everything carefully controlled, but what you're doing is having the opposite effect. We're all grown, mama. None of us want to be treated like babies who can't make their own decisions."

She lowered her head. "I *know*," she groaned, then brought her gaze to mine. I'm just… I'm *lonely*, son. You kids don't seem to need me anymore, and dammit I don't like it, so dammit you're going to give me my way!" She smiled at the scowl on my face, then stroked my cheek with her thumb. "But I guess it can't work that way, can it?"

I shook my head. "Sorry mama, but no. And if you're lonely, why don't you," – I cringed— "Start dating again?"

My mother shot me a scowl, then burst into a peal of laughter. "Roosevelt, do you really think I would find someone who fit my standards? Someone who would spoil the hell out of me like your father?"

"I don't, but maybe that's a good thing."

She scoffed. "Are you implying that he spoiled me too much?"

"Uh, no comment. I'm just saying, maybe thinking a little bit out of the box would be good for you."

"Is this your way of getting me to accept this *Lauren* girl?"

"It's my way of getting you to accept that good people come from all backgrounds, and don't have to have a pedigree to be worthy of your love."

Her eyes went wide. "*Love*? You're in love with this girl?"

"Did I say that?" I sputtered, swiping my face with my hands.

"No." She smiled. "You didn't. So I'm hoping that means I can introduce you to—"

"Okay, I'm going to work," I said, leaving her in the kitchen as I walked away.

Her heels clicked behind me on the tile floor. "Wait a minute, I was enjoying our talk!"

"Gotta get to work, seriously."

"But, I… we *never* talk anymore, Roosevelt. You kids just moved along without me, barely call, like I don't even…" She inhaled a deep breath, then exhaled, but didn't finish what she was saying. I put my keys down, and turned to her, pulling her into my arms.

"I love you mama," I said, then kissed her cheek. "We all do. But like I was saying earlier, you turned into somebody else after dad died. I know you were grieving, but you let *that* person stick around, and honestly it's hard to talk to you when you're on that bougie, tyrannical stuff. The woman we grew up with, who let us scrape our knees, and make mistakes, and color outside the line and still acted like we were the best artists in the world… *that's* the woman we want to talk to."

She sniffled, then dabbed her face again with her handkerchief. "I haven't been *that* bad, have I?"

"No comment."

"Roosevelt!"

I lifted my eyebrows. "Hmm?"

Her face was pulled into a scowl, but it slowly melted into a smile. "I love you too, son."

I kissed her cheek again, then grabbed my keys as a thought came to mind. "Hey, you want to come to work with me?"

Her eyes narrowed. "Why on earth would I want to do that?"

"Uhhh, because the library is a magical place with books?"

"What?"

I shook my head, laughing. "I was joking, mom. But for real, my job is laid back. You said you wanted to talk, so come hang out with me for a little bit."

"You're serious?"

"Yes," I said, nodding. "I'm going to be late if you don't come on. And I'll tell you what, it's a short shift, so I'll even take you to dinner afterward."

"Oh!" She adjusted the strap of her purse on her arm, and stood up straight. "Well you should have said that first!"

~

"MR. TYYYYY!"

I couldn't do anything but grunt as a blur of pink and yellow clothes and big curly hair flew at my legs and wrapped itself around me, tight. I'd just signed in for my shift, and made the mistake of introducing my mother to my boss – Blair Underwood wanna-be Franklin Geanes, library director – and had to sit through twenty minutes of overt flirtation before she let me pull her out of his office. *After* they exchanged numbers.

Guess my advice worked. *Shit.*

The glass-walled classroom reserved for the daycare kids was located right across from his office, and the doors were open because they were using the hall for their "book garden" event. I was barely out of the office before I was greeted by Harper.

"Hey Sparkler," I said, bending down to give her a hug. She was followed close behind by the other kids, all of whom I'd gotten to know from their weekly trip over here. Once I'd greeted everyone, she came back to me, poking me in the shin.

"It's *Harper*."

Behind me, my mother laughed. "And who is this delightfully sassy little flower?"

"This is Harper, mom."

My mother knelt down, like she wanted to give Harper a hug, but as I expected, Harper gave her a side eye, then looked at me. I gave her a subtle nod, and Harper turned back to my mother. Still no hug, but she reached out to gently pet the filmy layers of my mom's skirt.

"I like your skirt," she said quietly. "It's pretty, like a princess tutu."

My mother gave her a big smile. "Thank you, sweetheart. I think *you* are very pretty too."

"I am!" Harper nodded, showing deep dimples as she grinned, then finally gave my mother the hug she'd knelt down for. "Thank you!"

"You are *very* welcome."

Harper glanced up at me, then back at my mother. "This is your mommy, Mr. Ty?" I nodded, and she grinned again. "She's pretty, like a queen!"

A second later, Harper scooted off to be with the other kids, running and playing and my mother stood, turning to me with her eyes wide. I almost laughed at the childlike awe on her face.

"*Roosevelt*," she squealed, bubbling with excitement as she watched Harper. "Do you see that gorgeous, wonderful child?!"

"I do, mama."

She grabbed my arm, giggling as she leaned close. "How can you look at her and not want to settle down and have one of your own? I want one!"

I chuckled, then dropped my head to speak into her ear. "Guess what?"

"What? What?!"

"That's Lauren's daughter."

My mother turned to me with a haughty sniff. "Well… she's an innocent child, I guess I won't hold that against her."

I laughed again, shaking my head. "See there? There you again with that mess. You're playing around, but that sweet little girl you're so charmed by could have been your…"

I stopped, then swallowed hard, stopping short of speaking allowed that Harper could have been my mother's grandchild. Was I really that far gone over Lauren, that even if it was just in my subconscious… I'd actually thought about that? Something of that magnitude was way in the future though. It was crazy to think about, especially when we weren't even together.

It wasn't just crazy.

It wasn't even possible anymore.

nineteen

. . .

lauren

YOU'RE NOT A FAILURE.

You're doing the right thing.

I told myself that, over and over again, hoping that the repetition would make me actually believe it. Not even two weeks had passed since I hopped on a plane on a crazy impulse to go get Harper. Now I was hopping on a plane after thinking through every inch of the decision, to take her back.

I tried not to think of it as a sign of weakness, that I hadn't been able to handle the demands of school, work, and Harper. Other moms did it all at the time and kicked ass at it, but I wasn't those other moms. I was stressed, overwhelmed, exhausted, hadn't been doing particularly well in class lately, and honestly I was heartbroken – but that was my own doing. So, while I wasn't fond of the idea of accepting "defeat", it made more sense to me to simply put things back the way they were.

Harper had more room to grow and play with her grandparents, not in my cramped shared apartment with no yard. She wasn't at daycare 12+ hours a day while I went to class, and then worked so I could actually pay the bill for her tuition. Her grandparents could engage her in a way that mommy couldn't when she needed to study, or worse, when no amount of coffee or energy drinks could keep me from falling asleep.

I wanted, so badly to be one of those badass moms who held mothering through a stressful situation as a strength. I prayed, and cried, and prayed and cried a little more until I had to stop and realize that I wasn't doing myself any favors. Once I took that step back, I began to understand that I had limitations, which was perfectly human, and perfectly okay. I came to the conclusion that asking for, and accepting help when I needed it was simply a different kind of strength.

Strength in admitting that I *could* do it all by myself, if needed, but it came with a cost I wasn't willing to pay. My pride wasn't worth my health or Harper's well-being, so I had to grow up, and accept the fact that going to get her wasn't the best decision.

Maybe if I'd slowed down a little I wouldn't have made that mistake.

Ha.

That was a statement that could be tied to so much of what was wrong with my life right now, but it connected most immediately with Ty.

Four days had gone by, no text, no call, no nothing... whether or not I was within my rights to be mad about it was something I had yet to decide. After all, *I* was the one who'd let the words "I can't do this anymore" fly out of my mouth. I couldn't expect him to be the one to call first, or extend the first olive branch. That was probably supposed to be me.

But still, what did it mean that he hadn't even put up a fight? Or maybe that wasn't fair. I may not have much experience with men, but I knew Ty well enough to understand that he liked to balance my sometimes-craziness, and was always eager to make my life easier. So if I'd made him feel like his presence was the grand complication... why would he move to place himself back in that position?

So... no, it wasn't fair to place the responsibility for this on him.

It was mine.

"Mommy, I met Mr. Ty's mommy!"

I glanced down at Harper in the seat beside me, her pull-down tray scattered with paper and crayons. "What baby?"

She smiled up at me. "Your boyfriend, Mr. Ty. I met his mommy at the library!"

"Was she mean to you?" My guard went up immediately, and anger built in my chest. If that woman had –

"*No*, mommy," Harper giggled. "She said I was pretty, and she was wearing a big puffy skirt, like this!" She pointed at her drawing, of what appeared to be a person with long hair and a big white dress.

I raised my eyebrows. "So... she was *nice*?"

Harper bobbed her head up and down. "And pretty!"

With that final declaration, she turned back to her drawings, just as happy as she'd been before. Of course she didn't realize she'd just added to mommy's inner turmoil. Ty and I had only been together four months – not even time to begin talking about the possibility of step-parenting, marriage, kids of our own. Not that I was ready for any of that now, but still... it just felt like it was over too soon.

I pulled the chain that held my slipper pendant from my shirt and turned the warm metal in my hands, wondering if still wearing it even though we were broken up made me a crazy person. It was amazing that in less than a month, it had become a symbol of our relationship that it made me feel sick to my stomach to go without.

I turned the pendant over, and for the first time, noticed the tiny words etched in the flat bottom of the shoe. I held it close to my face, squinting, and my breath caught in my throat when I finally made out the tiny words: *Stop Running*.

Stop running? I knew it was our own little inside joke,

referring to the first few times we met, but... is that what I was doing now? Fear of the unknown, fear of failure, fear of heartbreak... maybe I was just subconsciously protecting myself.

Or maybe I was figuring out ways to justify my own bullshit.

How the hell was I supposed to know?

When Harper and I got off the plane, we headed straight for my dad's house. I hadn't spoken with Mekhi's mother at all, but Dad had served as a go-between to work out a schedule where Harper's time was split between them more evenly. I was still pissed about what she'd said to me, but had given up on getting an apology anytime soon. Despite the ugliness she'd thrown at me, I didn't give the thought of her saying negative things about me to Harper more than a few minutes of headspace. She wouldn't go that far – I didn't think.

I'd scheduled my flights for the specific purpose of getting home early enough to get some much-needed sleep and get to class the next day. With no delays, I would even have time to catch up on some school work. I hugged and kissed my baby goodbye, then left her playing in the backyard with her puppy and her grandpa. I held back tears, telling myself it was silly to cry about it, since in just a few weeks, the semester would be over, and I could be with her all the time.

Back in the rental I'd gotten from the airport, I let those tears go, still sitting in my father's driveway. Sadness that I was leaving my little girl behind again, disappointment that I hadn't been able to handle things myself, and guilt, that I felt so relieved. What kind of mother was *relieved* to leave her child behind?

I didn't get a chance to answer that question for myself before someone knocked on the window of the car. I quickly dried my face, and looked up to see who was trying to get my attention.

Tanya.

Reluctantly, I rolled the window down, and tried my best not to scowl at her.

"Hi Lauren," she said. "Are you okay?"

I nodded. "Just fine. You?"

"I'm good." She pointed toward the house. "Better now that I can see Harper in person. I appreciate you letting her call me, while she was up there with you, but seeing and holding her is different." Her voice choked with emotion, and I cursed the lump that built in my throat from hearing it. "Thank you, for bringing her back."

I shrugged, then swallowed hard, looking away from her. "I'm not doing it for you. I'm doing it for me and her."

"Thank you anyway."

"You're welcome."

There was an uncomfortable silence for a few moments before I turned the keys to actually start the car, and moved my hand to the gear shift. "Well, I'll talk to you later. I'm sure Harper will be excited to see you."

"Lauren, wait." She put both hands on the window opening, pleading with her eyes for me to leave the car parked.

I suppressed an eye roll, and moved my hands to my lap. "Yeah?"

"I'm sorry." –Wait, *what*? –"I had been encouraging Mekhi to bring his family back together, do the right thing, and marry you." – Again, *what*? – "But then he told me you had a boyfriend, and I got *so angry*. I kept pushing him, and pushing, and he said he was trying, but then every other time we spoke, you were mentioning this other man, and then spending time with him over the break, and your birthday, and I just… I built it up in my head, and twisted it, and made myself even angrier. And when you didn't answer the phone that night about Harper, it just all spilled over. I was wrong, and I'm sorry. And you have no idea how much I appreciate you not keeping Harper from me because of what I said to you."

Pressing my lips together, I swallowed hard to fight back the snarky response I wanted to give. I wasn't expecting an apology at all, so it was better to be cool.

"Did Mekhi tell you he has a girlfriend back on base?"

She looked down, then cleared her throat. "Recently, yes."

"So is *that* why you feel the need to apologize? Now that you know I wasn't the only one "whoring around"?"

Oops.

Couldn't help it.

"I'm apologizing because I said hurtful things that I shouldn't have."

"And because you were overstepping your boundaries?"

Her jaw tightened. "Yes."

I then turned to look back at the house. "If you feel like I'm not pulling my weight when it comes to my daughter, I need you to say something about it, instead of letting it build up to the point that you feel taken advantage of."

"I know that, sweet girl. My Harper is a joy to be around, and I've missed her like I would miss one of my lungs. I don't feel taken advantage of, I feel lucky. I spoke out of anger, and took things somewhere they didn't need to go. I am *sorry*."

I nodded, then swallowed down another lump in my throat before I put my hand back on the gear shift. "Okay. I have to go, before I miss my flight. Mrs. Tanya, you've always, before this, been really good to me, and you've *always* been good to Harper. I'm still upset right now, but we're family, like it or not. I guess I'm willing to move forward if you are."

"Yes," she said immediately, reaching into the car to clasp my hand over the steering wheel. "Yes. Thank you."

I shrugged. "No problem. Go ahead and go in and see Harper. We can talk later."

With a final smile, she waved, and turned toward the house. I took a deep breath to settle myself, then pulled out, racing to get to the airport on time.

I just barely made my flight, and fell asleep on the way back. When I got back into my own car, to drive home from the airport, I was exhausted, but restless, with so many things running through my mind. The car was too quiet, so I called my dad's house and talked to Harper until I got home. At home, the apartment was too quiet, so I called first Bianca, then Mina, but neither picked up.

Probably because they're with their men.

Something I no longer had, thanks to a stupid, *stupid* mistake.

I got into the shower, and stayed there until the water ran cold, and I had to get out. This would be the first time I'd had to sleep alone, in an empty apartment, since Ty and I broke up, and suddenly... it felt really, *really* empty.

And I felt really, *really* awful.

Once I'd pulled myself out of the shower, I dried off, moisturized, and pulled on sweats and a tee shirt. The sweats belonged to me. The tee-shirt belonged to Ty.

It was one I'd "borrowed", specifically for times like this. When I wanted to be close to him, to feel connected even when that physical connection wasn't possible. It still carried his scent, and that made it a little easier to reminisce about his touch.

But *damnit.*

That wasn't enough.

I picked up my phone and looked at his number. That was all I could make myself do, just look. Instead of dialing him, I dialed Bianca.

This time, she picked up, with a groggy hello that sounded like she had her head stuffed under a pillow.

"B... are you okay?"

She sneezed – a loud, wet, gross sneeze – then blew her nose before she answered. "Do I *sound* okay, baby sis?"

"No, you sound like somebody is holding your nose shut. Why didn't you tell me you were sick?"

Another sneeze.

"I don't think I'm really *sick* sick, just an allergy attack or something. It crept up on me a few hours ago. I took some medicine and I'm just now waking up. Fucking around with

Rashad and that camera out in the country. I'm not an outdoor girl, and I told his ass that, but – wait a minute, I doubt that's why you're calling me after midnight. What's going on?"

I sighed. "You know I took Harper back to dad's today, right?"

"Mmhmm."

"Well… now the apartment is too quiet, and I can't do anything except think about Ty. I want to fix it, but… I don't know how. I don't even know where to begin."

Bianca blew her nose again, and I cringed, but kept the phone up to my ear. "It's about time you asked. I was wondering what was taking so long."

I shook my head. I'd called Bianca from my car the night Ty and I broke up. It was the only place I could get privacy with Harper and Mekhi both there. She'd listened while I cried my eyes out, told me I was wrong as hell, then hung up when I tried to argue my point. According to her I didn't *have* a point.

"Are you gonna kick me while I'm down?"

She tried to laugh, but it came out as a weird sort of cackle with her stuffy nose. "I guess not, since you're still new to all of this. I'm about to tell you something really, *really* important, that I think is going to really turn this around for you. You listening?"

Hell yeah I was listening. The phone was practically plastered to my ear I was listening so hard. "Yes, B. Tell me!"

"Okay here we go," – she stopped to sneeze again – "You fucked up, so you should apologize. Don't wait on him to call you, because he didn't fuck up, you did. Don't try to be prim, or proper, or right. Don't try to explain unless he asks for an explanation. Apologize. Cry. Beg. Be genuine. There you go. You're done."

I rolled my eyes. "Bianca…"

"Don't you *Bianca* me," she said, sniffling. "I'm being playful, but I'm serious. You asked where to start, well there you go. Apologize to him, and mean it."

"But I don't know what to say!"

"Maybe try: I'm sorry."

"You know what I mean," I whined. "This is a situation that's going to need more words than *I'm sorry*."

"Says who?"

"Says *me*."

Bianca snorted. "Oh, because you're an expert at saying the right thing."

My mouth dropped open. "Low blow."

"It *was*, wasn't it?" She let out another one of those cackling laughs. "Sorry. But, seriously… there's no right thing to say, other than *I'm sorry*. Everything else will come naturally when you're actually there."

I groaned, then flopped back onto my pillows, inhaling Ty's scent from his shirt. "Are you sure Bianca?"

"Yes. Now get off the phone, I need to go in the other room and get Rashad to get me some more medicine. Let me know how it goes, alright?"

We said quick goodbyes and hung up, but I didn't move. I kept the phone clutched to my chest as I replayed Bianca's words in my mind.

You fucked up, so you apologize.

Before I could lose my nerve, I jumped up, slipped my feet into my flats, and grabbed my keys.

I just hoped my big sister was right.

twenty
. . .
lauren

I WALKED RIGHT INTO MINA.

She was coming down the hall outside our apartment, not paying attention to where she was going. Apparently, neither was I, according to the loud *smack* we created when we collided.

"*Ouch*, roomie. What are you doing here this late?" I asked, stepping back so I could see her. When I did, I realized that her face was wet with tears. "Mina… hey, are you okay?"

She nodded quickly, wiping her face with the back of her hand. "Yeah. Just got into it with Austin."

I frowned. I knew what Mina "getting into it" with Austin looked like. They had a mild disagreement, and twenty minutes later they were escaping somewhere to have makeup sex. This looked like something else.

"It must have been pretty bad?" I didn't want to pry too hard, but I wanted to know that my friend was okay, and that I wasn't going to need to fight Austin myself. We couldn't be going through it at the same time.

She shrugged, then looked down, and her hair slid forward over her shoulders, covering her face. "I'm pregnant."

"What?!" I yelped, them remembered that we were in the hall. I stepped closer to her and grabbed her hand, then repeated in a stage whisper, "*What?!* Mina *how?!*"

Like me, Mina was religious about her birth control pills, but it wouldn't surprise me to hear that she and Austin were no longer using condoms. They'd made things "official" before me and Ty, and spent a whole lot more time together than we could. If I imagined how I felt about Ty, Mina probably carried those same feelings for Austin, only three times over.

"I don't *know*," she whined. "I take my pills every morning, and I haven't been sick or anything to make them ineffective. Fucking super-sperm Austin I guess." She giggled weakly at her own attempt at a joke, but her pained expression was back a few moments later. "Lo, I don't know what to do."

I lifted an eyebrow. "What do you mean?"

"I'm not ready to have a baby! I haven't graduated yet, haven't gotten a first paycheck from a *real* grown up job. I'm barely not a baby myself, Lauren. How am I supposed to take care of one?"

Smiling, I took her by the shoulders and looked her in the eyes. "Uh, you realize who you're talking to, right? I was sixteen when I had Harper, and my life isn't ruined."

"Ah." She closed her eyes, shaking her head. "I'm sorry, I didn't mean anything by that."

"No, it's fine," I said, pulling her into a hug. "That fear and anxiety you're feeling is completely valid. How does Austin feel about it?"

If they were fighting about it, I was almost scared to hear this answer.

Mina rolled her eyes, then pressed her head against the wall behind her. "His crazy ass is excited. Talking about getting married and moving me to Texas. Lauren, I don't want to move to fucking *Texas*."

"There's nothing wrong with Texas."

"There's *plenty* wrong with Texas, do you watch the news?"

I groaned. "Can we focus here?"

"You're the one who brought it up."

I narrowed my eyes, giving her *the look*, and she grinned back. "Anyway, if he's excited about the idea of a baby, wants to marry you, and move you to the place he loves and considers home... not saying that you have to do any of that, but what are you fighting about?"

"Because I'm not excited. And I don't want him to marry me because he's "expected" to. And I don't wanna move to fucking Texas."

I shrugged. "Who says you have to do any of that right now? I mean, how pregnant are you?"

"Maybe five or six weeks. My period was weird this month, and I was feeling sick, and my boobs were hurting. It made me nervous, so I took a test, and here we are. Lauren, I don't know if I want to be pregnant!"

Nodding, I squeezed her arms again in an effort to comfort. "That's okay, to be unsure. You have time to think about it, and you have options."

"But it's not just about me, it's about Austin too."

"But it's mostly about you. You're the one sacrificing your health and body to grow a baby. Yes, you should consider his feelings, and there are things like providing and nurturing to think about, but there are physical considerations too. And I'm not talking about stretch marks or a loose tummy, there can be real medical complications, which can follow you for the rest of your life."

Mina cringed. "Are you trying to talk me into this or out of it?"

"Neither," I said, smiling. "I'm just giving you the real deal. You have a lot to think about – but you have time to do it. If you feel strongly about not wanting to be pregnant, if the negatives outweigh the positives, if you feel like not having a baby is the decision that works better *for you*, then maybe you shouldn't. But, from experience, I can advise you that having a baby is definitely not the end of the world."

She sucked her teeth. "You were like a zombie when I saw you last week, about to have a breakdown because you were so overwhelmed with Harper!"

"Because I was trying to do it by myself, and I'm still in school. We'll graduate soon. And you'll have – at the very least – Austin to help you. How will your family feel?"

Mina laughed, then rolled her eyes. "My grandmother, mom, aunts, sisters... all of them will be thrilled. They all just *knew* I was too vain to ever have a baby, so it would be a miracle to them. My dad would come around once the baby was here."

"So, *see*? You'll have support, which makes all the difference in the world. It's still up to you to decide, but that needs to be something you factor in, okay?"

She nodded, then pulled me into another hug, squeezing me tight. "I feel so much calmer now. I was ready to choke Austin, because he didn't seem to understand why I couldn't flip the switch and be over-the-moon excited about something that's going to drastically change our lives. Like, I have goals, and if I have a baby, they have to get put on hold."

"But that doesn't mean they won't get accomplished. Just a little delayed."

Mina smiled. "I guess you're right. I mean, you're out here kicking ass, so I guess I wouldn't have any excuse, huh?"

"Sure wouldn't," I laughed. "So take your time to think about it. And don't be too hard on Austin, I doubt he's *trying* to get on your nerves. And trust me, any annoying stuff he does now will be insignificant compared to the way he's going to annoy you through pregnancy and childbirth. Just try to enjoy it. Don't let the stress ruin what you have."

Mina squeezed me again, then pressed her forehead to mine. "Thank you Lo."

"You're very, very welcome."

Now if I could only give myself good advice, maybe I wouldn't end up making half the bad decisions I do.

"Are you going somewhere?" Mina asked, pulling me back.

"Umm, yeah."

"Without a bra?" She looked pointedly at my chest, which *was* looking a little "free" under the bagginess of Ty's tee shirt on me.

I wrinkled my nose at her, shaking my head. "I'm just going to see Ty, I don't think he'll mind."

"Didn't you basically dump him?"

I cringed. "Well, I wouldn't say it quite like that, but—"

"So, yes. You can't break up with somebody and then go crawling back with your titties roaming free, looking like you just rolled out of bed."

"But I did…"

Mina pushed out a heavy sigh, then grabbed my hand. "Come with me."

A minute later, we were in my bedroom, and Mina was hunting through my lingerie drawer. Tightness blossomed in my chest when she pulled out the gorgeous blue and silver lingerie Ty had given me for my birthday, with a low whistle. It was still wrapped in the delicate tissue from the box, because I'd been waiting on a special occasion to wear it for him. I didn't know if this could be considered a special occasion, but it was certainly a hail-mary mission. I was willing to do whatever.

Mina handed it to me as she sat down on the edge of the bed, and I stripped out of my frumpy clothes and slipped into the luxurious, lacy bra and panties.

"Whoa," she whispered. "You look *hot* Lauren. Like, Victoria's Secret angel hot. If I liked wimmenz, you'd have a problem on your hands right now."

I laughed, twisting back and forth to look at myself in the mirror. I *did* look hot, and I understood that men were very visual creatures, but I didn't really think that was enough. I still didn't know what to *say*.

"Okay, so now put the same clothes back on."

I turned to Mina with a frown. "What? Put on frumpy clothes over *this*?"

"Ah," she said, handing me Ty's tee shirt. "I forget this is your first time around. The lingerie is for if you guys make up. The tee and sweats are for in case you *don't*."

~

This scene feels familiar.

Storm threatening to start at any moment, waiting a long time for Ty to open the door, the slant of his eyes when he finally answered, and deliciously bare chest… yep, déjà vu.

Only this time, he wasn't high. There was no marijuana smell, just the very familiar smell of *him*, surrounding me as we stood inches away from each other in the door. I swallowed hard, but couldn't seem to open my mouth.

His eyes weren't just low, they were puffy with sleep, and his hair was smashed flat on one side. He scrubbed a hand over his face, squinting before he looked at me again, like he was making sure it wasn't a dream – I really *was* at his door in the middle of the night, staring like a crazy person but not actually saying anything.

The door moved, and his hand was on the knob.

The *door moved*, and for one gut-wrenching moment, I thought he was about to close it in my face, but then he grabbed my hand and pulled me inside. A few seconds later, the sound of raindrops pelting the door and windows filled the room around us. He kept my hand tucked in his, and drew me close. Even in the semi-darkness, I could see his eyebrows lifted, waiting on me to say something. To say *anything*. So I said the only thing I knew to say.

"I'm sorry."

As soon as the words left my lips, a lump built in my throat, and I looked away as my eyes started burning with tears. I'd acted on impulse again, instead of thinking through it before I made a decision, and now I was here looking stupid, with nothing to say. I turned my eyes back to him, and said *I'm sorry* again, because my mind wouldn't articulate anything else.

"I'm *so* sorry," I said, one more time, hoping that maybe that time would change the impassive expression on Ty's face. "I messed up. You worked so hard to make it up to me with your timing, and I know you can't control Jamila and your mother. I should have told you Mekhi showed up, and I shouldn't have gotten defensive about it, because you're right. If it was the other way around, it would have been a problem for me too. I'm sorry. You're not a problem. You didn't bring trouble into my life, and I shouldn't have said that to you, because it's not the case. If anything, you've made my life better… and I'm sorry for hurting you. So, so sor—*mmmph*"

My words got swallowed into a kiss as Ty cupped my face in his hands, pressing his lips to mine. His tongue probed the seam of my mouth and I immediately opened for him, pushing my body against his. It didn't strike me until then how much I'd missed him, missed his taste, his smell, and the feeling of his skin against my skin. He kissed me deeper, digging his fingers into my waist as he tried to drag me closer, and groaning when he realized we were already as close as we could get.

"Where's baby girl?" he asked, when we finally pulled away from the kiss, panting.

"With her grandparents. I… couldn't handle everything. I was overwhelmed. Exhausted, stressed. I took that out on you, when I shouldn't have. I'm sorry."

He pressed his lips to my forehead, the tip of my nose, and then finally to my mouth. "You said that already."

"I'm making sure you hear it. I miss you." I lifted my hands, running my hands over the low layer of stubble that dotted his chin. "Do you think we can...?"

He chuckled, then grabbed the hem of my shirt. "Do you *really* have to ask?"

I was suddenly grateful to Mina for turning me back to put on something sexy, because Ty's reaction was... *everything*.

His eyes went wide, and dark with desire as soon as he'd peeled me out of my leisurely clothes. His gaze was so intense I would have sworn I felt it against my skin if the touch of his fingers weren't so much hotter. Both – his gaze and his fingers – touched me everywhere, soaking me in like it had been years instead of just a few days.

"You are *so* goddamned beautiful," he murmured as he slipped the flimsy panties down over my hips, and tossed them aside. He did the same with the bra, leaving me naked in front of him, except for the chain around my neck and the pendant resting between my breasts. He backed me against the cool steel of his front door, and his thumbs brushed my aching nipples before he cupped my breasts in his hands and squeezed. I closed my eyes, sucking in a shallow breath as he slipped a hand between my thighs. He circled my clit with his thumb, then pushed a finger inside me. His teeth grazed my neck, then he kissed me in the same spot, sucking and biting and kissing more until I whimpered with pleasure. I gasped when he added a second one, and gave in to the urge to rock my hips against his hand until he abruptly pulled them away.

His boxers joined my clothes on the floor, and a moment later, he grabbed me by the ass, lifting me up and wrapping my legs around him. "I need to be inside you," he said, lips brushing my ear as he sank into me. My body was welcoming, gripping him tight as he burrowed as deep as he could, and I didn't even bother trying to suppress my contented sigh. He was comfortable, familiar, and wonderful as he began to move inside of me.

Ty's hands were all over, touching like he was committing me into his memory. Caressing my thighs, teasing my clit, squeezing my breasts, and getting tangled up in my necklace as he slid a hand up between my breasts, running his thumb over the hollow of my throat before he pressed his lips there.

He planted kisses all over my neck, some passionate, some sweet. I was so lost in the bliss of being with him again that when he mumbled something else in my ear, I barely understood the words, but they made my heart slam to the front of my chest. He kept moving – deep, intensely slow strokes that made me dig my nails into his back – but he pulled back so that we were face to face.

I opened my eyes, meeting his gaze because I felt him there, and he placed a gentle kiss against my lips.

"I love you," he repeated, and this time, his words registered. The room was mostly quiet, nothing but the sensual sound of wet skin against skin, the steady drumbeat of the rain, and the short moans I couldn't seem to help letting out. Perfect acoustics for a response. But he didn't give me a chance. Before there was time for the moment to stretch into awkward, he'd hooked his arm under my leg and lifted it, pushing himself deeper as he crashed his mouth onto mine.

He swallowed my sounds with kisses, stroking harder, and faster, until my legs began to tremble. I wrapped my arms around him tight, pulling him as close as I could as my body tensed into a climax. My scream of ecstasy was muffled by his tongue in my mouth until he pulled away, grunting against my neck as he released.

Neither of us moved for a long time, and then finally, Ty lifted his head. Immediately, I cupped his face in my hands, turning him so that his gaze would lock with mine.

"I love you too."

Christina C Jones

D<small>AMN</small>, <small>SHE'S BEAUTIFUL</small>.

That was a thought I was pretty sure I'd never get tired of having. Especially when it came because Lauren was naked in my bed, looking completely at peace as she slept. I didn't want to wake her, but I knew she had class in just a little bit over an hour. I was down with playing hooky if it meant I got to spend the morning in bed with her, but skipping class wasn't very *Lauren*.

I slid a hand between her legs, knowing that my attention there would promptly wake her up. Sure enough, her hips began a subtle rock against my hand as I played with her, and she slowly opened her eyes.

"Good morning," she whispered, then shamelessly spread her legs wider, opening herself for me. *That shit right there*, that sexual boldness that contradicted the straight-laced girl the rest of the world saw… that was just one of the things I craved about her.

She closed her eyes again, but not to sleep, biting her lip as I pushed two fingers inside of her. She clenched around my hand, tight and wet, and I was desperately thinking about how I could convince her she didn't need to go to class.

Her eyes drifted open again, and she smiled at me, then covered her face with her hands.

"What are you blushing for?" I asked, using my free hand to pull hers away.

Lauren's lips parted in a gasp as I sank my fingers deeper, and when she caught her breath, she met my eyes. "Just thinking about what you said to me last night."

I pressed my thumb to her clit, and her back arched away from the bed. "What, that I loved you?"

With her lip still pulled between her teeth, she nodded. "You said it during sex. Maybe you weren't talking to *me*." She flicked her gaze to where my hand was buried between her legs. "Maybe you were talking to *her*."

"Definitely wasn't talking to her," I said, moving closer so I could brush my lips over hers. "She's very special to me too, but I love *you*, Lauren. I said it, and I meant it. Did you?"

"Yes." There was no hesitation in her words, or in her eyes, and that made my chest feel hot. I kissed her deep, pushed my fingers deeper, devouring her sexy little moans as she came all over my hand. She watched with narrowed, lust-filled eyes as I licked those fingers, then kissed her again, so she could taste too, then cupped one of her chocolate-tipped breasts in my hand.

"Where do we go from here?" she asked, right when I was about to lower my head, and take her nipple into my mouth.

I pulled back, so I could look her in the face. "That's a pretty heavy question before we've even had breakfast. What do you mean?"

"I mean, *us*. Where do we go from here, in our relationship? I hate to make this moment heavy, but if we're back together, there are things we need to discuss, sooner than later."

I scowled. "*If* we're back together? There is no *if*. We're back together. What do you want to discuss?"

She dropped her eyes, looking distinctly uncomfortable about what she had to say. She swallowed hard, then shook her shoulders like she was steeling herself, and returned her gaze to mine. "Like... how you feel about kids. How you feel about *my* kid, specifically. How you feel about marriage, and family. How you see your future. We were taking things easy, having fun, but... the fact of the matter is that we're saying we love each other, Ty. We have to be on the same page about those things, or we may as well not take this further than it already is."

Wow.

We hadn't even been together five months, and she wanted to talk about marriage and kids? At twenty-one and twenty-five?

"Ty, please don't take that the wrong way, like I'm trying to pressure you into something too soon, because that's not what I'm saying at all. I have daughter that I have to consider. If you don't want kids, that's a red flag. I want a husband, eventually, and more kids, and a house. If you see yourself as a bachelor in a studio apartment for the next fifteen years... we aren't on the same page. I just don't want to get more invested only to find out that we didn't want the same things. Even if *we* don't work out, I need to know that we at least desired the same things."

Okay.

That made sense.

The tension left my shoulders, and I relaxed, pulling her against my chest. "Marriage, kids... those are things that I want too. And I have no expectations about the wife staying home, keeping her barefoot and pregnant, none of that. *And*, I happen to think Harper is pretty bad ass. So we're good."

Her mouth spread into a big smile, and she nodded. "Good."

"Are you going to class?"

Please say no. Please say no.

"No," she whispered, shaking her head.

I lifted an eyebrow. "*Seriously*? You, skipping class?"

Lauren bit her bottom lip, then pushed me back on the bed. She turned so that she was facing away from me, and a second later, my dick was in her hands. "*Oh, damn,*" I muttered under my breath as she gave me several soft kisses, then took me in her mouth.

She looked at me over her shoulder, smiled, and then said. "I think... I can break the rules just this one time."

epilogue

. . .

Lauren

IT'S FUNNY TO ME, how quickly your life can be one thing, and then suddenly very, *very* different, in a completely non-extraordinary way. Although more than a year had passed, it really felt like it had been no time at all since me and Ty exchanged those first *I love you*'s. But... you know, they say time flies when you're having fun, right?

I was relaxed.

Like, *very* relaxed, which was a strong contrast to the week before, when we'd been tired and sore and sweaty from moving everything into the new place.

Our new place.

After my graduation, I'd moved into a new apartment, since my place was considered part of the dorms. I couldn't stay there just for the hell of it, so my minimal belongings and I found a tiny two bedroom apartment, just for me and Harper.

While Ty started the research for his dissertation, I started training for my job. I'd been lucky enough to find a position at a local data firm, and was happy to go to that little cubicle every day for now, because I'd worked hard for the education that qualified me to be there. It wasn't exactly fun, but the paycheck made it infinitely better, because I could stack my little bank account with the funds to eventually do something I actually *wanted* to do. And I was only twenty one. I had time to figure it out.

But, things moved on, and time went by. I only signed a six month lease for the apartment, just in case. When that one was up, I asked for a three month lease. When *that* one was up, Ty asked me and Harper to move in with him, and I said no.

His place was entirely too small.

I paid my landlord a premium to allow me to do month to month rent until we found something all three of us loved. The day before my twenty-second birthday, we found this one, a pretty little blue stucco house, with white columns, and a big yard with swings, and a front and back porch, and grey brick accents. I almost refused to move in when instead of "throwing away money on rent", Ty insisted on buying it. But in the end, I used what I was going to pay in rent to stack more money into Harper's college fund and my personal savings. It wasn't *my* ideal set up, but I was okay with that, because this place felt like home.

Beside me on the porch swing, Mina sat silently, with four month old baby Dallas in her arms. Me and Ty had teased them mercilessly about the Texas name, but once we saw her, with her big brown eyes, cinnamon skin, and head full of curly black hair, it seemed blasphemous to call her anything else. Now, Dallas was covered by a lightweight blanket while she nursed, and I was shocked she hadn't done her normal thing, of snatching the cover off, exposing Mina to the world. I shifted backwards, peeking under the blanket, smiling when I saw that her eyes were closed. When I looked up, Mina's were too.

The sight of those two was so sugary sweet it made my teeth hurt, and a different, familiar sort of longing fill my chest. I'd experienced that same feeling many times since Mina brought

Dallas into the world, and every single time, I pushed it away. It definitely wasn't time for *that*.

I stood carefully from my seat beside Mina on the swing, not wanting to disturb her rest. On the other side of the yard, Austin was flipping a slab of ribs on the grill, and further back, Ty pushed Harper on the swings.

Excuse me – Mr. Ty, as Harper still called him. She *loved* her Mr. Ty, and Mr. Ty *loved* Harper, and that made me love him even more. He was good with her, patient and kind, but firm when her little mouth or behavior got out of control. Their interaction was natural, and always the same, even when he didn't know I was watching, and that was exactly what I'd needed to see to confirm what I already knew about the type of man he was.

I stopped to tease Austin about not burning the food, and when I looked up again, Mekhi was opening the gate to my backyard, followed shortly by a pretty woman I recognized from pictures as Talia. A *pregnant* Talia.

Once again, I pushed the desire for a baby away.

I caught a glimpse of the wedding bands on their hands, from the small ceremony they'd had on base last month. They didn't see me from the grill station with Austin, and headed straight back to where Ty and Harper were.

I just watched, as Harper got scolded for jumping out of her swing, then ran to hug her daddy, then Talia. I was beyond grateful, for growth and maturity when I saw Ty and Mekhi not only shake hands, but actually *embrace* each other. Two men who loved Harper. Two men who loved me, in different ways, able to move past the mistakes we'd made.

Actually… it made me a little misty.

Ty left Mekhi and Talia with Harper, then looked across the yard to find me. When he headed in my direction, I waved to Mekhi and Talia, then went with Ty when he motioned for me to follow him inside.

We'd barely made it in when he pulled me into the hall that

led to our bedroom, just far enough that we were out of sight of any prying eyes. He pushed me against the wall, then lowered his mouth to mine, giving me a kiss that, if we didn't have company waiting outside, and more coming, would have made me drag him into the bedroom.

"What was that for?" I asked, draping my arms over his shoulders when he finally let me catch my breath.

He shrugged, then pressed his lips to my forehead. "Just because."

I grinned, and he kissed me again, deeper this time, then grabbed my hands.

"And what was *that* one for?"

He chuckled. "That one was because I think you're beautiful."

"What are you doing?" I asked, shaking my head as he stepped away from me. He wiggled his eyebrows, then dropped to his knees in front of me, gripping my thighs. "Ty, *no*," I giggled as he lifted my dress and put his head under. "We can't, our families are going to be here any second!"

We were still waiting on Bianca, Rashad, Roger, Roslyn, and Raquel, plus all of the parents. All of the siblings got along well with everyone, and the parents did as well… mostly. It was Ty's mother that I was still a little worried about.

She and I had gone toe to toe a few times, and I'd asked Ty not to interfere. If she was ever going to respect me, it had to be because I'd earned it, not just because he asked her to behave. If my suspicions were correct, it was working, because the last time, I'd gotten the distinct impression that her jabs were meant in fun, and we'd even had a good time together more than once. And she *loved* my baby, which counted for about a million points in my eyes. Still, I wanted to put off a good impression, and sex-rumpled clothes wasn't the way to do it.

Ty sucked his teeth, then lowered my dress back into place. "*Fine.* Spoilsport. That's not what I'm down here for anyway."

The Right Kind Of Trouble

"Oh, whatever," I said, rolling my eyes up to the ceiling. "What, checking a loose tile on the floor then?"

"Uh uh. I got down here to ask you to be my wife. Will you marry me, Lauren?"

When I looked down, he was holding a ring in front of me, and my heart swelled in my chest. I barely felt like I could breathe, let alone answer, but somehow I managed a frantic nod.

"Yes. *Yes.*"

My hands were shaking as he slid the ring – an intricately engraved band, with a large diamond flanked on either side by smaller stones – on my finger. He gripped my hands tight as he stood, then cupped my face in his hands. "Surprise," he said, grinning as he brushed my lips with his.

"What do you mean?"

He chuckled, then used his thumbs to brush freshly-sprung tears from my eyes. "You really think I wanted to invite all these people over here just for a house warming?"

My eyes went wide. "This isn't a housewarming?"

"Not anymore," he quipped. "It's an engagement party now."

I shook my head, smiling, just as the doorbell rang. I started to go answer it, but he caught me by the hand, turned me around, then lowered his head and gave me a kiss that made me weak in the knees.

"What was that one for?" I whispered, when he pulled away.

"*That* one was because I love you."

the end

If you enjoyed this book, please consider leaving a review at your retailer of choice. It doesn't have to be long - just a line or two about why you enjoyed the book, or even a simple star rating can be very helpful for any author!

Want to stay connected? Text 'CCJRomance' to 74121 or sign up for my newsletter. I'll keep you looped into what I'm doing!

Check out CCJROMANCE.COM for first access to all my new releases, signed paperbacks, merch, and more!

I'm all over the social mediasphere - find me everywhere @beingmrsjones

For a full listing of titles by Christina C Jones, visit www.beingmrsjones.com/books

about the author

Christina C. Jones is a best-selling romance novelist and digital media creator. A timeless storyteller, she is lauded by readers for her ability to seamlessly weave the complexities of modern life into captivating tales of Black characters in nearly every romance subgenre. In addition to her full-time writing career, she co-founded Girl, Have You Read – a popular digital platform that amplifies Black romance authors and their stories. Christina has a passion for making beautiful things, and be found crafting, cooking, and designing and building a (literal) home with her husband in her spare time.

Made in the USA
Middletown, DE
18 September 2024